Game Trail

A Jessica Anderson K-9 Mystery

by D. L. Keur

Book 7 of
The Jessica Anderson K-9 Mysteries

NO AI content, guaranteed. All original D. L. Keur.

Published by D. L. Keur, Sandpoint, ID 83864

D1523105

Dedication

To Bailey, my wonder mutt, and all the other dogs in my life,

To my dad,

And to Laura Belgrave, who made me do it.

Acknowledgements

Huge thanks to my editors. Without them, this book would be 'less than'. Thanks to Ann Davis, Mitch's 'mom'. Original Landon Reid portrait by Steve Merryman of Sigmadog.com, copyright owned in entirety by D. L. Keur, adjusted by D. L. Keur. Photo credits go to: kuzmaphoto (shutterstock.com), Emile Guillemot, unsplash.com, Asoggetti, unsplash.com, Jakub Kriz, unsplash.com, dog photo credits go to Ana Arroyo, unsplash.com, and Luzelle Cockburn, unsplash.com.

Copyright

D. L. Keur

TABLE OF CONTENTS

Game Trail

A Jessica Anderson
K-9 Mystery

by D. L. Keur

Book 7 of
The Jessica Anderson K-9 Mysteries

NO AI content, guaranteed. All original D. L. Keur.

Published by D. L. Keur, Sandpoint, ID 83864

D. L. Keur

1 – Shots Fired

MONDAY

A SHOT RANG OUT close by, startling Jessica Anderson and making her dogs, all six, jump up on full alert. A fifty-something lady they were working on, Linda Allen, jerked and let out a little yelp as Jessie, Deputy Tom Hudson helping, worked to set a vacuum splint on the lady's compound fracture.

"That was close," Tom muttered.

"It was."

"Maybe a .9mm."

Now came a burst, then two more shots, one similar and one a bigger, slightly different sound, perhaps a hot-shot loaded .357. Acer and Sumi, Jessie's German Shepherds (GSDs), Mitch, her Malinois, and brown and white Milo, the giant Wonder Mutt on Stilts, all had their hackles up. Queenie, half Irish Setter, half Golden, whined with worry and snuggled in close to Jessie's hip. Oso, a Norwegian Elkhound who was Jessie's premier air scenter, moved nearer, his ears pricked and quivering, his nose working …working.

"It's all small caliber fire," Tom whispered, one hand still helping steady the lady's arm, the other unsnapping his holster. Then the young ex-soldier pulled his Glock.

Jessie focused on getting the vacuum splint around the woman's fracture, then engaged the splint's small pump. Though the splint wouldn't apply undue pressure to the fracture, this was often where fear of pain would cause the victim to shift.

Quite coherent and calm, the lady braced herself, though her face constricted—worry. "Okay, Linda. Worst part's over now," Jessie told her.

The woman gulped a breath. "Those shots," she whispered.

"It's okay. Tom's the best."

"Shh," Tom said, signaling for silence as he released his hold of the woman's arm and shifted his crouch, eyes scanning. Jessie's dogs began growling, low and soft. Jessie drew one of her SIGs, left hand steady on the woman to physically keep track of her just in case Jessie had to cover.

Long moments of silence. The morning bird sounds had stopped. Nothing stirred but the dry autumn leaves rustling in the gradient winds. Then, all at once, the snap of branches breaking.

Jessie's dogs, even Queenie, moved to defensive positions around Jessie, Tom, and the woman. Jessie twisted her squat toward the direction of what now sounded distinctly like hoof-falls from some heavy animal. *Moose?* The three shots prior worried Jessie. If it was an angry or wounded moose, it meant trouble.

Tom holstered his Glock and brought his rifle around.

Moments later, the dark brown body of a horse broke through the brush and onto the trail, a man slumped over in the saddle. The horse turned toward them and slowed. That man slumped more, then toppled off, the horse stopping, then dropping its head to put its nose on its fallen rider.

*

THEY WERE finishing up the breakfast dishes when Bitterroot County Sheriff Landon Reid's blonde German Shepherd, Britta, sat up, ears alert. Landon took note. Frowned. *Something's up.*

Moments later, the newly installed computer system that was connected to the S.O. (Sheriff's

Office) chattered code. Out in the living room, Landon's cats took off to rip around the room like crazy animals, their tails stiffly curled under in a rigid arch of feistiness. Somehow, the radio chatter from the system's speakers always set them off.

Britta stood. Landon listened, and so did his housemate, Dr. Sol Preston, an achondroplastic dwarf who stood barely four feet high. "Well, that's me," Sol said, once the details came through.

Landon rolled eyes toward the county's brilliant, if mischievous, criminologist. "You want a ride?"

Now, the house security system went off, and they both looked toward its monitors. Britta trotted off to the window, Landon's cats leaping to the top of the overstuffed chairs to look out, too. Both men said "Martin" simultaneously. A few seconds later, the honk of a car horn gave notice of the undersheriff's arrival.

"I'd better get my stuff," Sol said with a grin and marched upstairs.

"This means trouble," Landon muttered. Went to the kitchen and filled a mug with coffee, then went out to call off the guard dogs.

Slipping the dogs each a couple of treats along with praise, he asked the big GSDs to *'Platz'*. Only then did Martin open his window a crack.

"You're safe," Landon told him. "You can roll down your window now."

"You're sure?" Martin asked, eyeballing the dogs.

"I'm sure."

Martin did, but, eyes still on the dogs, he rolled it down only just enough for Landon to hand in the mug of coffee.

"Thanks," Martin said, taking a sip. "Thought you should know. Jessie's out there."

Uh-oh. She who finds trouble.

Landon begged 'more' with a tip of head, and Martin responded with, "She was on another SAR call-out for an injury accident when a guy—don't have an ID yet—dropped in her lap, and the guy said 'shot me'. And he *had* been shot, but, get this. Tom says he's been shot with what they suspect is a high-velocity paintball gun. Sent the victim into arrhythmia, maybe. Jessie's not sure. Said ask the docs. Medivac is already on its way. That's all I got."

"So Deputy Hudson is with Jessie?"

D. L. Keur

"Yep. He sticks to her like white on rice, now."

Landon nodded. "Good. You think it's an accident?"

"Paintball gun?" Martin shook his head. I don't think so. Tom said they heard three small caliber shots. He thought one was a .9mm. The other, Jessie says, is maybe a .357 hot-shot. One of the dispatchers says that paintball guns sometimes sound like .9mms. He plays."

Martin's eyes went to the house. "...And here comes the man," he said as Sol marched up, then stowed his gear in the back. "Can I keep the coffee?"

"Bring the cup back next time. Be safe, both of you," Landon told them.

"Of course!" Sol came back, his squashed, child-like voice all happy and perky.

Martin nodded. "Later, Reid."

Landon gave a nod. "Later."

*

THE MAN had numerous blunt force trauma injuries, center chest, and a few a bit lower. His BP was low, but, overall, he was holding, despite shallow, elevated respirations and an irregular, fluttering heartbeat. To Jessie, he felt clammy, and she didn't like his color. The ER doctor on speaker with her, a new woman, decided against IV fluids in case of internal bleeding, just kept Jessie monitoring and ready in case of cardiac arrest or the victim going further into shock. "Rapid transport," the doctor kept telling her.

"Medivac on the way," Jessie kept repeating.

The injured woman was sitting by the man's feet, her good hand rubbing his leg. She was keeping out of the way, but talking away at him as if she knew him, though the man wasn't responding. He was only borderline coherent.

Jessie appreciated the woman's efforts. Hearing a sympathetic human voice speaking to them was good for the injured and even for the comatose or dying. The brain registered their presence and, possibly, even understood their intent, if not their words.

Tom got on the radio to the Medivac chopper, which brought the knowledge that their ETA was now two minutes and that they would take both victims in one trip since the woman was ambulatory.

Suddenly, the man sat up and gasped, his hands grabbing his chest, his eyes coming wide open. All the dogs' heads came up. "I *shot* her," he said.

"Came up to finish me off, and I shot her dead. I killed her."

The man's heart converted right then, returning to normal sinus rhythm as he reared up. Jessie, who had her hands and her stethoscope on him, heard and felt it happen.

"Easy, easy," Tom said, hands supporting. "Ease back down, now, please."

"Oh, Lord, I *killed* somebody!"

***

2 – No Body

THE MAN'S NAME was Homer Garrison—a local—and Linda Allen, the woman with the broken arm, knew him. They were neighbors, in fact.

Linda's presence got Homer to quit stressing so much. "Maryanne's not going to let anything bad happen to you, Homer. Honest."

"I killed somebody, Linda!"

"You just shut up. You'll see. It was all in your head."

"Cover," Tom said as the chopper came overhead, he and Jessie protecting both civilians with their bodies from the downwash as its paramedics descended, one with the basket, the other with an extra harness.

The injured successfully lifted into the hovering Medivac chopper, Jessie and Tom stowed gear. Done, Jessie asked her dogs to backtrack the horse's trail, something she'd taught them when a fifteen-year-old kid's mount had come back home without its rider in what was later determined was an attempted kidnapping.

Jessie's dogs took off, and, about two, maybe three minutes later, Jessie and Tom chasing after, the wonder mutts alerted, their barks and yips coming from their collar mics to Jessie's phone. About a quarter of a mile of Tom and Jessie threading their way through timber, leading the man's saddle horse, they broke out into a small clearing. There, they found the dogs all downed. Found a tagged, hanging deer, half gutted, and saw another horse fitted with a pack saddle, that animal tied to a tree. The pack horse nickered at the one Tom led.

Jessie praising her dogs, then inspecting the ground, careful not to disturb things, she and Tom discovered both paint and blood along with a fallen .357 near where the deer carcass hung. There was no dead body, so whoever the guy thought he'd shot got away. "Or has been carried off," Jessie said.

"So, is the blood deer or human?" Tom asked. "And where's the woman's body our vic- supposedly killed?"

"Milo, Mitch," Jessie called, her two HRD (human remains detection) experts coming up all wags.

Jessie pointed to the blood around the hanging deer carcass. Both dogs glanced once, then just kept looking up at her, ignoring her point. "That's deer," she said to Tom.

He chuckled and grinned big. Raised a finger. "Kinda sorta got that."

Then, wagging off, both Mitch and Milo put their heads down on one spot where there was scant sign of anything but for a bit of scuffed duff.

"My good, good dogs," Jessie said, squatting down.

Examining the ground, Jessie saw what looked like tiny, dark gray plastic shards and what might or might not be blood. Without a forensic light or reagents, there was no way to be sure, though. "I've got to mark this."

"Guess we're going to have to carry both med stuff and crime scene kits, now, huh?" Tom said.

"Probably would be a good idea," Jessie agreed, ringing the spot with gauze.

"Yeah, well, what's another twenty-some pounds, right?"

Jessie groaned.

11

"Look here. What's your Mitch and Milo doing now?"

Both the dogs were stock still, their heads angled oddly.

Easing over, Jessie saw mangled bone, mush, and a fingernail. Some inches away were two more partial fingers, those mostly intact below their severance points. "Ah, Tom?"

"Yeah."

"There *was* somebody else here, and, yes, they were shot. The dogs just found fingers. I'm going to process, then collect in case we find the injured and reattachment is possible."

"It's evidence, you know."

"Yeah."

And, taking photos, making a quick sketch with measurements on her phone's touchpad, she wrapped the fingers in gauze, the tissue still warmer than the late October air temperature, stuck them in a plastic bag with some saline, then catalyzed a cold bag and wrapped it around the lot. Dropped it into a small tissue container and put it in her pack. If the person was found soon enough, doctors might be able to salvage enough to give them back some use.

Mitch, the Marvelous Malinois, started crawling along on his belly again as soon as she signaled the go-ahead. His head was pointed sideways. Milo, a dog Jessie guessed might be pitbull and Great Dane with, maybe, some pointer or some other hunting dog thrown in for good measure, got up and slowly paced, one step at a time on the other side, his head also angled. Dropping gauze pads as she went, Jessie followed, casting her eye where they pointed. Saw what could be a series of shoe or boot tracks, including a faint blood trail. *The paintball shooter's?*

She called a halt, and the two HRD dogs downed where they were.

"What's up?" Tom asked.

"We've got a blood trail."

"Let's go, then."

Jessie didn't dare let the pack run to track fast. If they needed this for evidence, her SAR dogs would contaminate it. *Okay. So we do it slow,* and, putting the rest of the dogs on down-stays, she and Tom began following the two dual-trained SAR/HRD experts ...for over two miles through wild country before getting to a road, Mitch and Milo now indicating that the trail had ended.

"She …or he got in a vehicle?" Tom suggested.

That was Jessie's guess. "I think so."

"So the guy who got shot *didn't* kill anybody."

"Don't know," Jessie said. "Depends on how badly injured. Definitely wounded, though."

"Better keep a check on the hospitals and clinics. Calling it in."

*

GETTING IN The Rhino, his refurbished and highly customized moose of an old 2006 Hummer, Landon called in.

Told Dispatch he was headed out to the murder scene. That's when he was told that it probably wasn't a murder scene. "No body. Not yet, anyway. Just somebody's fingers. Anderson and Hudson are doing another search. We've got a BOLO out to all law enforcement, clinics, and ERs."

"All right. I'm going out there."

"Yes, sir."

Beside him, riding shotgun, Britta kept watching him, her warm brown eyes giving him the impression that she knew way more than she was telling. "Your mom has found something, hasn't she, Britta?"

The dog's eyes blinked, and that was enough for Landon—*Yeah. I'd bank on it.*

***

D. L. Keur

3 – Nail on Head

JESSIE AND TOM gave their run-down to Undersheriff Doyle, Deputy Dr. Sol Preston, and newly certified CST (Crime Scene Technician), Deputy Sinclair.

Jessie handed over the fingers. Then, at Sol's request, him handing over sacks of evidence markers, Jessie had Milo and Mitch retrace the blood trail they'd found, she and Tom dropping markers at every spot the dogs again indicated as significant.

"So, you studied under Dr. Preston?" Tom asked as they worked.

"Yeah, I did."

"He just doesn't seem like a criminologist to me. He's so happy and …well, such a joker. I would expect him to be all serious, even mopey. Grumpy, for sure."

Jessie laughed. "Um, my bosses in Blaine? One of them was serious, but not mopey, at all. Sharp *and* sharp-tongued, though. The head guy was all upbeat and jovial. I think people just think that CSIs and criminologists are that way because of all the bad stuff they see."

Tom nodded. "Yeah. I sure wouldn't be very upbeat. What we do is bad enough. I can't imagine getting into the nitty-gritty stuff like they do."

Jessie totally got Tom's thinking. She had never developed a shrug-it-off, even humored attitude about crimes, not like Sol. She had gotten that way about evidence processing, but not about the crimes or the criminal mind. They gave her chills and willies down her spine. Unlike Sol, she didn't *want* to know how criminals thought, much less why.

Done with dropping markers when they reached the road, they backtracked, stringing sheriff's-line tape on both sides. Tom took one side, Jessie the other, a tedious job that used rolls and rolls of the thousand-feet-per-roll, bright yellow, plastic ribbon marked 'SHERIFF'S LINE' and 'DO NOT CROSS'. "Good thing this stuff's cheap," Tom said.

They were just reaching the working team when Sheriff Reid appeared, white hat a beacon. Jessie's dog—ex-dog, now—Britta was glued to his side. Britta wagged, and Jessie had to stop herself from calling out. The dog looked more relaxed than ever she had when she was Jessie's.

Sheriff Reid turned to them. His pockmarked face a mask, he nodded once. "Jessie. Tom," he said, acknowledging them in his deep, soft, so slow grumble.

"Sheriff," Jessie answered formally, and her resentments immediately stirred.

Still on down-stays, Jessie's dogs were practically beside themselves. They all wanted to greet their old pack mate. Landon must have noticed, because the next words out of his mouth were: "Is it okay if Britta goes to say hi, Jessie?"

Relief. "Yeah. It'd be great." And she almost choked up saying it.

He looked down at the shepherd. "Well, go on. Go see your pals," and Britta bounded toward Jessie's pack, the dogs begging release from their down-stays …which Jessie gladly gave them, then watched the joy of reunion among friends.

*

LANDON WATCHED the dogs. He watched Jessie's face. Yeah. She was still upset about Britta 'choosing him', as Jessie called it. It hadn't broken their working relationship, but there was noticeable strain.

19

Landon hadn't asked for Britta. Jessie had done it all herself, turning the dog loose to make 'her own choice', as the Andersons called it. The fact that, yeah, he really felt a genuine affection for the dog, the fact that, yeah, the dog seemed to like him, too, was beside the point. Landon would have never accepted the animal …or any dog. He just didn't have enough time in his life now to give a dog the kind of attention it deserved, though he admitted that having the sentinels coerced on him had already proven invaluable protection. Nobody got past the big, burly shepherds that guarded him and his property …except, of course, for the Andersons, him, and Sol. Even Howie, his powerhouse tac team commander, stayed in his unit until Landon gave the okay.

Landon worried, though. Guns stopped dogs, and Landon did not want that on his conscience, never mind how valuable the animals were. Jessie's dad, Oli, wasn't listening when Landon brought it up, though, so Landon had some heavy-duty, highest-level protection Kevlar® on special order for all the dogs in his care—the four sentinels and Britta.

"Sheriff, sir?"—Deputy Sinclair's voice.

"Yes, Deputy?"

"Would you come this way, please, sir? Deputy Dr. Preston is asking for you."

*

BRITTA CAME all the way down with them to where Jessie had parked the XV, Britta and Acer bounding along, the big heritage shepherds pulling at each other's ruffs and chasing each other back and forth, the other dogs joining in, all wags and play growls.

Once down at hers and Tom's rigs, Jessie opened the XV's doors and back hatch, then watched to see what would happen.

Her dogs jumped in, but Britta didn't. The blonde shepherd gave one last wag, then bounded away, heading back up the trail they'd just come down.

"You miss her, huh?" Tom asked.

"Yeah, I do. So does Acer. So do the rest of the dogs." She shook her head. "She's the sheriff's, now. It's what she wants."

"I saw that. I find that kind of a surprise. He's such a reserved guy until he gets testy. Then he's all

21

hardcore gruff and growl. I wouldn't think a dog could get along with him."

Jessie almost blew it by laughing out loud. Managed to choke it back in time. But Landon, hardcore? Not hardly. Obviously, Landon had Tom fooled, and she wasn't about to blow her dad's friend's cover.

*

HAVING LISTENED to Dr. Sol Preston's reasoning as the patient man pointed out evidential details that, honestly, Landon couldn't discern, Landon took his criminologist's word for it. Boiled down, they either had someone wounded or a corpse to find. "If a corpse, that means somebody or several somebodies moved it, right?" he asked.

"Well, unless zombies are real," Sol said, grinning up at him.

Landon rolled eyes as his undersheriff and head investigator, Martin Doyle, chuckled. "Are you guys done with the horses and the deer?" Landon asked.

"Why?"—Martin.

"I was going to finish dressing the carcass out, then load it on the pack horse and take it and the horses down."

"Why?"—Sinclair.

Landon wanted to shake his head. *Because it's the right thing to do.* Sighed. Gave reasons these guys would understand. "Because there's no reason to waste the meat. The deer is tagged and belongs to Homer Garrison. That meat needs to be processed in a timely manner, its tag reported, and the horses need to go home to their pasture. Waiting for the family or friends to get out here just adds hours."

"Go for it," Martin said. "We're done over there."

"Good."

Landon went at it, Britta showing back up to sit and watch him as he worked. Then she followed along beside as he rode the saddle horse down, the pack horse now loaded with the deer following behind.

Once he got down to where Garrison's truck and horse trailer were parked, another deputy meeting him there to drive it, he opened The Rhino, waited till

Britta jumped in, then called in to see what else was
going down around his county.

"Just a sighting of some adult-sized Halloween
tricksters hitting early," his sergeant told him. "They
were wearing what the lady called spaceman suits. We
figure they're high schoolers by how she described
them in age, height, and weight—'fresh-faced, tall,
and skinny', and 'brat-faced, short, and round' is what
she said."

"All right. Anything on the BOLO for somebody
missing fingers?"

"Not yet, sir, but word just went out an hour
ago."

"All right."

"Oh. Something else, sir. There's a television
crew hanging around town. Northridge P.D. called
about them. Wanted to talk to you about it."

"Why?"

"Why what, sir?"

"Why is a TV crew hanging around, and why does
Northridge want to talk to me about it?"

"I don't know, sir."

"All right. Heading home to clean up, then I'll be in."

"Ten-four. 10:13."

*

FINALLY BACK at the S.O., Jessie finished her report and hit 'save', printed it out, then hit 'send'. Watched as the system cleared her screen and gave her a confirmation code. Copying that code into an email to herself, she wrote it down, too. Her phone chimed moments later as the same confirmation code—a proof-of-filing—came in from the system and, right on its heels, her email to herself. She logged out.

"How did you do that report so fast?" Tom griped.

"Just the facts, sir," she quipped, grinning.

He shook his head and gave her a scowl. Went back to tabbing and typing.

She looked down at her dogs all laying around the room. "Okay, boys and girls. One more stop, then we'll go home!" And up her dogs all jumped, wagging up to her.

She squatted down and gave hugs and strokes all around—her wonder dogs. Stood, gave Tom a "Later," and headed to her last objective before signing out. She swore she'd seen Tank's name lit on the duty roster.

Heading down 'the quiet hall', FBI agent Andy Newsome was just coming out of his leased suite of offices. Despite being newly promoted and an even bigger gun than ever, he gave her a nod. She smiled and nodded back, the dogs giving small wags of recognition, too.

Getting to the hall's far end, she saw that Tank's door was open. Grinned. *About time!*

Stepping in, the dogs crowding around her, she saw the lieutenant speaking with an elderly woman in a wheelchair. "Oops. Sorry. I'll come back later."

The mountain-sized man looked up and smiled big. "Jessie! Come in. Come meet my mom."

Introduced to a Mrs. Ellen Sherman, the woman practically just skin stretched over bones, Jessie's eye picked out the signs of malnutrition and all but starvation. She frowned, seeing it. *What gives?*

"Mom's agreed to give Idaho a try. She's going to be living with me," Tank said.

And, instantly, Jessie knew there was a lot more to the story than that.

Niceties done, which had not been her goal, Jessie headed back toward the front to sign out. From there, it was down the hall to the back exit nearest where she'd parked the XV.

Passing the break room, Jessie stopped to grab a snack and a drink. Then, her dogs reacting, she turned to see Tank standing there, watching her.

"You didn't come down to my office just to say 'hi'," he said, quiet voice gentle. "What's up, Jessie?"

She felt her face flush, but tried to cover it with, "You snuck up on me. You shouldn't do that. I'm armed, you know."

He dropped his eyes, grinned, and shook his head, then extended a hand to one of the tables. Waiting for her to sit, he sat down himself once she had and folded his hands over each other—his waiting pose, as Jessie thought of it.

"And, actually, I did," Jessie said, unwrapping her goodie and taking a bite, then chewing and swallowing to give herself time. "I saw your name lit on the day roster. We missed you and are so glad you're back."

Again, Tank shook his head. "Not buying, Jessie. And who's this 'we'?"

Darn him! "Well, me, for one. And Land— ...The sheriff mentioned it. So did Captain West and quite a few others."

"I can wait you out, you know, and, were this a session, I would."

Yeah, he would. Successfully. *Oh, bite it.* "So, it's that obvious?"

"Not obvious to the casual observer, maybe," he offered. Then, "Tell you what. Come by when you feel comfortable talking about it again, okay?"

She nodded. "Okay." Then, "Ah, Tank ...Deputy Lieutenant, I mean. Um, your mom. She needs some heavy-duty nutrition and a lot more food intake."

"Working on it. It's not Mom's fault, but it's part of the reason I had to take leave, and all of the reason why, despite her not wanting to leave her home of thirty-five years, she's now agreed to come on a trial basis to live with me here in Idaho."

"Oh." The way Tank said it sounded ominous, and Tank never, ever sounded ominous.

"Where's Britta?" he asked, looking down at the dogs. And, as usual, Tank had just hit the nail square on the head.

***

4 – Oh, Mondays

LANDON PULLED into the S.O. to find a big van with two satellite dishes mounted on its top sitting on premises where it shouldn't be. He frowned. "What in the world?"

Beside him, Britta sat up very straight, a low rumble starting to roll in her throat. "My sentiments exactly," Landon muttered, and the dog glanced his way, then put her attention back on the van. That van's signage read 'Actuator Studios' and had California plates. It was parked on the wrong side of the sign and the clearly marked line, both of which said 'Authorized Vehicles Only', and it was half-blocking the entry/exit. If the APC (Armored Personnel Vehicle) had a code run, the van was in the way.

Landon pulled up beside it. Saw people inside. Flipped his lights and burped his siren. That seemed to wake somebody up, because the side of the van opened, and two men climbed out, one short and skinny, one taller and of a more normal weight, maybe one-sixty. The normal-sized one had a camera on his shoulder, the 'live' light on.

31

Landon lowered his driver's side window. Britta stood up, and he signaled to her.

She sat back down, but the low rumble got louder. "You're parked in a restricted zone," he told the men.

"Oh, is that so?" the skinny guy said, his voice too cheerful. He started to approach. "You're the sheriff, right?"

Beside him, Britta's rumble now turned loud and menacing for just a second of warning to the stranger before she went absolutely silent, her attention riveted on both men, but especially on the one moving in. Britta's head slowly lowered, body leaning forward, her eyes keen, ears stiffly pricked.

The guy saw it, too, and stopped.

Landon studied both men, especially the guy who'd spoken. He didn't respond to the question. Finally said, "Move your vehicle to the public parking area, please. ...Now."

That brought objection—"We have a right—"

He pressed the switch, the window rolling up, then turned on a directed LRAD (Long-Range Acoustic Device) pulse for just one second. That seemed to do the trick. They scrambled back into their van, the skinny guy jumping into the driver's seat. The van moved out.

And stay out.

Watched them park in the public lot. …Grumbled under his breath.

So did Britta.

*

THE DOGS STOOD up, tails starting to wag. Acer went to the door just as Jedidiah Blackthorne came in view, his long, black hair tied back and him dressed in jeans and a white shirt. "Red said he thought you were back here! He let me come on back," Jedidiah said, smiling down at Jessie, his beautiful, dark eyes sparkling.

Jessie got up, and Tank did, too. She extended her hand toward Jed. "Deputy Lieutenant Sherman, this is my friend, Jedidiah Blackthorne. Jedidiah, Deputy Lieutenant Thomas Sherman, a.k.a. 'Tank'."

"Pleased to meet you," Tank said, extending a hand.

"Likewise," Jedidiah responded, shaking.

"Lieutenant Sherman is our go-to guy for dealing with job meltdowns," Jessie said. She looked at Tank, then added, "And meltdowns, in general, too."

"Good to hear there's that available," Jedidiah said. Then his eyes caught on Jessie's. "I thought I'd see if you were free for lunch."

She grinned. "I am. Perfect timing. I'm starved."

Jedidiah looked over at Tank. "You're welcome to come, too, Lieutenant. I'm buying."

"No, thank you. My mom's due at her new doctor's in about an hour. We'll take lunch afterwards. Thanks for the invitation, though."

"How about dinner?" Jedidiah asked in his oh-so-pleasant, mellow voice. Jessie gave him a grin.

Tank paused for a second, then nodded. "We can do that."

"Good. Tanner's?"

That got raised eyebrows. "Whoa. High end. I'm not even unpacked. Neither is Mom."

"The Hereford better?"

"You're not going to take no for an answer, are you?" Tank asked, chuckling.

Jed's black eyes went mischievous. "No, I am not, and it's my treat, no argument. Good company is hard to come by."

"All right, then."

"Seven good? That's the earliest Jessie gets free from her dad to play."

"Seven is great."

"See you then," Jedidiah said, and Jessie picked up her day pack, her wonder dogs giving escort out the door, Mitch and giant Milo in the lead, as ever.

*

WATCHING AS THE VAN finished reparking itself over in the public side, Landon put The Rhino in gear and headed around back. There came surprise number two—Jessie leaving with Jedidiah Blackthorne, Jed's arm hovering near the small of Jessie's back as the two crossed the lot, Jessie's dogs all wags around them.

Britta stood up. Gave a little whine. "You want to be with them?" he asked her. "You can. I won't stop you."

The dog gave him a look …and he swore it was a 'Jessie look'. The dog sat back down, her eyes on him.

"Your choice," he said, and pulled in to park. Watched as Jessie loaded her dogs, handing out something to each as they got in. Then she opened the windows and got back out, Acer with her, him carrying whatever she'd given him, probably Anderson dog jerky. She and Acer got in Jedidiah's fancy sports car.

Landon gave a wave as they passed, but they didn't seem to see him. *Jedidiah and Jessie?*

He shook his head. Got out, Britta with him, secured the vehicle, then made his way inside …only to see surprise number three coming out of the break room. "Tank!"

His lieutenant stopped. Turned. "Sheriff."

They shook. "Glad you're back," Landon said.

The big man grinned. "Me, too."

"Watch out of the way, please," came Sol's voice from behind.

Landon turned to see Sol struggling with a box that was way too big for him. He stepped toward and came to the rescue, surprised by the heft of it. "What in the world is in this?"

"Thanks," Sol said as Landon took the box, his squashed voice happy. Answered, "New toys."

Next came Martin and Sinclair, both of them packing similar boxes.

"Where to?" Landon asked.

"My lab," Sol said, pointing to the hall wall in the direction where, in a parallel hall, his lab/office resided. "Just put them on the big table in there. I'm going back out for the last one."

"Use a dolly," Landon called after.

Sol turned around, walking backwards. "Right. Good idea, but I want to get this done, and rounding up maintenance would take till the next ice age."

Landon laughed. It wasn't quite that bad. Didn't say so.

"I'll go with him," Tank offered.

"Take this one, and I'll go with him," Landon said, handing off the box. He wanted to talk to Sol.

Catching up outside, Landon asked, "So, what's the status on the Garrison case?"

"Like I told you up there, we've potentially got a missing, injured suspect …or a corpse. The attack on Garrison was purposeful. The weapon used on him shot paintballs. The shooter walked right up, the footprints showing a decided stride by their impressions."

"You're sure."

"Not a hundred percent, but yeah. Whether wounded or corpse, it has to be one or the other, probably the former. Found one spent bullet from the fallen .357 and one empty casing in the revolver's cylinder, which was loaded with a total of five rounds. Then there are the fingers. I doubt anybody was packing still warm human fingers around with them just for fun and lost them. And a quick field test says the blood type in the blood in the fingers is the same as that on the retreat track."

"All right. Thank you. …So, what's in the boxes?" Landon asked for a second time, lifting this last one out of the back of Martin's unit.

"I told you. New toys." Sol said with a conspiratorial grin. "You'll see …when I'm ready to share."

In other words, butt out.

"Can I get a ride home tonight?" Sol asked, jumping to grab and close the back hatch. For a really short guy with bandy legs, he was pretty capable.

"Of course. You don't have to ask."

A long, loud buzzer went off, a warning that the APC was on the move and coming through.

Britta backed herself around to beside Landon's knee. "Now what?!" Landon grumbled. It was turning into one of those Mondays.

***

5 – Snagged Straggler

JESSIE DIDN'T like the idea, but didn't say so as Jedidiah parked in back in one of the diagonal parking spots that bordered the river walk. She knew why he did it—less chance for somebody to scratch or dent his car, but she still preferred peopled areas. Less chance for trouble.

This isn't Denver, she told herself, just like she did almost every time she came to town. *Not even Blaine County. Get over it.* And, yes, she wasn't over it, much as she wanted to be. She still wasn't over Blaine or that terrible night in Denver related to it. She wasn't over being trapped downtown and having to run for it with Acer through the back alleys of a hostile city full of angry, rioting people. She also wasn't over the damage that whole case had done to her psyche. She was getting there, though, thanks to Tank Sherman. And now he was back. But Tank's mom bothered her. The woman was frighteningly thin.

"Let's take the alley, rather than going all the way around," Jedidiah said, pointing as he got out.

Acer jumping out, Jessie grabbed a leash from her day pack and looped it through her belt. Left the day pack. Nodded. "Okay."

Halfway through the alley, the sound of sirens reached Jessie's ears. Acer's head came up. Ahead, on the main street, the S.O.'s APC passed, all lights, warning sirens, and buzzers ...on the wrong side of the street. "That's odd in town," Jessie said, turning to Jed, who walked just beside and behind.

Behind them, a car sped off, tires squealing. Then another. Jessie turned to see too late.

"Watch out," Jed yelled, pulling her sideways into him as somebody crashed right into her as they came flying around the corner from the street. That someone was dressed, head to foot, in black—face, body, hands, and feet.

The guy, gray-blue eyes angry-looking, tried landing a weak-by-half, back hammer fist on her—all he had in that moment as Acer launched himself, toppling the tall form, who let out a yell as the dog connected to grab an arm. A green, cloth shopping bag the man carried fell to spill two boxes of paintballs and a box of ammo all over the pavement. A gun—tiny—skittered across to land out of reach.

Jessie pulled her SIG. Jedidiah threw himself across the stranger's legs as the man went down, Jessie trying to get her act together enough to do something useful. Reholstered and hooked the struggling man's free arm with a quick loop of Acer's leash as the man punched at Acer, who had the other arm held fast. Moments later came pounding feet, and the most famous hat in all the Bitterroot was suddenly right in it with them, Britta there, too, snarling in the face of what, once they got him secured, then pulled off his black stocking mask, seemed to be a Black guy.

Jessie squinted at the face once she and Landon got cuffs on him. Wanted to touch the skin, but didn't have gloves on, so she didn't. "Pull off one of his gloves, Landon," she suggested.

Her boss looked at her like she was nuts. "Why?"

"He's got gray eyes, and weird nostrils, eyelids, and lips. I think he's wearing one of those hyper-realistic silicon masks. Let's see if the hand matches the face."

And he was most definitely wearing a mask, because, when they pulled a glove off, the hands were white, the short fingernails painted green.

Getting to skin underneath a padded paintball jacket, some cheap IIA body protection under that, then a t-shirt, Jessie found the mask edge about a foot down the back. The silicon seemed stuck or suctioned against skin. She pulled …peeled, and the 'Black man' mask came off to reveal the real perp underneath—a young, shorn-haired, flat-chested, blonde woman.

Cursing and accusations flooded the air as Landon recited Miranda rights to her.

More pounding feet—Howie, another deputy with him. "Everybody all right?"

'I think I bruised a knee," Landon said, grinning.

"Well, at least you snagged one of them. The rest of them got away."

"That was all Jessie and Jed," Landon said as two city cops came running up, too. Landon let them have the perp, along with the two masks and glove they'd stripped off of her.

"And Landon, Jed, Britta, and Acer," Jessie said. "Acer got first take-down!"

An hour later, statements and reports completed, Jessie, Jedidiah, and Acer, a happy dog at Jessie's side, finally got to go to lunch.

Landon and Britta came with them on Jedidiah's invite.

✳

"HOW DID YOU know we needed help?" Jessie asked Landon as they waited for their burgers and home fries.

"Britta," he said, looking down, laying a hand on her, and smiling. *His* dog—she really was amazing. He looked back up to see Jessie watching him. "She knew somehow. Some sort of sixth sense or something. Was going nuts. I let her out, and she flew down the street to the alley. I followed."

"Good thing. I didn't even have zip ties with me," Jessie said.

Landon purposely gave her a look-down. "I thought the Andersons were always prepared," he said.

She grinned, taking it. "Hey, I had on my Kevlar® and was armed. Plus, I had Acer and his leash."

"About that," Jedidiah said, turning to specifically address Jessie. "Are you always going to go around armed like Annie Oakley or something?"

Landon watched Jessie give Jed a glancing grin. "Yep."

"That's going to make it real hard to go out somewhere fancy."

Landon ducked his head down and focused on Britta.

"It's called an ankle holster, Jedidiah," Landon heard Jessie return.

"Right."—Jed.

They get along.

"Did you notice the caliber of rounds the guy …er, woman stole, Jessie?" Landon asked, raising his head and turning the subject to something that was bothering him.

Jessie's dark blue eyes instantly brightened. "I did. .380 ACPs. The gun looked like a Stinger®."

Landon nodded.

"I found it odd," Jessie added. "A tiny, two-shot gun."

"So did I. Not the usual gun of choice for a robbery."

"She didn't strike me as your typical thief, either, and, with the get-up she had on, it reeks 'first timer' and a TV fantasy idea of how to commit a crime."

Landon's thoughts exactly on the 'first-timer' analysis. Not so much about TV ...but, then, he didn't watch it. Hadn't even had one until Sol brought one into the house.

"Your hamburger, Jessie," the server said, setting Jessie's plate down.

"Thank you."

Then came Jedidiah's plate, and, last, Landon's three.

"Three hamburgers? Are you trying to win our weight gain contest, Landon?" Jessie asked with a laugh. "It won't work, you know. I'm five pounds ahead of you, now."

He groaned. "Don't remind me."

"What's this?" Jedidiah asked, his eyes full of laughter as they moved from Jessie to Landon and back.

"Dad made it a wager to get us both competing against each other since neither of us were gaining what both our doctors insist we have to. Whichever of us reaches our target weight first gets dinner at

Tanner's paid for by the loser. And I'm winning, of course."

"She only has to gain thirty pounds to my forty-two, though, is what she's not telling you," Landon grumbled.

"That doesn't sound fair."—Jedidiah.

"Of course it is," Jessie came back. "I run all day. He sits all day and night. I burn a lot more calories."

"I do not sit all day and night," Landon said, carefully stripping off the buns for himself, and cutting two of the burgers—plain, nothing but meat and cheese—into bite-sized pieces.

The table went silent, and he looked up to find both Jessie and Jedidiah watching him intently. "What?"

"You're going to eat your hamburgers with a knife and fork, too?" Jessie asked, her voice breaking with choked-back laughter.

"No," he said.

"What do you mean, too, Jessie?" Jed asked.

"It's how he eats pizza. And he also told me he eats chicken that way."

Yeah, Landon had slipped up admitting to that. "Only out in public," Landon corrected, eyes going to Jed's. "Mom."

"Oh. Yeah. Your mom is kinda like that, if I remember right."

Landon looked down. *"Sitzen?"* he asked, and Britta sat up from where she lay beside him. He put her plate down, sliding the other to Acer.

"Landon!"

He turned a look on her. Knew what was coming. "What, *Jessie?*"

She huffed at him, but didn't follow up, and he grinned. He already knew the 'what'. "Britta and Acer both deserve it. They got the bad guy."

"Bad woman," Jessie corrected.

"That whole double mask thing was weird," Jedidiah said.

Landon agreed. Took a bite of his hamburger. And, of course, he got more flack from Jessie when he got both Acer and Britta a scoop each of vanilla ice cream, him having a root beer float.

Leaving The Soda Shop, he had to admit to himself that Jessie looked happy with Jed. And Jed looked happy, too. "She looks contented, doesn't she, Britta?"

The dog just glanced his way, then jumped up in The Rhino when he opened the door. "She looks happy," he muttered.

*

"DON'T FORGET dinner tonight with Lieutenant Sherman and his mom, Jessie," Jedidiah reminded her as they headed back to the car, Acer bumping along at her knee between Jed and her. They were taking the long way around since Northridge P.D. had the alley blocked.

Everything with Jed was breakfast, lunch, or dinner. Or a horseback ride, maybe. They'd gone on one of those on Sunday last ...and it had been okay. Her dogs had approved, even little Duchess, who got to ride, not in her carry pouch, but laying on Jessie's lap most of the way, harness tethered to Jessie's belt.

Jed seemed to think that Jessie had all this free time, though she kept reminding him she didn't. "You know that I don't go out except sometimes on Saturday night, then Sunday afternoons, Jed ...unless we're out on a SAR op. And when I'm not out on a search, I've got dogs to train. And tonight and every weeknight, I hit the shooting range with Dad and Landon as soon after five now as possible."

"I know. I know. In bed by eight, up at 3:30 in the AM, and it's train, train, train. When is fun time?"

"I'm sleeping in till almost four, now. And dogs and running *is* fun time for me. I told you. Dogs are my life."

"There's more to living than work, running, shooting, and dogs, Jessie."

"Not for me."

He turned on her, his dark eyes smiling down into hers, something that unnerved her. Jed had one of those magnetic personalities that made people melt to his will. "I'm going to change that," he said.

"We've had this discussion. Remember, Jed?"

And he repeated himself, voice going even softer: "I'm going to change that."

***

D. L. Keur

52

6 – No Reprieve

TIDYING UP his desk, Landon thought he was done for the afternoon, his goal being to make it to the shooting range before Oli and Jessie Anderson. After that, Sol and he would head home, fix dinner, do chores, then he'd settle down to do his workout, a game of chess against Sol to end the day.

He got a call from Harvey Mueller, the town of Northridge's chief of police. "Need to transfer our newest prisoner to your facility," the man said.

Landon frowned. "The woman who robbed the sporting goods shop?"

"That's the one."

"I thought you said you were keeping her overnight."

"Was, but, now, ah, no. Can't. She's being ...ah ...difficult."

"Explain 'difficult', please, Harvey."

"She ...and she's ...well, she's sort of a she. Got most of the right parts, according to ...never mind. But she says she identifies as a 'he'."

Landon quelled his urge to huff out an exasperated sigh. He'd made a contingency for this based on troubles in other places around the U.S., but he'd never thought he'd have to use it in Bitterroot County. At least he hadn't so far in his year-and-nine-plus months in office. Rainbowers didn't tend toward violence or felonious pursuits ...except for, maybe, using weed. At least not in his county. But, then, they didn't have that many of them here. He knew of four adults and six kids, most of whom were doing it because it was popular to be one. "All right. Will you transport, or should I send deputies?"

"Captain Compton and another officer are en route. They just left."

"All right. I'll call the jail and warn them they're incoming."

"She's a handful, Reid."

"Right."

And, of course, his captain in charge of the jail was also not pleased. Landon went over there and waited for Compton and company to appear ...which took a bit longer than what Landon thought it should. He found out why once they finally pulled in, both Compton and the woman officer with him looking a bit worse for wear.

"She laid over and started kicking at us," Compton said as Landon's deputies went to get the prisoner out of the vehicle …or tried to. The woman was anything but compliant.

"Watch out," Compton said. "She bites, too."

"HE!" the prisoner screamed.

Landon stepped away. So did Compton and the other Northridge officer. "Why didn't you shackle her up?" Landon asked, getting a little ticked. Compton was an old hand. He knew better than this. Or should.

"Didn't think it necessary."

Landon rolled eyes toward. Didn't say what he thought. But, then, as much problem as the woman was giving his deputies just trying to get her out of the sedan, Landon doubted that shackling her normally would have done much good anyway, especially without a cage …which Compton's unit didn't have installed. "Should have trussed her up like a turkey," he said to Dirk.

"Chief doesn't want the hassle of the ACLU coming after him. Women, even those like this one who identify as men, *can* be pregnant, and shackling pregnant women is hotly debated now."

"Well, let's see. They can alley fight, mud wrestle, ride horses and motorcycles, even enter MMA bouts when they're in the family way, but they're too fragile to be slapped in irons? I don't buy it, Dirk. It's an excuse to avoid consequences, and it's used every time it's convenient to get them out of something they don't like."

Dirk actually chuckled. Sobered just as fast. "Shackling her like you're talking about so she couldn't move, that would *really* get them going, Reid."

"Even when they're violent?!" Landon came back, voice heavy with sarcasm.

But Dirk seemed to either miss it or dismiss it. "Even then," he replied.

"Well, not in Idaho. If it's ever a question, we have plenty of evidence to support our use of them and prove that it's to protect them from themselves as well as protect everybody else. Best, though, would be locking up the folks objecting to the practice with some of those violent offenders they're going to bat for and see how they feel after they get hurt, maimed, or killed by them."

"They'd still make some excuse."

Not if they're dead. But, in fact, Landon knew that, especially in some jurisdictions, what Dirk said was too true. He was glad he didn't live or work there ...*wouldn't* live or work there.

"Where are you putting our Jane Doe who says she identifies as a he?" Dirk asked. "Just curious."

"You still don't have an ID on her, then?"

"No."

"Well, biologically, she's a female, so she goes on the woman's side, but in solitary. We're doing it 'PC'—protective custody."

"Tried that. She pitched a fit."

"Let her. We'll hand out foam earplugs to everybody. Then, she can scream to her heart's content."

"Well, good luck," Compton said, now that the deputies had successfully extracted the struggling prisoner from the back of Compton's unit.

"Thanks."

*

"WHERE'S LANDON, Dad?" Jessie asked when he pulled in his last target, his shots center bullseye, every one.

Her dad turned around, pulled off his ear protection, and grinned, his blue eyes happy. "He called. He's running late because of a problem prisoner intake or something like that," Oli said.

"Oh."

"Said he was on his way."

"Too bad," she said, grinning back. I love it when he's got to suffer demerits. Let's me beat him easy."

"Be nice."

"I am. You should have *seen* him and Britta in action today. Showed up just in time. I was not prepared for a perp to come around the corner and ram right into me and Jed."

Her dad's mien changed just that fast. "What do you mean, Jessie?"

Uh-oh. Shouldn't have said that. Now, he's going to put me through worse training on the mat. "What I meant was that Landon did his hero thing again, and just in time. Acer went into action, but I didn't have cuffs on me. The woman …who looked like a guy—no boobs—wasn't particularly strong, but, well, she wasn't easy, either. Got her sort of under control using a leash and leverage, but, between Acer, me, and Jed, it was all we could do to control her without breaking something. Then your best bud and Britta showed up. That tipped things in our favor."

"One of my best buds, Jessie."

"Yeah." She started setting up. "Anyway, I found out Jed isn't the best when it comes to hand-to-hand situ-s."

"He's a knife fighter, Jessie."

Shocked, she turned on her dad and just stared. "What did you say?"

"He's a knife fighter. Look at the way he moves."

"You're sure."

"Yes."

She watched her dad's eyes, so steady on hers, so sure. "…I didn't have a clue."

"I know."

"I'm here," Landon said, walking up and sounding slightly out of breath.

Jessie turned to him. Grinned. "You're late, Landon."

"I know. Sorry."

She calculated …wanted to tease him sooo bad. Did, but just a tiny bit. "Don't do it again!"

"All right, you two. Fifty push-ups. Now," Oli said, pointing at the floor."

Landon looked askance. "Really?"

Oli nodded. "Get on it."

"I'm in unifo—"

Oli jabbed a finger at the floor. "Now!"

*

"SLOW YOUR HEART rate down," Oli said as, push-ups done, Oli ordered both Landon and Jessie to pull their weapons and fire. And, of *course*, neither of them was as accurate as usual. But they both were hitting inside the sevens and eights.

"On the exhale. Slo-ooow …your …heart …rate …way …down. You can do it."

Not without being some sort of East Indian yoga expert, was Landon's thought.

"Slow your exhale," Oli repeated over and over, his voice measured.

And, after a couple of commands to, it actually started to work for Landon as Oli counted shots, Oli telling them when to fire in a steady rhythm, rather than his usual irregular one.

Then he had them do it again—this time, forty push-ups, then immediately fire twenty rounds. Then thirty, where Oli stuck, having them do it over and over.

Landon was flagging after the sixth series. So was Jessie. Landon wanted to beg reprieve, but a glance at Oli showed him no deal. The man was as hard as he'd ever seen.

"And again," Oli said, his voice calm, but resolute. "Thirty push-ups, then fire on command."

There would be no reprieve. *What's set him off?* Landon wondered. It had to be something Jessie did …or didn't do, was his guess, but they both got to suffer the punishment.

***

7 – Go!

FLYING HOME at over the speed limit, Jessie barely had time to feed her dogs, then shower and dress before Jedidiah arrived. She managed, but just. Then it was off to The Hereford, which, they discovered, was busy tonight. That was strange for the last Monday in October, but the countryside around the Bitterroots was in high color, the mountains above already blanketed in snow—very picturesque—so fall color visitors could explain the crowd. "A lot of out-of-state license plates," Jessie mentioned. They were mostly from Arizona and California. A few from Nevada and Utah.

Jedidiah chuckled. "You notice stuff like that. I didn't even see it."

"It's part of being an ex-cop, I guess," Jessie said.

"You're not an ex-cop, though. You're a full-on cop."

That was true …though Jessie didn't think of herself as one. "I'm a Special Deputy, Search and Rescue, not really a cop, Jedidiah."

"If you say so." Again, he chuckled. "Think you'll ever quit?"

"Search and Rescue?"

"I know you won't ever quit that, no. Being a cop."

Jessie didn't want to wear a badge anymore. She'd never have thought she'd be back in one—ever again—but here she was. Landon, with his tricks, was responsible for that. "I don't know. I guess I take it one day at a time."

"That's how I take what life throws at me, too."

"What do you do, Jedidiah?"

He shrugged. "Keep the family holdings in order and on track, mostly. And play with the horses."

"What does keeping the family holdings entail?" And Jessie was all ears, because, honestly, she had no idea what Jedidiah did for a living …or if he had to do anything at all. She knew he had a master's degree from Harvard in business, but there was nothing in her snooping that indicated he held a job.

"Watching our investments, mostly," he said.

"The stock market?"

"That, plus," he said, getting out.

'Plus what?' she wanted to ask. She didn't get the chance to pursue the question, though. Tank Sherman and his mom were making their way toward the restaurant's front door. Jedidiah and she rushed to catch up with them.

*

"THAT WAS A *TOUGH* session, Oli," Landon told his taskmaster as they sat in the shooting range's cafeteria sipping pop and munching nachos and cheese. "What set you off tonight?"

The man chuckled. Shook his head. "It's time you and Jessie both step up to the next level."

That hadn't answered his question. Oli had just deflected. "I'll repeat my question. What set you off tonight?"

The head dropped and didn't lift for long seconds. When the face did raise, the eyes were bright and hard. "Jessie is the future of Anderson Working Dogs."

Landon knew that.

"Things are getting serious between her and Jedidiah Blackthorne."

Landon sat back. Swallowed. Reached to touch Britta, who sat beside his chair. What did he say? ...*The truth.* "I didn't even know they were going out until today, Oli. She just met him, what, three weeks ago, maybe?"

"Something like that. Maybe four. And he asked her out but a couple of days after that. And she went. And has been going more and more ever since."

Landon was listening. Carefully. Heard, not just irritation, but something else in the tone underlying Oli's words. Said what next his mouth decided to: "Jedidiah isn't a fast mover, Oli. Never has been. He pretty much shuns people except for a scant few ...like Tucker Rohrbache. Jim Stanton. Sometimes me, though we rarely get the chance now with my job. And, of course, Shane Bremmers. Jed prefers horses. When it comes to dating, he's always been a 'one date, move on' kind of guy."

A frown came down, Oli's eyes dead-reckoning. "You say that, but he's been nothing but underfoot since the first time he asked her out. And Jessie's never taken an interest in anyone. *Never.* ...Until now."

"And you don't like it," Landon said, speaking the obvious.

"I think he's a good guy. But I am worried. I can't afford for her to suddenly decide she's a woman."

Landon double-blinked at that. "But she *is* a woman, Oli."

The man's eyes rolled to his. "She's my daughter."

Landon's phone chimed, saving him. He read the message. Sighed.

"You have to go?"

He shook his head. "No. But our newest lockup is causing issues. It's going to wind up with her put in restraints in a padded cell, and that's not going to go down well with her public defender or the human rights people."

"What's she doing?"

"Trying to kill herself. Used her jumpsuit to try to choke herself."

"Wow. What's wrong with people today?"

"She's just a kid, Oli. Barely out of high school is my guess. Maybe twenty, at most?"

"Maybe she's suffering a mental condition."

"Possible. We have no idea who she is. Won't tell us, and fingerprints got us nowhere. We're running her mug shot too, but no hits there either, as yet. Terri—you know Deputy Corporal Terri-the-Techi Macleod, right?"

Oli nodded. "Jessie and she are friends."

"She's running facial recognition, but she hasn't gotten hits back. Takes time to go through all the DMV and social media photos on file in the federal database. That's *if* Jane Doe has an ID, a driver's license, or an online presence. Northridge P.D. managed to get a DNA swab, but I doubt that will bring anything."

"Why isn't she cooperating?"

"I have no idea. Could just be what they term ODD."

At Oli's look, Landon said, "Oppositional Defiant Disorder, a mental health problem that comes from a combination of genetic and environmental influences. The Grierhausen case was where I first encountered it."

Oli shook his head. "Glad we don't have *that* in our family."

The man stood, and Landon helped pick up their mess, taking it up to the tray return station, Britta at heel beside him. Oli gave him a quick pound on the back. "Time to go, Cowboy. Dinner won't wait forever."

Landon smiled. "We're having leftovers tonight." Then he remembered. "Oops. I was supposed to give Sol a ride home."

"Oops," Oli repeated, giving him a grin. "Thanks for talking, Landon. Somehow, it helped."

"You're welcome …and anytime."

He packed up his own stuff, then helped Oli pack weapons, ammo, and the rest of Oli's gear out to the man's Caddy. Oli gone, he called Sol. Found out that the man was still working in his lab. "Pick you up in ten or so, depending on traffic."

"Okay."

Sol sounded distracted.

*

JEDIDIAH BLACKTHORNE was a most charming host. Jessie had to say that about a man she'd first taken for a grimy weirdo and a possible candidate for being the worst kind of criminal megalomaniac, akin to Jim Jones and Charles Manson—charismatic sociopaths. But, in fact, Jedidiah came off like one of the gentlest, kindest, most benevolent people she'd ever met. She was having a tough time reconciling what her dad had just told her with the man sitting across from her at their table.

As if aware of her thoughts, Jedidiah's dark eyes touched hers. The long, black lashes lowered a little. Then he slow-blinked. And he smiled.

She smiled back.

Yeah, she liked him. Best, her dogs liked him, and *that* she trusted most of all. Tank's mom sure liked him, too. Jed had her laughing and sharing life anecdotes within a few minutes of their appetizers arriving, and Tank had a bemused smile on his face as his mom told stories on him.

"Don't you hate when parents do that?" Jessie whispered, leaning his way.

Tank chuckled. "Can't stop them."

"I know."

"What's worst is when they get out the baby pictures. Mom actually has some of me lying naked, belly down on a fuzzy white rug!"

"Oh, I'd love to see that!"

"Not happening, Jessie."

"We'll see."

"Not happening."

*

"YOU'RE QUIET tonight," Landon said as Sol got in The Rhino, Britta jumping in back to accommodate.

"I just finished running the numbers on the damage to Homer Garrison's innards."

"You got that information back from the hospital?"

"We did."

"Is he going to be all right?"

"His heart converted while he was still in the field. He's going to be fine."

Landon nodded. He'd seen that Homer was still kicking, down-listed to stable. The man was still undergoing tests at Landon's last check on things. He did not envy the man what was coming from the medicos.

"Garrison was shot from only some five feet away …which matches the evidence at the scene and on his clothes, which the hospital sent over."

"That close, huh?"

"That close. And there's evidence that a gun muzzle was stuck right up on his chest, the ring it produced identical in every measurement to something called a Charper Pro 2. That happened *after* the paint was already on Mr. Garrison. I also think the gun …or 'marker', as they seem to call them, wasn't industry standard. It took me a while to figure that out …because the numbers just weren't working."

"Did you use the computer?"

"No. I used my brain, a piece of paper, and a pencil. Anyway, even at point-blank range, it shouldn't have done that kind of damage to Homer Garrison. I'm just glad it wasn't a real gun."

"A paintball rifle is a real gun. It fires a high-velocity object."

"Yeah, but a bullet shot at that range probably would have gone through Mr. Garrison completely. Instead, it just bruised his heart, liver, and, well, his thoracic area in general. He was lucky Jessie was there."

"Lucky," Landon muttered. "I don't think he was lucky, at all. He got shot."

"Well," Sol said, his voice brightening. "He wasn't as lucky as Jessie when she got shot in Blaine, and he definitely wasn't as lucky as you when you got shot in the butt, that's true."

Landon shook his head. Groaned. Finally said, "You know, Sol, sometimes private information should stay private."

The man turned a quizzical look on him. "I visited Jessie in the hospital after it happened. She told me all about it."

"Fine."

"And yours is part of the Grierhausen case."

Landon knew that, thank you. He'd been there, Sol hadn't, and Landon still had the painful-to-the-touch scar and muscle twinges to prove it.

Landon's onboard bleeped, the screen going live. "Audio, please, Computer."

"Injury incident, 28778 East Raleigh Road. Neighbor on scene, Deputy David Long en route.

Ambulance dispatched. Single gunshot to the throat to one Richard Raymond Orr, twenty-eight-year-old male."

Bullet to the throat—that meant dead.

"Matthew Orr, six, son of Richard, plus one dog were thought to be in the vehicle and are assumed missing and possibly abducted."

Oh, no!

"Dog is reportedly a large, pitbull type. Deputy Long requesting CSI assist. Special Deputy Captain Nelson Remmers requesting Special Deputy Anderson and her dogs take it."

*

HER PHONE erupted. Remmers …and Dispatch. "I've got to go," Jessie said, excusing herself.

"Let me pay for this all, and I'll be right with you," Jedidiah said, getting up.

"No. A deputy is on his way," Jessie told him.

Jedidiah gave her an odd look. Then, "Be careful, Jessie."

She raised a hand, turned, and headed for the door, dodging customers and wait staff. Outside, the

S.O. unit was just pulling in. It flashed its lights at her. Came to a stop.

She climbed in, slammed the door. Said, "Go!" as she grabbed the seat belt.

***

8 – HADAR

JESSIE'S DAD met her at the intersection of Highway 95 and East Raleigh Road as agreed during a quick phone home. He had her dogs, plus all of his, in her XV, the dogs already geared up in their radio collars and Kevlar®. And the dogs were hyped, already panting and bouncing up and down, tails up and going.

"You're coming?" she asked, jumping out of the deputy's unit and getting in the passenger side when her dad motioned her to. Jessie was surprised that her dad was sticking with her and not getting a ride back home with the deputy.

"I am. I called Landon, and he gave me the scoop. Clothes, boots, and heavy body armor on the passenger side floorboard."

Of course, her dad would have called Landon, right after she called Oli, begging her dad to meet her with the XV and the dogs. "Okay, thanks."

The deputy tore off around them and, lights blazing, preceded them down the East Raleigh county road as her dad put it in gear. Jessie changed from pants suit and heels into work clothes, body armor, and boots. Hit the button that exposed the onboard.

Turned it on. Turned on the radio, too. Listened to chatter as she read through the known facts. Shook her head. "Bad country. Lots of hazards. Six-year-old missing kid, a boy." Turned to her dogs. "You ready?"

Milo stuck his nose in her face, tail-wagging-dog as said tail thumped against the window beside him as well as her other dogs who crowded close. Queenie blew happy dog cheek bulges, the rest all ready to go and enthused, as well—her wonder mutts. "Got a bad one, guys and gals."

More tail wagging with accompanying thumps.

*

LANDON WATCHED as they loaded the man into the ambulance. Amazingly, he was alive. Deputy Long had been within a mile when the call came, had gotten there and done an emergency tracheotomy using his pen. And the man hadn't been shot, not shot with a bullet, anyway. Just like Homer Garrison, he'd been shot by a paintball. Whether his brain had suffered irreparable damage from lack of oxygen was the question.

"Shot at almost point-blank range, the paramedics say," Sol said, coming over. "Crushed larynx. I'm guessing that Mr. Orr came home and surprised a burglar."

"How do you know this?"

"Mr. Orr's driver's side door is open. The garage door is up, garage side access door broken. That, along with the nature and disposition of the footprints, tells me that this wasn't a calculated attack. Garage looks ransacked. I'm guessing the burglar was looking to snag the expensive toy guns Orr has. Mr. Orr is himself a tournament-level paintball enthusiast."

This last piece of news Landon's deputies now on scene had already reported. So, a burglary in progress, the thief surprised, maybe, when Richard Orr opened the garage door. He frowned. Garrison, then the Northridge robbery. Now this. *Paintball, again. Not happenstance.*

"Footwear on the suspect looks like the same as we cast up at the Garrison scene, only a lot narrower. These footprints are smaller by about two sizes," Sol replied, not even pausing. "I'm guessing a woman's foot, by the shape, length, width, and estimated weight."

"How can you tell that?"

"That rainstorm we got two nights ago? The dirt drive—can you say mud?—gave us some good impressions."

Landon had meant, how did Sol know it was a woman's footprint? *Men can be slight and have small, narrow feet, too.*

The growl of a big engine and the crunch of gravel…. Landon turned to look. Jessie was here. So was her father. He gave them a nod.

*

"OF COURSE, Landon's on scene!" Jessie groaned.

Her dad chuckled. "In all our twenty years of living here, I have never seen a more conscientious effort by a public servant."

"Yeah, but you only had his dad, Clyde, to compare Landon to, right?"

Oli nodded. "True enough. Clyde did a good job of keeping the lid on things, though."

"Yeah. Through pure cussedness."

"The threat of the big stick serves its purpose, Jessie."

"Right!"—all sarcasm on purpose, but her dad just chuckled again.

Most of Jessie's irritation with Landon now was perpetuated and even exacerbated by the fact that standing right beside him was Britta, the dog that had been hers, Britta abandoning her, the pack, and Acer, for a man the dog adored for no known reason. Jessie had to admit one more time, though, that the blonde shepherd truly looked happy. Britta had found her person.

Getting out, Jessie strapped on her extra protection and weapons, then, setting her backpack on the tailgate, backed into it and anchored the chest and waist straps. Tightened everything up and watched as her dad started to get on his body armor and weapons. "You're arming up heavy?" she asked.

"We're not just looking for a missing kid, Jessie. Landon thinks there's the strong possibility that the shooter is also out there and might have the kid." Her dad handed her a helmet. "Here. Take this. *Wear* it."

"You know I hate wearing night vision goggles, much less a full helmet and face shield!"

"*Wear* it. It's a new development called HADAR."

Her dad's face read, 'brook no argument', so she gave it up and took it. "Yes, Dad."

"You can patch your phone display to it, too." He showed her.

"Okay." That would help. The thing would still interfere with her peripheral as well as lower and upper vision fields, though.

Landon approached, Britta with him, of course. The dog wagged, seeing her, but stayed at Landon's knee as Jessie braced herself for more interference.

And, sure enough, here it came: "You will wait for Deputy Hudson," Landon said, his eyes hard on hers, and, of course, her dad gave his nod of approval. "Tac Team is also en route."

Jessie toyed with the idea of sending up her drones during the wait. Time was critical in finding a lost, possibly traumatized, even injured, child. "Why do you think the shooter is out there?" Jessie asked.

"Just a gut feeling," Landon rumbled back. "Cam on, including audio, please. And set it to broadcast. Also make sure your radio is working."

Jessie agreed to do as bid.

"And, by the way, the kid has no mom. She died when he was two. So no help there."

"How's the dad?"

"Alive. At least he was when he left in the ambulance."

He motioned, and Jessie's old mentor came over. "Deputy Dr. Preston, would you go over what you know for Jessie?"

"Sure thing," Sol said, and Jessie followed her long-time friend over to the area near the scene of the incident and squatted down, studying the ground.

Sol squatted down beside her. "There, and there," he said, pointing.

"I see."

Following the sign, Jessie went over to the car, careful to avoid treading over evidence. "So, to me, it looks like the child was dragged," she said. A chill went down her back. *By whom ...or what?*

"That's what I see, too," Sol said, his voice dropping to soft.

"By the burglar or the dog, do you think, Sol?"

"I don't know. There *are* paw prints, but it's not clear what actually happened yet. Working on it."

The partial and few full paw prints Jessie saw were hit-and-miss. "Do we have any idea of the weight of the child?"

"According to his grandparents—" Sol pointed to two people being spoken to by one of the deputies on scene. "He was a little over forty-five pounds at his last doctor's visit, which was mid-September."

"That's a lot for a dog to drag."

Sol showed her a picture on his phone. "Took this of a framed picture in the house. It's a big dog."

And it was. Jessie frowned. "On the readout, it said large pitbull. That looks like a purebred Bull Mastiff. The two are distinctly different in temperament."

"Again, according to the grandparents, the dog is a rescue. Got him as a puppy when the boy, Matthew, was four. They don't know what he is. 'Just grew up to be big', and 'the dog loves the boy', is what they said."

"Bull Mastiff, I'm betting. Full or a part-blood, by the looks."

"Dog weighs over a hundred-and-fifty pounds, Jessie."

Then, it was definitely feasible that the dog could drag the kid. *Protecting the child?* That was Jessie's bet, whether pitbull or mastiff.

There was blood on and around where the drag marks suddenly stopped. The perp picked the kid up?

The blood trail continued, but no tracks were apparent as they crossed the shoddy backyard lawn to where the woods started. Jessie sucked in a long breath. Exhaled slowly. They could, in fact, be looking for a wounded or dead child. "Okay."

*

LANDON WATCHED Oli finish gearing up, his dogs, two very big German Shepherds and three Malinois sitting or downed around him. He stepped over to the man, the older Malinois, named Numa, coming up to wag and touch noses to his Britta. "You don't need to go, Oli. Tac Team is on its way."

"I need to go, Landon. I'm not letting Jessie go out there alone. If the shooter is there, and if he makes a lethal move, my dogs and I will take him out. Just warning you."

And, yes, Oli *was* warning him.

"The suspect is armed with what is probably only a paintball gun, it looks like, Oli." Then remembering the blood trail Sol had mentioned, he added, "But he or she could have a gun, too. There was a blood trail. Sol said it doesn't test as human, so we think the dog is injured."

"That paintball gun almost killed that guy who got hauled out of here, right?"

"True."

Landon thought about it. It took less than a moment to decide. "Be right back," he said, and walked over to The Rhino, got what he needed, then went back to Oli. Handed him the badge. "You're still sworn," he advised. "Emergency deputy status. Understand me?"

"I do."

"Don't use lethal force unless you absolutely have to."

"Got it."

More crunching gravel and a slamming door. Tom Hudson was here. Landon had hoped the Tac Team would have arrived by now, but they were still ten minutes out. At least, now, with Tom here, Oli would stand down. The longer they stalled the search, the worse the potential outcome.

"You got here," Oli said to the young deputy, then handed Tom a helmet similar to the one he held.

"You don't need to go now, Oli," Landon said.

The blue eyes—hard eyes—raised and locked to his. "I'm going."

Landon watched Tom fiddle with the helmet, Oli explaining things about it to him. The units were something Howie was pushing Landon to secure for the S.O., though still experimental. The way they worked, though, could be well worth the investment. How Oli had gotten his hands on some had never been revealed, but Landon was impressed by the tech.

"A word when you're done, Deputy Hudson," Landon said.

***

D. L. Keur

9 – Night Search

"ANYBODY GOT scent articles for us?" Jessie called, heading back to the front yard.

Deputy Long walked over. "I got these," he said. He held out bags containing a pair of dirty underwear, another with dirty socks, and one last with some beat-up shoes.

"Thanks," Jessie said, taking them all. "Good going on the emergency trach job."

"I never want to do *that* again."

"Yeah. It's scary. You 'done good'."

He grinned at her 'mangle-ish', stress still making his face muscles twitch. "Thanks."

Jessie touched her camera on, including audio. Set it to broadcast as well as record. Made sure her radio was working. Called her dogs as Tom and her dad trotted up, Numa at his side, prowlers bounding around.

"Find it. *Such*," Jessie said, her voice light, encouraging, even happy-sounding, this after having opened the scent bags and let her pack sniff their fill. And Jessie's 'happiness' was real. It had to be …for her dogs' sakes. They needed their person confident and absolutely sure of a happy ending. It couldn't be 'fake', and Jessie had a special technique she used to put herself in a genuine place of mental cheeriness by remembering their best successes, her with her wonder mutts—the happy, non-traumatic rescues they had accomplished together.

Jessie's dogs now backed up and turned to start fanning out, their noses working, sifting air currents. Then, they started to cast, scenting both ground and air, moving from near where Jessie stood beside the pathway of the apparent drag sign, Sol having given his go-ahead for the dogs to violate that part of the crime scene.

Her dad held his dogs back, those dogs sitting around him, waiting until the SAR pack began to move. The prowlers' jobs were not to seek the child. Highly trained fugitive apprehension and attack dogs, their specific task was to protect the SAR pack and the humans in situations like this. Only if 'sent' would the prowlers take down a target.

At home, Oli and Jessie put the dogs through this scenario maybe about once a month now, but only just enough to check that the dogs maintained their self-developed coordination, a coordination that the two packs had employed during a search for a missing marathoner discovered to have been abducted. The dogs had worked out this strategy themselves, and, after showing her dad the cam of that search, her dad had become a whole-hearted proponent of Jessie's mindset when it came to dogs—dogs knew their jobs best ...at least intelligent dogs did, dogs that had been schooled, but not trained into robots, dogs whose bodies, brains, and temperaments hadn't been ruined by bad handling and bad selective breeding.

It had been a huge turning point in Jessie's long campaign to win her dad and granddad over to her theories about dogs and their innate skills, plus to her pack training techniques. It had been a personal breakthrough for her with her dad and was paying big dividends for training Anderson Working Dogs. Even Darby, Jessie's granddad, had been won over, which was nigh on, in Jessie's opinion, an impossible feat. But she was grateful ...for the dogs they raised and trained.

No longer was implicit command obedience the rule. Now, it was communication and request—a willing partnership and understanding between human and dog, each respecting each other's skills and contributions.

"*Such*. Find it," Jessie urged again, then put on the helmet her dad had given her to wear and turned it on.

Night turned to day—a bright, hyper-colored 'day'. Jessie's brain balked …but, after a moment, she adjusted to it. She brought her wrist with its strapped-on phone near the helmet face, pressed the connect, and an inset appeared, showing her phone's display in a translucent overlay. She took off as her dogs did, her dad beside her, the prowlers leaping to join her wonder dogs as they headed into the woods behind the garage.

*

LANDON WATCHED the dogs disappear into the forest, Jessie, Oli, and Deputy Tom Hudson with them. And he fretted. Located in the low foothills of the Bitterroots, this area was known for some treacherous terrain that could surprise the unwary. Landon had ridden it horseback. He knew this country, and he was glad that Oli had shared the HADAR helmets. "Please, no broken legs or worse," he grumbled.

"What?" Sol said, coming up beside him.

Landon shook his head. "This area. It's a worry. It might not be that steep, but it's rough country to travel if you're moving faster than slow. A lot of ground disturbances and obstacles."

"And Jessie never goes slow on a search, so you're concerned. Got it," Sol said, the seemingly ever-present grin broadening. "Good thing Jessie knows what she's doing, then, right?"

Landon groaned, then squatted down to share the tracking app he was watching on his phone with the short-statured man. "She's going full out, Sol."

*

MILO IN THE LEAD, the dogs were in a closed arrow formation, ranging around a single, direct-line track, the fastest ahead, the slower behind. The speed with which the dogs were taking the search indicated strong traces of the target. That meant one thing to Jessie. The kid had been really stressed, his adrenals kicking hard.

Jessie set a fast pace, pushing it more than she usually did with Tom or when training with her dad. And both of them stayed with her. And now she blessed the HADAR helmet. The terrain was a series of trip-falls with pits and lifts, downed trees, exposed roots and rock, plus sudden drop-offs. They weren't steep or deep, but they weren't easily predictable and were enough of a hazard that breaking a leg or even a neck could be the result if you failed to see them, and, at the speed the dogs were traveling, Jessie was pushing hard, not quite long-sprinting, but just under. Milo was getting farther and farther ahead, Mitch with him. He was out a half a mile and pulling away.

Dodging through the tree cover, clambering over the outcroppings, Jessie paced her breathing, maintaining an even rhythm, despite being forced by the terrain to irregular strides and footfalls.

Behind her, Jessie heard somebody go down. She slowed and stopped. Looked. It had been Tom, but he was back up and running strong right at her, her dad with his Malinois, Numa, beside him.

An odd shift, then audio chatter:

Oli—"You okay?"

Tom—"Roger that."

Then the helmet went silent again, the sensation like someone had closed something off, making a sudden sensation of claustrophobia. *I hate helmets.* She loved being able to see in the dark, though. *Worth it.*

Jessie took off again as they closed, but kept it slower. No sense having injuries to the rescue team. And the terrain was getting rockier, the trees more mature, the branch hazards as well as ground hazards increasing. They were three-quarters-of-a-mile out, now.

Milo's deep-voiced woof, but quieter than usual.... Mitch didn't audibilize. That was different. Both dogs had stopped, and so had one of her dad's prowlers—Wolfy.

Seconds later, the rest of her pack, plus the three other prowlers, caught up, the icons indicating the dogs all clumping up. *What's happening?*

A branch caught her, glancing across the helmet, and she almost went down herself, but managed not to. *Stupid. Pay attention to where you're going!*

The dogs were a quarter of a mile away, a two-minute run on good, level ground, maybe three or more in this terrain. Jessie so much wanted to kick up the pace. Didn't.

*

"SHERIFF, Sir?"

Landon turned to Howie's voice, his Tac Team captain, Captain Howard West, fully geared up. "The dogs just reached target …I think," Landon told him.

"Any sign of the perp?"

"Not that I know of. Both Jessie and Tom have their cams going with audio on."

"I know. I'm monitoring, too. Thanks for that. Is that Oli Anderson out there, too?"

"It is."

"Deploying," Howie said, and turned to signal his team.

Landon frowned.   More and more, law enforcement, even in the Bitterroot, seemed like a military op …even to the jargon. That bothered Landon. *It shouldn't be like this. Not in America.* Technology was the reason …and more informed and skilled criminals, never mind weaponry. When would it stop? And he already knew that answer, too: *Never. Not until the end of the modern world as we know it.*

The icons indicating Jessie, Oli, and Tom Hudson were now closing on the SAR dog packs' position. Behind them, Howie and his team were hustling, but they had a ways to catch up.

"Second ambulance is here," Deputy Long said, coming up on him.

"Thank you, Deputy. And thank you for your service. You saved a man's life today."

"Thank you, sir."

*

ON HER HEADS UP display, Jessie watched a shift in the icons that identified the dogs, her dad's prowlers moving to surround hers—defensive positioning. Except for Milo. Mitch, however, had retreated from Milo's side, and that was unusual. More icons now moved in far behind on the tracking app. Whoever they were had connected their transponders. She guessed the S.O.'s Tac Team was on the move. *Go, Howie!*

Milo was stock still, standing ground, Wolfy just behind and off his flank. This was *not* normal—not at all. What had they found, Jessie's worst fear being that the shooter had the kid?

Stretching stride, she honed her attention to the ground she traveled. Paced her breathing to slower and deeper. She needed to oxygenate in case of an emergency encounter with the shooter.

Her fingers touched one of her SIGs, the one on her right hip. And she was glad for both Tom and her dad being there. She was doubly glad for her new body armor laid over her standard Kevlar®—the new foam stuff.

Light and made of a metallic foam composite developed by a North Carolina State University professor, the foam vest supposedly would stop a high caliber round, disintegrating bullets that hit it. Jessie did not care to test its effectiveness, not that she had the choice. That would be all on the perp, because, just like her dad, Jessie was betting the assailant had, not just a paintball gun, but a real gun, too. *Could be a knife, though. Guess we'll see, won't we?*

***

10 – Big Dog

AT HER FATHER'S and Tom's urging, Jessie pulled up, stopping short of her dogs. Coming up beside her, Oli, his visor up, was already scanning with night-vision binoculars. So was Tom.

"I see the kid," Oli whispered. "I see the dog—big—and, yes, he looks like a mastiff. The dog's laying down, the kid beside him. Get your eyes used to the dark, people. Helmets off. Don't want to scare the kid or trigger the dog to attack."

Jessie removed her helmet—Tom already had—and had the shock hit her eyes of going from enhanced, utterly false hyper-daylight to all but blind in the dark. She fumbled in her pack's side pocket for her binoculars, switched them on, switched them to IR, and looked, too. She saw the forms of both a kid and a dog.

"I don't see anybody else," Tom whispered.

"All right. Let's move out," Oli muttered after about four more minutes to get their eyes somewhat acclimated to the faint moonlight they had. "Keep it slow, quiet, and careful," he ordered.

Clipping the big, but surprisingly light helmet to her med pack, the pack's weight heavy on her sweating back, Jessie accepted a hand up from Tom. "Thanks."

Pulling up their headlamps from where they were slung around their necks, they kept them off as they moved toward the boy's position, Jessie's dogs wagging as they approached.

Jessie put her hands out, touching the heads and backs of her wonder mutts. "My good, good dogs," she murmured. "My good, good dogs. Down-*Platz*"—the English and the German for both the English-trained and the German-trained, though all the dogs now recognized both. "Stay-*bleib*."

The dogs obeyed.

Reaching Milo, who turned his head toward her just slightly as she came next to him, she called, "Matthew?"

Jessie called the boy's name softly. Then, "We're here to help you, Matthew. I'm Jessie, a deputy with the Sheriff's Office, Search and Rescue. This is Deputy Tom Hudson and Oli, my dad." Then she repeated, "We're here to help."

She got within twenty feet, Milo creeping forward with her, her dad beside, Tom just behind, flanking.

Then the mastiff shifted, and Jessie heard a low growl. Stopped. "Matthew?"

No answer.

Touched her radio. "Landon? What's the dog's name?"

*

"LANDON, WHAT'S the dog's name?"—Jessie's voice.

Ah.... He had no idea! "Deputy Long? Do you have a name for the dog?"

"Grandparents said the dog is called 'Brown', sir."

Landon relayed that.

Jessie: "Thank you."

*

"BROWN?" Jessie called, then eased forward a small step.

Again, a low growl.

"Jessie, let me try," Oli said. "I bet he's used to men." And, to her dad's voice, him trying English

101

first, then German, the dog's ears relaxed some at the German command to *kommen Sie hier*, but he didn't move. And that's when Matthew finally spoke—"My dog. He's hurt. Bad."

*

"WHERE'S OUR paramedic ground team?" Landon barked to Dispatch.

"Five minutes out, sir." *Get here, get here.* "They'll need two baskets, one for a dog. Relay that."

"A dog, sir?"

"A dog. The boy's dog."

"Yes, sir. I'm not sure they can do that, sir."

"They'll do it."

"Yes, sir."

*

"ARE YOU HURT, Matthew?" Jessie asked. They'd had a breakthrough. Jessie breathed a little easier as soon as the boy said, "No. Not really. Just scared. My dad...."

"Your dad is on his way to the hospital. He's going to be okay,"...which Jessie didn't know for sure, but you didn't tell a traumatized child that. "He's going to be so happy to know we found you."

"He was shot."

"I know."

"Brown is shot, too, but by a real gun."

So, they'd been right. The perp had a gun. "Okay. Can we come there?"

Finally, the boy said, "Yes," and both Jessie and her dad approached …slowly, ever so slowly, the boy standing next to the downed dog, the small hand stroking the big head.

Checking out the child while her dad got the dog used to him, Jessie found the boy uninjured except for a scrape to his forehead and a cut on his hand.

"Dog's friendly, Jessie, but in a lot of pain. Looks like the hind leg."

"Matthew, can you ask Brown if I can look at him."

The boy nodded. Went back to the dog and squatted down to run his face into the big animal's neck. "My Brown-Brown. Let them help, okay?"

A grumble.

Jessie eased in, gave the dog her scent ...which he ignored, then slipped sideways toward the wounded hind leg. "Dog has been shot, Dad. By a bullet, not a paintball. Small entry and exit. Bones are fine, and bleeding has stopped."

Jessie pulled an ampoule of ketamine out. Sighed. The dose was right for a one-hundred-pound person. Did she dare? "Brown? I'm going to give you a shot, okay?"

"Jessie?!"

"Dad, it will be fine. Just get the boy, please."

Easing off her pack, she waited till Oli got the child out of range. Then, ready to move, with one quick jab, delivered the dose, starting sympathy sounds and encouragement as she did.

The dog's head came around, but he didn't move much. And his eyes read suffering. "It's okay, Brown. You're going to be okay. You did awesome. You kept Matthew safe. You're a hero."

The dog moaned, then, within minutes, lay his head down and sighed. The painkiller had kicked in.

"Good, good dog," Jessie murmured.

Looked up ...to find her dad, Tom Hudson, Captain Howard West, and eight other Tac Team members standing there watching her. She hadn't even been aware of their arrival. *Great awareness!* she scolded herself.

***

D. L. Keur

11 – Saving Brown

THE BOY wouldn't leave his dog—Landon watched that through Jessie's and Tom's live cam feeds. And he hoped. He didn't want to have to step in if he didn't have to. The fact that the boy was adamant and getting upset, that forced the paramedic ground team's hand before Landon had to. Without further fuss, they loaded the boy into the basket, the boy coaxing in the dog, who managed to get himself up and in, despite his weakened condition.

Jessie helping, they strapped the two secure, the dog allowing it. With the two onboard, the basket weighed no more than a good-sized adult man—easy transport for the three-man and one-woman team. "Who's going to help us with the dog when we get to the unit?" one of the paramedics asked.

"I'm coming with," Landon heard Jessie say.

"Good girl," he muttered. Now, where was Oli?

With Howie and company, he found out on the ask. The prowlers had a human scent line and were on track. "Blood trail," Howie told him in a huffing whisper.

"Be careful," he muttered, and sent a prayer heavenward. Landon hated these situations.

Beside him, Britta got up and started to wag, ears snapped forward.

"Teams are incoming," a deputy near him said. Landon turned to look at the speaker—a big woman, her rifle angled down in her hands—one of his babysitters assigned by Howie. This was one of those women whom Landon never wanted to rile. She was like something out of the Norse legends, hard-jawed and muscular with a deadly humorous glint to her eye. *Nope. Stay on her good side. Always.*

She pointed. He looked. Sure enough, he thought he saw movement in the dark by the light of their partial moon—mostly because of Milo's big white patches of hide.

"Load the dog in my XV," Landon heard Jessie say, and headed over there to help, his babysitter tagging along.

*

GETTING TO her XV, Jessie put up a barrier, snapping it into place. The paramedics held the basket, and, coaxing, she actually got the dog to get himself into the rig all by himself. "Such a good dog, Brown. Thank you."

The dog groaned and laid himself down, then actually rolled onto his side. He was not in a good way. *Probably blood loss*, was Jessie's guess.

"I want to ride with you," Matthew said.

Jessie knew that wasn't happening.

"Let's get you checked out," a paramedic named Kyle said. "Come on."

"I'm going to take Brown to a vet," Jessie assured the kid.

"Dr. Caldwell," the kid said. "She's his vet."

Oh, good! "She's my dogs' vet, too," Jessie told him, nodding. "He's going to be okay,"—also something of which she wasn't sure. "Meanwhile, you get to ride in an ambulance and go see your dad, okay?"

Matthew didn't answer. Just looked like he was about to cry. "Don't let her kill my dog."

"I won't let anybody kill your dog, Matthew."

"Promise?"

And, despite not knowing if it was a lie, Jessie promised.

*

THE AMBULANCE transporting the kid pulled out.
Jessie pulled out right after. Landon got back in The
Rhino, watching cam live streams. His babysitter
…and he was surprised he only had one, where
usually Howie sent two, stood outside until he invited
her to sit in the unit with him. She wasn't the
friendliest, but then she was new. They hadn't
bumped into one another very often …except in
times like these. He remembered pinning a badge on
her, he remembered she was ex-military, but that's all
he knew, except her name—Amy Vandertil. *Time to
familiarize myself with new faces*, he told himself.

"What's that, sir?" the deputy said, her finger
pointing to something on the cam feed.

Landon looked. Didn't see anything significant.
"What did you see, Deputy?"

"I thought I saw a shadow move."

Pretty much everything was shadow, though.

Landon got the computer to put up another
instance of that feed, then had it back the duplicate up
several minutes before replaying.

"There," the woman said again.

And, this time, Landon saw it. It was one of Oli's prowlers. "Good eye, Deputy."

"That's a big dog," she said.

"Yeah. They are. And very good at what they do."

*

FINALLY UNDERWAY, her dogs' attention on Brown, who lay too quiet in the back, Jessie called Kathy, her vet. "I'll see you when you get here," Kathy told her.

Jessie took the back way—the shortest distance possible by road between two points—and was rewarded with a fifteen, instead of twenty-five, minute drive. By the time she got to the clinic, Brown was extremely lethargic. Jessie, Kathy, and her husband got the dog loaded on a stretcher and into the treatment area.

"He's crashing," Kathy said. "He needs blood fast. I've got synthetic—"

"Milo. Acer. They're almost his size, and they have the same blood type."

Kathy turned to watch her. "You're sure you want to do that?"

"You told me a dog could take a blood transfusion from any other dog, any blood type, the very first time they have to be transfused. After that, no. Is that still true?"

Kathy nodded. "That wasn't what I was asking."

Jessie knew that. "Then, let's do it."

Milo, of course, who, though bigger than Brown, weighed twenty-pounds less, was a dream. Acer wasn't quite as go-along-get-along. Between the two dogs, though, they got enough on a dog-to-dog transfuse that Brown's BP came up, and his heart rate and breathing stabilized.

Kathy hooked up IV drips on Acer and Milo, plus gave them injections. "I could top them off with synthetics, if you want, Jessie?"

"Recovery without?"

"About a day."

"Then, let's just pretend they're like me when I give blood—wimpy for a couple of days. I'll just leave them home if we get a call out."

"They won't be happy about that."

"No, but they'll do it."

"I've got to get Brown into surgery and repair what I can," Kathy said. "Can you tech for me?"

"I can, but I'm not trained."

"You'll do fine."

An hour-and-a-half later, Kathy had repaired the nick to the caudal branch of the lateral saphenous vein, as well as reconnected a minor branching of the same. "He is so lucky," Kathy said.

"He's lucky you're a surgeon and know your stuff," Jessie agreed. "I'm not sure how lucky it is to get shot, though. I've only been shot once—a flesh wound—and it was not fun. Getting shot by an arrow was no fun, either."

"Comparatively speaking, he was lucky," Kathy came back. Then, she tipped her head. "Frankly, I'm surprised he lost that much blood."

"He dragged a fifty-pound kid for a good fifty feet, then herded or hazed that kid almost a mile to safety, all the while bleeding."

Kathy nodded. "That explains it, then."

Jessie watched Kathy get the dog comfortable, then check the IV drip. "He's going to be here a couple of days," Kathy told her.

"As long as he survives. I don't think Matthew could handle losing him right now."

"That boy does love this dog," Kathy said, smiling. "And this dog loves that boy."

"I'm going to take a couple of snaps of Brown for him, okay?"

"You bet. Take a video, in fact. That way, Matthew knows he's breathing."

"Okay. Oh, and I may have to kennel him, because Matthew's dad got injured, too."

"I figured something had happened. I'll keep him here. Brown knows this place. Stays when they take a weekend trip."

"Sounds good. Thanks."

"Thanks for caring," Kathy said. "Really."

"Hey, it's a dog. Of *course,* I care. Humans?" Jessie grinned. Shrugged. "Eh!"

"Not true."

"Shhh. No giving away secrets."

Kathy laughed. "Then, no telling lies."

*

OLI'S PROWLERS came through, tracking a faint blood trail through broken terrain in heavily timbered, rolling countryside with lots of potential places for someone to hide. For Landon, it was terrifying to watch.

What they finally came upon was a maskless woman dressed all in black, her upper body wrapped in a loose-fitting, low-quality protective vest, and she was in dire trouble. Under the headlamps, she was visibly gasping for breath and had what looked like the end of a pen pinning the vest to her side, blood apparent.

One of Howie's people, who was now also a certified EMR, went to work, him on the horn with the hospital. Punctured lung was the tentative field diagnosis, and, once they got the woman stable, they transported via the same ground team as had answered before. Of course, this patient got handcuffed and leg-cuffed to the basket, something that Landon did have to step in on. Paramedics did not like their patients hog-tied—too bad. This was a law enforcement decision. A deputy—Long, again—went in the ambulance with her.

Landon got a call from Jessie moments after the ambulance pulled out. That surprised him. "The dog's leg was a through and through," she said, "but was definitely caused by a small caliber round."

"Okay. Thanks, Jessie. We found a Stinger®."

"You're welcome."

"Your dad's already gone home. I had a deputy transport him and his dogs."

"Oh, good. Heading that way myself."

Landon didn't get to go home, though, not until long after midnight. When Sol finally declared the scene processed, they took the evidence back to the S.O., then, finally, Landon could head The Rhino toward the ranch. It had been way too long a Monday.

***

12 – Pest Control

TUESDAY

BOTH HER DAD and Landon having wimped out of the morning run, Jessie decided to take her most challenging distance run on the property, out to the Cliffs of Long and back. She still got willies running it, but, as Tank, their professional crisis expert, pointed out, you didn't get over things until you faced them. Still, Jessie sincerely doubted that she'd ever go up the cliff trail again, not with the memory of the voices, then the screams, coming from on top as fresh as yesterday. Just being able to run through here was enough, at least for now. And, yeah, both her dad and Landon were right. She wasn't law enforcement material. Not like the undersheriff. Not like her dad's bud, Howie. Murderers gave her chills. Not having Acer and Milo with her this morning, them showing the lethargy of having donated blood, was playing on her nerves, too. Today, she felt especially vulnerable. And, of course, Britta was gone forever—super-protection dog Britta.

Britta is happy. And the dog was. She wagged her tail like never before, and that was all Landon.

Silly dog. It irked Jessie some, seeing it. The change in the dog was astonishing—staid Britta turned 'happy dog'.

As if catching her thoughts, Sumi came up beside her and bumped her on the hand. She looked down. Slowed and gave a stroke. "My good, good dog, Sumi." That got her a Sumi grin, plus a tail flagging and flogging. "It'll all work out, right?"

And, with that, Jessie stood back up, let out a whoop, and put on the speed, the dogs powering on and bounding out ahead of her, all joy. The sun was coming up.

*

"WE HAVE an audience," Landon said as Sol came downstairs.

"Oh?" The man went to the big window and looked out. Turned and went over to the surveillance monitors.

"That's a TV crew."

"Technically, a film crew. Yesterday, they were parked at the S.O. in the 'authorized vehicles only' area. I ran them off out to the public parking lot.

Now, they're parked on the county road. Were out there when I went to do chores."

"So they're interested in you, then," Sol said.

"I don't know why."

"Well, I do, but that's beside the point, right?"

Landon ignored that. "How do you want your eggs?"

"Whatever way you're doing yours is fine, thanks." Then, a frown came down. "That's a bit invasive, privacy-wise, especially with today's camera capabilities. Can they legally do that? Park there?"

"Yes, they may. They may not block the drive, inhibit ingress or egress, impede traffic, or endanger others, but, yes, they may park there for a limited time."

"Oh." Sol went quiet as he got out plates and flatware. "What about filming you …or me?"

"In public spaces, they may. And they may record when we're engaged in our public duties, but they cannot violate our privacy in places where we have a reasonable expectation of it. Nor may they interfere with our law enforcement duties," Landon replied. "Bacon is done. Eggs coming up. Want to get the hash browns served up?"

119

"You bet," Sol said, doing it. "So, you didn't go running this morning?" he asked, hash browns and bacon gravy served up from pans to plate. Then, pans stowed in the sink, the man grabbed the buttered toast, a jar of jam, and sat down at the table as Landon brought the rest of the goodies.

"No. I didn't run this morning …and I'll pay for it, but I begged off, and Oli said that he wasn't going today, either. None of us got enough sleep."

"I sure didn't, but I bet Jessie ran."

"Yeah," Landon agreed. "I'm sure she did." He chuckled. "You do know, Sol, that Jessie is actually a robot, right?" he said as he served up the eggs and bacon, first theirs, then one egg, plus a piece of bacon as a top-off to Britta's regular breakfast.

Sol had turned startled eyes on him. Then, obvious realization dawning, Sol's grin broke out. "You know, don't you, that, for me, it's before coffee."

Landon put the pan in the sink, then came and sat down.

"Second, you shouldn't pull on just one of a dwarf's short legs. It makes us walk lopsided."

And that's what Landon liked about Sol. The man knew when he was kidding around. "Sol?"

"Yes?"

"Consider the ranch your permanent home, if you want."

Startled eyes came up to his. "Are ...are you sure?"

"Positive. You think I put in that raised floor in the bathroom upstairs for fun?"

"Thank you. And for the kitchen rolling riser, too."

He smiled and nodded. Hoped his Christmas present for Sol would be built and shipped in time.

*

WITH RIGOROUS TRAINING sessions full on with the coming yearlings, Jessie was glad they had their extra help. The recruited trainers, all ex-military dog handlers, had settled into the program well, their attitudes relaxing out of the alternating stiff and reserved during work time and loose and rowdy off-hours that had been so apparent their first weeks after arrival. Their one woman trainer, Twilla, was becoming friendlier, and Jessie and she actually got along really well.

From the South, Twilla, a Black woman, had, once she 'let her hair down', a lot of laughter and gentility in her heart, especially toward dogs. That made her A-number-one in Jessie's book. And the puppies absolutely loved the woman. When it came to the tough training is where Twilla showed true merit, though. With patience beyond what would be called upon to qualify for sainthood, the woman was meticulous and exacting, but always gave it her all. Plus, she always gave the dogs, not just the benefit of the doubt, but her absolute best effort to bring them success.

Twilla was a star. Even Jessie's granddad mentioned it. John, who was now dog trainer manager, thought the world of her and of a man named Stan.

Today, Jessie would be handling alongside John, Darby, and her dad, plus two of the new hires. It would be four of the new trainers who worked in the bite suits, responsible for correcting and finessing the training. It was their maiden flight in this part of the work. Today, they would emphasize subtleties, getting the dogs to read human feints, distractions, and diversions—tricky. …At least, that was the plan.

Oli came through the mandoor promptly at 7:00. "All right, everybody. Let's get to it."

Jessie recognized the mood. Her dad was in 'military mode'. *Must have gotten a call from the brass, and it made him happy.* She sighed. She so much wanted to move the company completely away from war dogs to SAR. Knew that wasn't going to happen. But at least maybe she could nudge it to part SAR dogs. *Next year, maybe?*

…Maybe.

*

"THAT VAN'S following us," Sol said.

"Yeah. I see that," Landon answered. Sol was again riding in with him, and, idly, Landon wondered why so much these days. Sol was pretty darned independent. Asked.

"Um. …Well, I almost got run off the road a couple of times by this old Cadillac. I think the driver is laying in wait for me. Does the flashing headlights thing, passes, then swerves close to pull in front of me, and flashes taillights by braking. Luckily, I haven't been hit yet."

Landon cast a glance. "If you see him as we drive in, point him out to me."

"It's a 'her'."

"Same applies."

"Okay."

Landon watched his rearview as he pulled out on the 95. Sure enough, the van followed. *Okay. Definitely being tailed* ...which he already knew. *Let's have some fun.* All he needed was an excuse. *God will provide.*

"There she is," Sol said, pointing to a car when they'd gone south down the 95 about three miles.

It was an older Caddie—a 2000 Deville DTS—parked at the mouth of a county road. Landon noted the plate—local—as they blew past. Typed it one-handed into the computer as a query. Up came the stats—frowned. The driver was a woman in her sixties, a Mrs. Lindholme. She'd lost her son on this stretch a couple of years back. Landon remembered the wreck. Verbalized the last name to the onboard and asked for fatality collisions on Highway 95 in the last four years, pertinent milepost to milepost from here to Northridge, which is what he remembered from that incident. Got an answer. "Hmmm."

"What?"

"Her son was killed on this stretch. He drove a lime green 2003 Chevy Spark."

"Oh dear."

"Yeah." God had provided.

Warning Britta to down and Sol to hang on, he abruptly flipped The Rhino around using the median, but not bothering to get to a paved emergency access. In his mirrors, he watched the van try to do the same thing—illegal for all but emergency vehicles—and the van wound up nose down, bumper ground into the turf. "Gotcha."

Called the ISP and had the computer send them the vid-recording of the act. *Go get 'em, cowboys.*

"You're having fun," Sol said with a smirk.

Landon smiled. Got back to the road where the Caddie was still parked. Did a left across a legitimate, paved emergency vehicle turn-around, turned on 95 south again, then turned onto the country road, coming to a stop beside the car. Got out and, touching his hat, waited.

The lady's driver's side window rolled down.

"Ma'am?" he said, voice friendly, eyes, too.

"Yes, Sheriff?"

"Are you waiting for someone?"

"Yes. My son. I keep seeing him drive by. I can't believe it."

"All right, Ma'am. May I see registration, proof of insurance, and driver's license, please?" he asked, keeping his voice soft, a carefully gentle smile on his face.

The woman handed him the requested. To Landon, she seemed perfectly cogent. This was odd. He expected signs of dementia or Alzheimer's.

He nodded. "I'll be right back." Got back in The Rhino, Britta wagging. Brought up a picture of the woman, then the woman's deceased son …and knew. "Look at this, Sol."

"Wow."

The woman's deceased son had a face very similar to Sol's. "Okay, Sol. Here's what we're going to do." Outlined his plan, then got out and gave back the woman's paperwork. Told her to have a good day.

Turned around using the next wide spot and headed for work …only a half-an-hour late. Passed the ISP officer still dealing with the film van's driver, the cameraman sitting in the passenger seat, his head leaned on his hand. Gave the statie a nod. "Have a good day, Actuator Studios," Landon muttered.

***

13 – Under Fire

THE DOGS were performing well. A couple of times, her dad stopped things, her granddad going up to demonstrate a finesse that Jessie paid attention to. She was still learning this stuff. The dogs had been especially keen today.

Afterwards, putting their heads together, they went over specifics of which dogs were showing themselves especially good at 'reading human'. Those would be separated out for top-level training, the others kept to the regular program. "We're being asked to take them all the way up," Oli told them once they'd finished business. "All the way."

"That's good, isn't it, sir?" Twilla asked.

Oli nodded. "It is."

Not in Jessie's opinion. This was the opposite way she wanted things to go.

"Jessica Marie?" her granddad asked.

She shook her head. "Nothing. Just listening."

He gave her a sideways glance that told her he knew better.

What did she say? That she didn't like it? Would it matter? Knew it would. It would get them straight back to the same old arguments, and she didn't want to let her dad down with objections she knew he wouldn't accept …and, now, neither could Jessie, if she was honest. But she loved these dogs. Couldn't bear the thought of them going to war or into law enforcement.

But, if not ours, then someone else's who were less prepared, less able. Always the dilemma. Always bad choices. She hated it.

"With me, Jessie," her dad said, coming up behind her as she headed for her kennels to take advantage of the free hour she had to work her rescues, most of them almost ready to be certified.

"What?" she asked.

"With me," Oli repeated, and she went along. He took her into the new K4 barn that was almost finished. "So, this barn will be dedicated to your SAR trainees, Jessie."

She almost tripped over her own feet. "What?"

Oli looked sideways at her and grinned. "The dogs that we used to cull? And those that aren't quite as sharp as they could be for war and police dogs? They'll be under your training protocols. What say, Jessie, my Jessie?"

She didn't say anything. Just grabbed a hold of him and hugged him with all her might, him chuckling and tousling her hair. "Thank your granddad and grandmother, too, now," he said, returning the hug.

"I will."

Then Jessie's tracking app went off with an EPIRB (Emergency Position Indicating Radio Beacon) alarm. That was weird.

Jessie looked—Grant Evans. She ran for her dogs, even as she called Dispatch.

*

LANDON'S ONBOARD began running a line of bold text as he was sitting in the left turn lane, waiting for the light. He ignored it. Next thing, his radio squawked. "Must be important," he muttered. *A commissioner is upset about something petty.* He picked up the mic. "One Alpha One," he responded, then listened.

"Grant Evans and Sandra Darstead, SAR. Under fire. Special Deputy Anderson and Deputy Kins en route. S.W.A.T. deploying to Air One."

Landon frowned. *Tac Team deploying—good. ...What's Jessie doing there?*

Hung up the mic and told the computer to put him on audio. Broke in. "What's Anderson doing out there?"

"Evans' Emergency Locater Beacon went off. Jessie called it in as she was deploying."

"Where?"

"East side of Fox Meadows at Green Creek."

Bordered on the edge of wilderness and very near his home. "En route," he said.

He flipped on lights and siren and, watching as traffic gave him the right-of-way—"Thank you."—took the available break people gave him to flip a U-ey and head back north.

"My, we're busy," Sol said softly, his hand on a grab handle.

"Yeah," Landon agreed. "Monday on Tuesday, too." And tonight was Devil's Night.

Grant Evans and Sandra Darstead under fire.... He pushed up his speed.

*

"I'M COMING along," Oli said, opening the passenger-side rear door, his prowlers and Numa jumping up and in to crowd her dogs. Everybody shifted to accommodate.

He stowed his gear and weapons, then got in, Acer jumping in back to let him have the front passenger seat.

"Thanks for coming, Dad," Jessie said, and, putting it in gear even as he pulled the door shut, she lit out.

*

"WHERE ARE WE going again?" Sol asked as Landon wove through traffic, some of the drivers completely oblivious to his presence despite his light bar strobing and alternately flashing head- and fog-lights, plus screaming siren on wail, yelp, and piercer. Luckily, most moved to give him right-of-way. "I can't find it on the maps."

Landon smiled, despite his worry. "Locally called Fox Meadows. Look on the map about eight miles east of the Anderson place. You'll see a creek and a string of three open patches along that creek. Those are the Fox Meadows."

"Oh. ...Found them. Thanks."

"You're welcome."

"Do you have a map with local names, by chance?"

"No. Anybody local who plays outdoors pretty much knows them ...unless they're—"

The computer jabbered out Dispatch traffic again. Air One was lifting off. E.T.A. twelve minutes.

"Unless they're newcomers," Landon finished.

"Like me."

"Like you."

*

GETTING TO the Fox Meadows trailhead, Jessie didn't bother to park, just headed the XV up the trail, brush scraping paint. Her dad was silent beside her, his face hard.

She drove as far as she could, gaining them a good half-mile till she reached the rocks pushed up to stop ingress. She shut down, got out, and grabbed her med pack and a rifle. Oli was already climbing up and over the boulder pile, all the dogs with him, save Acer and Milo, which Jessie had to restrain with stiff commands, then lock in with little Duchess, pack mascot. Then, Jessie followed, got over the rock barrier, and, stretching stride, ran hard to catch up with her dad and her dogs.

The prowlers were ranged ahead, noses high, Jessie's four dogs with them. Then, as one, the prowlers stopped and turned, eyes on her dad.

Jessie's dogs slowed and then stopped, too. Watched, as well. He signaled, and the prowlers took off, disappearing from view. So did Jessie's dogs. And Jessie took the cue from Oli's use of hand signals only. It was her dad's way of saying that this would be a silent run.

On her phone app, it showed that the dogs were taking it fast as usual, Mitch and Sumi in the lead, and Jessie let them …until they got to the third meadow. The distinctive sound of intermittent light caliber gunshots began to transmit through her and her dad's phone mics. The dogs were heading up into the trees on the hillside north of the lower meadowland, a winding trail she often rode on horseback. That trail switchbacked up and through this low hill country.

Ahead of her, Oli signaled again. Jessie whispered a recall to her dogs, the becoming-too-familiar sensation of super-cooled, super-hyped, and 'ready for deadly' taking over her brain and body, her heart slowing, her vision sharpening, her brain honed. Ever since Blaine, and especially since going after the Grierhausen kid, then the drug runners, this had been happening. Something was different, though. She wasn't 'icing down'—going into zombie mode—not since her dad included her in his once-a-week training sessions with Howie and the guys on the mat and the once-a-month sessions in the pit. *Something's happening to me. I* am *getting better.* And it made her feel good. Maybe she was finally getting over Blaine. She knew one thing, though. She was never going to get over losing Jameson.

Sumi, Mitch, and the rest bounded toward them, swapped directions, and went to running heel around her, Mitch at her knee, Sumi in Britta's old place to her right, Queenie and Oso behind her. She blessed them for their obedience to recall and the fact they wore their Kevlar®.

Again, her dad signaled, and Jessie dropped even as Oli grounded, the dogs dropping to *Platz* with them. The gunfire was close, now, but only occasional. She heard Oli send the prowlers. Moments later, voices yelled. More gunshots. …Screams.

***

D. L. Keur

D. L. Keur

14 – Well-Oiled Machine

THE SILHOUETTE of Air One blotting out the rising sun brought Landon some ease, the big Huey's chop pummeling as it passed nearby overhead. His personnel were on top of things. Meanwhile, he was just coming to the turnoff to his county road. "Hang on, Sol."

"Hanging."

And he took it too fast, but The Rhino held the turn. "Good boy, Moose."

"You shouldn't call it that," Sol said. "The Rhino will get a complex."

"It's a rig, Sol. Don't anthropomorphize."

"Why not? It's fun. And, besides, you just did." Then, "Well, technically, you zoomorphized, of course."

Landon groaned under his breath. Sol was worse than he was. Thought about it. Chuckled. That's why they got along so well. ...But, no, for Landon, the anthropomorphizing wasn't just fun. It was something else ...at least for him. Stress relief and, sometimes, safe company—poking at something that you couldn't hurt and that couldn't poke back—something to talk to where you didn't have to worry about consequences, could just vent or joke or even just chatter at will, no worries. *Worry if you start hearing it talk back to you.*

"Air One on scene. Personnel deployment imminent," the onboard told him.

"Thank you, Computer."

"You're welcome, Sheriff, sir."

"I thought you broke it of appellations," Sol said.

"I did. The latest software update brought it back. Now I've got to retrain it all over again."

"Fun."

"Not."

*

HER DOGS led her straight to Grant and Sandra, their dogs hunkered down around them.

Grant was stripped down, blood running down his chest and right arm—cuts, bruises, and scrapes. He had paint splatters all over him, and so did Sandra. Their dogs did, too.

Grant was bent over Sandra, holding his bloody shirt on her, her pants cut down to her knees to expose the thigh. Jessie slid in beside. "What do we have, Grant."

"Femur. Broken. Compound fracture. We fell hard down this slope when they started blasting us with paintballs. Sandra hit that boulder—"

"Stop talking about me as if I can't hear you," Sandra cut in.

"They kept shooting us even after we fell. I think those guns are way over regulation impact levels," Grant added. "I used to paintball. They never hurt like this."

Already having put the call in, Jessie was waiting for a doctor to pick up as she stripped her med pack and, with a nod to Grant, took a quick look. It was a clean break, not splintered, one bone end just poking through the break in the skin, no blood spurting, but lots of it welling. No swelling yet, though. Muscle tissue was pulpy. "Okay. Pressure, again," she told Grant, then got out a cuff and stethoscope. Sandra's color was decent. She was shocky, but not dangerously so.

Dr. Moynihan's voice came on, and Jessie blessed the fact it was him. Told him status and stats.

"Start an IV." Told her what he wanted exactly— isotonic sodium chloride. And, her hands dead steady, she hit the vein, taped the catheter in place, and had fluids running in seconds as, overhead, the S.O.'s big Huey came to hover, trees tops whipping.

"Get that leg immobilized, Jessie."

"Um … it's going to be tough without painkiller," she said.

Moynahan approved a local and a super-light dose of more painkiller, IM.

"Administering." She pinched skin hard on the lower belly to divert Sandra's attention as she stuck the local right in the gap between exposed bone and tissue.

"Set that splint, please."—Moynahan.

"Okay, Sandra. Hang on to Grant. This is going to hurt a bit," Jessie told her, getting her biggest vacuum splint ready.

*

RADIO CHATTER live on speaker, Landon kept his eyes on the road, pushing speed as he listened.

Howie's growl came on. "We've got visual." He went on to report the status of the incident field:

Jessie was working on Sandra Darstead. Grant Evans was okay and working with Jessie on Sandra. "Anderson apprehension dogs on two suspects. Anderson male approaching. Deploying now," Howie said, cutting the connection.

Landon frowned and nodded. So, Oli was there, and the shooters were down. That meant Oli had taken the prowlers and gone along—not surprising, considering it was his daughter out there *without* Tom Hudson, who was presently deploying from Air One. *Gotta fix that.* But how? And you bet Oli would have gone along. *I'm going to have to make him a special deputy, too—criminal apprehension, maybe.*

Oh, the commissioners were going to love this! He was the authority, though. It was his call. But, then, actually, the commissioners would probably be all for it. Oli had a good rep with the county, the state, and the country, all—a national hero. So did Jessie, now, her national prominence in SAR playing well for Bitterroot County. *Like father, like daughter.*

*

"HOW ARE YOU feeling, Sandra," Jessie asked, taking a BP reading again. Jessie had an oxygen mask on the woman, but had shut the volume down. Sandra retained good color and was calm and lucid. Sandra was a trooper.

The woman nodded. Jessie was very glad Dr. Moynahan had okayed the light shot of morphine and a wound-local shot of lidocaine. Sandra was out of pain. "I hope this doesn't mean I'm going to miss my daughter's Christmas wedding in Hawaii."

"Me, too."

"How are my dogs?"

Jessie gave a glance to the two Border Collies that lay panting, eyes worried. Called them over, the dogs wagging up all sympathy to their person, and Sandra immediately brightened.

The dogs laid down next to their 'mom', their stress less.

Tom came up and slid in next to Jessie. "Can I do anything?"

"Grant," she said. "His chest and arm. Saw some bruising and scrapes on his back, too."

"On it."

Grant, of course, played typical tough guy, but Tom ignored that and cleaned and bandaged him up.

*

"MEDIVAC canceled. We'll take the injured and the perps aboard Air One," Howie reported. "Jessie said she'll keep the dogs with her. Alpha Four One."

"08:23," Dispatch came back, then things went silent.

"We might as well turn around, I guess. Everything will be tied and tidied by the time we ever get there," Landon grumbled.

"Ah, Sheriff, sir?" Sol said, startling Landon with the sudden formality.

"What, Sol?"

"We need to process the evidence."

He rolled eyes at himself. "Right."

"You can just drop me off. Somebody will give me a ride back."

He had the computer put a phone call into his undersheriff. "Martin? You coming out?"

"Already on my way."

Ended the call and, turning, headed up past the trailhead parking lot where Grant Evans' and Sandra Darstead's rigs were parked, then on up the Fox

Meadows trail, brush busting as he went, following fresh laid tire tracks in the turf. Jessie had obviously gone in ahead of him. So had somebody else. Rounding a bend, he got confirmation. There sat Kins' unit behind the XV. "We hoof it from here, Sol. I'll take your kits for you."

"You take the cameras. I can handle the rest."

The S.O.'s Huey was just leaving. They had the injured and the guilty all headed to Northridge Hospital. Deputies would meet them there to take charge of the suspects.

Landon breathed relief. His personnel, every one of them, were working like parts of a well-oiled machine.

*

JESSIE SET evidence markers and took pictures, Dave Kins and Tom Hudson helping as her dad checked over his dogs.

"They okay?" she asked.

"Not a scratch," he said, his voice happy. "Got some paint on them, but it smells like typical non-toxic paintball goop."

146

Jessie glanced his way after labeling the picture she'd just shot with her phone. "The prowlers look happy."

He turned. "They always love a good takedown," he said, grinning. "And those two more than deserved it."

They had. They'd resisted. They'd tried to shoot the dogs. The guns they were using niggled at Jessie. Both the shooters were using Stingers® identical to the one the woman had with her in the alley yesterday. Their outfits were similar, too—dressed in black paintball uniforms, their paintball rifles scattered, both guns broken. They weren't wearing silicon masks, though. Still.... *This is just weird.*

"Coming up, your position," a voice said— Landon's.

The dogs had already warned them that someone known was approaching. Jessie turned to look. "Landon," then, "Sol," she said, nodding to them, Britta hugging Landon's leg, her ears up. Then, with a glance up and Landon's nod of 'okay', Britta bounded up to Jessie's, Grant's, and Sandra's dogs, all of them doing happy dances. Then the blonde shepherd, all the dogs with her, went to say hi to Oli and his prowlers, not one dog posturing because of the canine newcomers, even Oli's GSDs, Wolfy and Trounce, even the Malinois, Grit and Cobra.

Her dad's Numa wiggled all over.

Dogs greeted, her dad stepped to and grasped Landon's hand. Then Sol's. "Glad you guys could make it to the party."

"Late as usual," Landon grumbled. His eyes came to Kins', then Jessie's. "I'm parked behind you and Kins."

"Okay." Then she gave him and Sol a run-down on what she had witnessed and what she knew, her dad putting in his two cents.

"You're all almost done processing the scene," Sol said, his eyes proud.

"Not even close. Tom and I have to trackback to see where the perps came from."

"You didn't wait for Tom," Landon grumbled.

Jessie noted the critical tone. Ignored it. So did Tom, who was now standing by. "Dad came. Couldn't wait. Sorry." But she knew she was going to hear about this later. She'd promised Landon. Personally. And she'd kept that promise. So far, anyway. Well, not today—not when one of her own was in trouble. Nope. Not happening. *Too bad, so sad, Landon*.

*

JESSIE AND OLI had heavy body armor on. Jessie looked like she had put on an instant twenty, thirty pounds over what she usually looked like wearing protection, and, of course, all in the torso. Oli, a big guy, all hard muscle and hustle despite his fifty-three years, looked even broader and thicker than usual, too. "What are you wearing, Oli?"

"I don't trust that new foam armor. We'll wear it, but we're sticking with what we know, as well, at least until it proves itself not to fail in the field, something I do *not* want to test in live action."

"And I never argue with Dad on these things," Jessie said with a short laugh.

"Mmm." That was a lie. She argued with her dad a lot, according to Oli. But what Oli had just said about the new metal composite foam armor gave Landon food for thought in considering whether or not to buy some for his personnel. Still, if it *did* work, the cut price for those who purchased while it was still in the trial phase would save his budget a lot of money.

Decisions, decisions. More information required. *...On more than equipment.* Landon wanted answers as to why somebody was out shooting people with paintball guns, and he wanted them before anybody else got hurt.

***

15 – Persistent Snoops

FINALLY GETTING to the S.O., Landon touched fingers to his hat brim in mock salute at the Actuator Studios boys parked neatly in the public lot as he went through. They saw him, but turned their faces away, acknowledgement enough for him. He quelled a smirk, but, beside him, Britta opened her mouth in what Landon thought of as a dog's version of one. *You're anthropomorphizing*, he scolded himself. Then he did laugh out loud. Britta's tail tip—just the very tip—was wiggling, so she was amused, too.

After Landon parked in his usual spot in back, Britta escorted him in, and he was grateful for the company. She was comforting and fun to have along. He felt like he wasn't alone anymore when he was out and about, and that was soothing. He now had three somebodies in his life that he knew loved him—his cats, Pine Tree and Owl, plus Britta. That mattered. The nice thing was that the two cats and the dog all got along. The cats actually adored the big shepherd, curling up against the dog's stomach and under her chin when they all went to bed. Of course, Landon was now limited to one side of the queen-sized mattress, and, while he didn't mind sharing, he didn't particularly care for feeling pinned down on one side by their weight on the bedding. He was coping, though.

Already wise to his patterns, Britta turned into the break room to wait while he nuked an egg, sausage, and cheese breakfast muffin and got himself a cuppa. Then, tossing her a piece of the muffin innards, they headed toward the front to check in.

Rounding the corner, there stood the Actuator boys, camera lit. He scowled. Britta soft grumbled. Continued toward destination—front desk—the cameraman backing up as he approached.

The deputy at the desk grabbed something and stuffed it under the counter as he walked up. "What was that?" he asked.

The deputy flushed.

Odd. He waited.

"That was ...ah ...one of the old embossers, sir. I was using it for a paperweight because, today, with the wind, every time someone comes in as somebody else is going out the outer door, papers fly everywhere."

Landon knew the problem. Still, that hadn't looked like any of the old brass embossers they still had stashed—too big. Shrugged. *You're micromanaging*, he chided himself. *Leave them alone.* "I have arrived," he said. "Finally. Only two hours late. I'll be in my office."

"Ah, Sheriff?"—Red's voice, or, formally, Captain Pete 'Red' Wheeler.

He gave his administrative captain, the S.O.'s third-in-command, his eyes. "Yes, Captain?"

"Judge Laird called. She asked if you would come to chambers as soon as you have a free minute. She said it wasn't urgent. Sometime this week is fine."

He groaned. He liked Laird, but she could be a hellcat if you got on her wrong side. Luckily, she seemed to like him ...mostly. He suspected it was because he dotted his 'i's and crossed his 't's when it came to search warrant applications and arrest warrants, along with his office doing due diligence in evidence procurement and processing. That, and she liked that he was at least somewhat familiar with the laws of the land, both Idaho's and the federal statutes. "Will do. Let me scrape off whatever is pending my attention here, then I'll give her a visit if I don't get waylaid."

"Yes, sir."

He started to leave, then stopped. "Oh. What did I miss at briefing, Captain?"

"It's all on your laptop. I've run up the briefing notes for you, plus the video is queued on your system. I left some paperwork for you to look over and sign, too."

"Thank you."

"You're welcome, Bossman."

…Turned around and there stood the Actuator boys way too close, Britta facing them, dead-staring them down. He had missed their having closed in on him and also missed Britta going on guard. "Good, Britta," he muttered. Glared at the Actuator guys and headed down the hall to his office where they couldn't come without an appointment, Britta with him, her head constantly glancing behind.

They followed as far as the public lobby area let them and, in the convexes, Landon watched them keep filming him until he made his doorway. *What gives?* It made his back twitch.

Got in his door, closed it, something he didn't usually do, hung up his hat, and went to work.

*

BACKTRACKING the assailants wound up being pretty much a cakewalk for the dogs, Grant's five and Sandra's two joining her four as if they belonged there. Pack training worked well with well-socialized, well-mannered SAR dogs. The trail wound them up on a Forest Service road, a car parked there. It was part of a fleet, according to the sticker on it, and had an Arizona license.

Tom called it in, and then, of course, they got to hang around till more deputies got there, Jessie and Tom munching down on trail mix and power bars, water as chaser, dogs getting water and dog jerky treats to gnaw.

"Eleven dogs all working together," Tom said. "That's something."

Jessie grinned. "It's great, isn't it?"

"Wish people worked that well together. We did a combined training with Northridge's guys, and it was a tough go. Howie just told us to keep our mouths shut, follow their protocols, and do the job, so we did. Never so glad when that was over."

Thunder on the road. "Tow truck's coming, finally, I bet," Tom said, getting up.

"I hear that."

Sure enough, two S.O. units, a tow truck with them, rounded the switchback, and Tom got to sign over responsibility. Then, Jessie and he headed back the way they'd come. Got back to find everybody gone, including Landon and her dad.

"Looks like Kins has cleared out, too. Can I get a ride, Jessie?" Tom asked as they jogged the last leg to the XV.

"Of course. You think I'd leave you for a grizzly bear snack, the remains something for the crows and turkey vultures to pick clean?"

He grinned. "You might."

"Never. You're too much fun to tease."

"Back at ya, Deputy."

"Don't rub it in."

"Deputy."

"You're rubbing."

"Yep."

*

JESSIE FILED her report from the XV after loading the dogs. So did Tom. Saw that her dad had filed one under Landon's unit number. Had to laugh.

Landon's meticulous hand was evident in it. Her dad would have just been short and to the point, no attention to correct grammar.

A text from Oli told her he was home, that Landon had dropped him, Numa, and the prowlers off while she, Tom, and the dogs were still working the backtrack. "The best buds," she muttered. Recognized resentment and scolded herself. She'd felt that way about her dad and her brother Erik's relationship, too. *Why?* "Because I'm always second best."

"What was that, Jessie?" Tom asked, glancing over.

"Just mumbling under my breath."

"Yeah, it is weird, isn't it?"

"What is?"

"This paintball connection between four incidents yesterday and today."

"Four?"

"The Northridge Sports Shop smash-and-grab? That's what the thieves grabbed. That and small caliber ammo."

"Oh. Right."

"Yeah. Could be just because of this being the new go-to weapon because it's considered less-than-lethal, so not carrying the legal jeopardy of firing a, quote-quote, *real* gun at somebody. There's a lot of traffic about it online."

"But these people did have 'real guns'—those Stingers®. So did the one in the Northridge incident." Stingers®, again…. Three incidents with four of the cheap little two-shot mini-guns.

"These two suspects had speed loaders on them, too," Tom shared.

That was new. "Caliber?" she asked. "I didn't hear."

"Jacketed .22 shorts."

Her radio crackled—Dispatch calling her. *Oops. Should have turned it off.*

She touched on audio. "On audio, Dispatch. Deputy Tom Hudson in the unit with me."

"Ten-four. Please report to the undersheriff when you return to base."

Jessie groaned. She hadn't planned on doing more than dropping Tom off. "Copy that."

"Deputy Tom Hudson, too," they came back.

"Will do," Tom said, then gave her a grin. "Are we on the carpet or up for an award, do you think?"

"I'm betting the former …for me, anyway. I didn't wait for you. You'll get a pat on the back, though."

He gave a headshake. "I don't think so. I think this is gonna be a 'pick-our-brains-for-missing-pieces-we-didn't-think-were-important' session."

And Jessie knew he could be right. Groaned again and headed out, first stop home to kennel up Grant's and Sandra's dogs, then onto the S.O. to face whatever awaited Tom and she with Martin. Then, later, it would be back here to pick up Grant's and Sandra's vehicles.

***

16 – Cloudy Water

DONE WITH pressing tasks—all but paying the requested visit to Judge Laird—and having listened …and sometimes even watched the recorded morning briefing, Landon made his way toward Martin's office once his undersheriff and Sol came through the back.

Happily, maintenance was finally working on the wall outside Sol's lab and office. "Finally."

Tools were apparent. A ladder. Warning cones. Of course, nobody was presently working, but at least the wall would soon be patched, all embarrassing evidence of his temper getting loose finally eradicated.

He grunted approval, nodded …smiled. *Finally.*

*

LANDON LOOKED as pleased as a dog who had successfully stolen a bone when he stepped into Martin's office, and Jessie guessed why. She hid a smirk and started to excuse herself, but Martin barked at her to sit down, her dogs stalling mid-stand, then sinking back to the floor. *Darn.* Tom glanced a grin her way and winked.

"Don't even think 'I told you so'," Jessie mouthed back at him, and he grinned bigger. *Brat.*

Landon was giving her the hairy eyeball, too, and her dogs started to tail thump as Britta, all doggy grins, eyed them and wagged big.

The blonde shepherd looked up at Landon. Nosed his leg.

He looked down at her. Looked where she then pointed her nose, only to look back up at him. "Well, go ahead," he said, his voice going indulgent.

Britta trotted over to greet, and even let Jessie give her a stroke, but Jessie wanted to roll eyes. Britta had Landon completely locked up and in tow, pandering to her any whim and wish. Shook her head and saw that Landon caught it. Luckily, he didn't do more than give Jessie the slant eye and a guilty grimace.

He knows. At least there was that much satisfaction.

*

"SO WHAT do we have?" Landon asked the room, casting eyes around.

"Not a whole lot," Martin told him. "But there's a potential for a second victim in the woman, Linda Allen, who suffered a broken arm around about the same time that Garrison was assaulted. We've just been quizzing Jessie and Tom about details that they might have encountered, but don't realize are significant."

"And?" Landon asked, eyeing the two deputies. Tom was relaxed; Jessie was looking like she wanted to squirm.

Martin turned to Jessie. "Want to tell us about the lady's comment?"

Now Landon really saw her squirm. Calculated. Yeah. She had something. "Jessie?" he asked, keeping his tone very soft.

She raised pained eyes to him. "It's stupid," she blurted out.

"Try me."

"And we said there's nothing stupid, remember, Jessie?" Sol piped in.

Audibly, Jessie groaned.

Martin was about to bark again. Landon raised a hand, and his undersheriff settled back and kept quiet.

It took about a full minute, but then Jessie shut her eyes, tipped her head aside, then dropped it, and gave a single nod. Opened her mouth and said, "Mrs. Allen said she'd been toppled. 'Was toppled' was what she said exactly. Not that she toppled over or just toppled, but that she *was* toppled. And she had two kinds of different …splotches of dirt on her that were …more ground in on the sleeve of her jacket, the same arm as was broken. Then there was the bright wood on the upper bank on the other side of the puddle."

Martin sat up. Scribbled something on a pad. Typed madly on his computer.

"…Bright wood on what was maybe an old log or an exposed tree root. …Like it was freshly scraped by something."

Jessie's eyes came open—now bright blue with stress. She looked around. "I had my cam on. What Allen said exactly should be on there." And Jessie's voice held a mix of hope and desperation.

She's so afraid of being wrong …of not being credible, and that one Landon knew too well. *We've got the same injury—called out for getting it wrong until we're afraid to fail.*

"Found it! Both Jessie's and Tom's cam footage confirm that," Martin said, looking up, then glanced toward Landon. "And, no, we haven't gone inch by inch, frame by frame, through the cam shots. Our bad, I know. Guess we will now."

"I guess you will."

"Good job, Jessie," came Sol's voice, no humor, all pride. Landon shared that sentiment.

*

ROLLING THE FOOTAGE of both Jessie's and Tom's cams of the rescue soon showed other details. Martin's eye was quick to point out scuffs apparent on approach before Jessie and Tom had disturbed the ground. "Look there," he said, pausing both recordings at the same time-stamp on both on their approaches to where the dogs had found Linda Allen.

"Let's zoom in," Sol suggested.

"We'll lose clarity," Martin said.

"You don't have that enhancement algorithm on your system?"

Martin glanced a 'huh' at Sol.

"I bet you do."

A sigh. Martin did a quick search. Found the app, and, tapping it, tried to get it to work.

"Just drag it onto the recording," Sol said, and Landon heard Jessie chuckle. That irritated him. *We're all not trained in crime tech programs, Jessie.*

"Okay. There it is. I'm going to mark that for Terri to enhance," Martin said.

"I'll do it. Terri is busy enough. Besides, it *is* my job," Sol said.

"So where did the assailant come from?" Landon asked. "We know where he or she went to, right? The road a couple miles from the location of the attack?"

"Correct. At least according to Jessie's dogs. But we don't know where she came from. We don't even know if those are human footprints we're seeing in the cam recordings."

Silence around the room.

"Moving on," Martin said, starting the cams from where they were. Now they watched as Tom and Jessie checked Linda out where she sat hugging her arm. Watched them carefully lift her out of the trampled hole she was in, the local flora spoiled, the pool of water that trickled down from a small spring above, cloudy from being disturbed.

"Did Ms. Allen fall in the water?" Landon asked.

"No," Jessie and Tom said simultaneously.

"So, she wasn't wet?"

"No," Tom said. "Cold, maybe a few damp spots, but, no, not wet."

"Did one or both of you step in the water?" Landon asked.

Both Jessie and Tom shook their heads.

"Then, why is the water cloudy?"

***

D. L. *Keur*

17 – A Question of Why

Everyone grabbing to-go lunches from the break room, Martin, Sol, Landon, Jessie, and Tom, plus the dogs, all piled into Landon's and Jessie's rigs, Martin and Sol with Landon, Tom with Jessie and the dogs. It was one by the time they headed back out to where Ms. Allen had been found yesterday morning.

"Look at that, Tom," Jessie said, pointing to the feed from her XV's top rear cameras. "That film van just pulled out and is trailing the sheriff's unit again."

"Yep. Wish we were behind him."

Jessie pulled into the S.O.'s fueling station on the auspices of getting diesel, then pulled immediately back out after The Rhino passed, sandwiching …almost *ramming* the van to get herself in between the back of The Rhino and said Dodge van, the van's nose dipping as it braked hard and the driver Laying on the horn.

She grinned. "Didn't like that, huh?"

"Guess not," Tom said, grinning.

The van pulled a daredevil move and tried to pass and push in ahead of her on the two-lane in a no-passing zone, but Jessie paced him, riding almost up on Landon's bumper.

"Road rage," Tom said.

"They're definitely serious about being on Landon's tail, aren't they?" Jessie muttered.

"Yeah."—Tom. "Terri's been surveillance tracking them on the traffic cams. Pretty much, they've been following him everywhere he goes whenever they can. Have been since Monday, but they started in earnest today."

"Anybody quizzed them about what they're doing?"

"Howie said he sent Marty out there and the twerpy-chirpy guy told her they were doing a documentary on Sheriff Reid."

"Did Marty finally make Tac Team?"

"Yep. She wore Howie down."

"Good."

"She's a go-getter, that's sure!"

"So how are all you ex-military mighties getting along with her?"

Tom chuckled. "Just fine, thanks."

"Also good. Okay. Hang tight. Here they come again," Jessie said, as they hit the 95.

"Glue yourself to Sheriff's bumper, Jessie."

"Oka-aay."

And so it went all the way out to the road leading to the Brinker Ridge trail.

Getting there, they parked beside Landon who touched fingers to his hat at her. Jessie gave him a thumbs up and a grin, then let the dogs out, even Duchess, Milo, and Acer, since this walk wouldn't stress them.

The Actuator Studios van now pulled in to stop and shut down.

"Persistent buggers," Tom muttered.

"They are."

As she geared up with evidence kits and cameras, Tom, too, a tall guy got out of the van and hoisted a camera onto his shoulder, then pointed it at Landon as Landon got out of The Rhino.

Jessie frowned. These guys were definitely serious about getting footage of him. And she wondered what the slant was—pro or con. She bet it would be a negative spin. Hoped not. Landon didn't deserve that.

"I'm going string tape across the start of the trail so they can't follow us," Tom said, grabbing some.

"Can't?" Jessie said with a laugh. "Or won't?"

"They can't legally cross it," he said with a scowl.

"You think that will stop them?"

"No, but it's grounds for arrest."

"I'll help you string it."

Tom scowled again. "Let me get authorization."

"The sheriff himself is authorization," Jessie pointed out.

"Still going to call it in. Can I use your radio, Jessie?"

"You don't have to ask."

"Thanks. And thanks for giving me permission to access the XV without the machine throwing a fit all the time."

"Hey! We're partners, right?"

Tom grinned.

*

RETRACING JESSIE'S and Tom's run up the trail, though at a much more leisurely walking pace to accommodate Sol's short legs, they made their way toward the scene of Ms. Allen's accident.

Jessie's dogs led the way, tails up and flagging, and, thinking of how Jessie ran so effortlessly with him and Oli every morning, Landon was once again reminded of just how much stamina he'd lost. *Need to get stronger.*

Jessie might be onto something with her long-sprint training, Landon mused. She didn't get winded; she didn't get tired. *Or else she really is a robot.*

He chuckled. Oli wouldn't like him for that thought. Oli hated the growing use of lethal autonomous weapons systems (LAWS)—robot soldiers—in the military and robot dogs in both the military and law enforcement. Of course, at least in law enforcement in the U.S., those very un-dog-like contraptions were mostly just surveillance tools. They couldn't compare to the jobs a real dog did. *Not even close.*

He glanced down at Britta who was sticking by him, despite her long-time pals trotting along ahead. He'd expected her to join them and was surprised when she hadn't. But, then, neither had Acer, Jessie's big GSD, who trotted along at Jessie's side as she and Tom led up.

Behind him, Sol hollered, "Whoa-ho. Looky here." Landon turned to see the criminologist pointing to a series of scrapes up the rising trail-side bank. "Wonder if that's important?" Sol asked, eyes gone wicked, and, joining Sol and Martin, Landon was surprised that, while Martin was huffing a bit, Sol wasn't even breathing hard.

Sol didn't train …that he knew of, other than using Landon's weight machine. *I've really got to get in better shape.* Maybe Jessie was right. Landon mostly sat all day, either in his office, in his reading chair at home, or in The Rhino, his Camaro, his granddad's pickup, or on his tractor. *I do chores. I run five days a week. I push weights every evening.*

Groaned. Obviously not enough, but then there wasn't enough time in the day, never mind in life, even though, other than the S.O., he had no life.

Martin, who was clearly out of breath, squatted down next to Sol and the two men put their heads together. Sol took some shots with both cameras he carried. "Could you tape this off, Tom?" Martin called, standing up.

"Sure can," Tom answered, trotting back down to them, Jessie and the dogs coming, too.

"Can we get up on top without disturbing things?" Sol asked.

Not easily was the consensus.

"Your thoughts on this?" Landon asked.

"I think someone used that as a lookout," Sol answered.

"Really. A lookout for what?"

Sol shrugged. Martin gave him a scowl. "We don't know. ...Yet. May never know. Could be nothing but a bird watcher's perch or a deer hunter's watchpoint."

Landon itched to go up and look ...but that would destroy what footprints and other evidence might be there to give them clues to the who and what. "What do you *think* can be seen from up there? According to the topo map, there's just more sidehill above."

"Hard to say without getting up there."

"My drones," Jessie said. "Let me go back and launch the drones while you guys go on up to where we found Linda. We'll meet you here on your way back down."

Martin gave his go ahead, and Landon nodded agreement. "Let me take your evidence kits and cameras, Jessie," Landon offered, and, without argument, for once, she handed it all over.

Tying off the tape, Tom scrambled to join them. "Going with you, Jessie."

"Okay."

And, just that quick, Jessie and Tom, her dogs with her, took off back down the trail …of course at a run.

She's only a year and five months younger than me and, for her, this is like nothing. The thought depressed him.

*

RUNNING DOWNHILL was always harder on the body than running up. It was especially hard on the knees. Jessie wore light compression knee supports as standard gear under her jeans, and both Tom and her dad had taken up the practice, too, after she'd gotten them both a set to try.

Getting them to give them an honest trial had only taken a small forever of teasing and logic. "Just try it once. I mean, nobody is going to see that you're wearing them under your pants, are they? If it doesn't work for you, give them back. I'll wash them and give them to the physio- to give to someone who's not suffering too much he-man ego."

That last had done it, and both her dad and Tom had finally tried them and, surprisingly, had seen the benefit of wearing them …grudgingly.

Today, Jessie was especially happy that both Tom and she were wearing them. Though the trail had a gentle grade of only about eleven percent, it was popular and, therefore, hard-packed from heavy use, and, after her stiff morning long-sprint training, then running hard to get to Grant and Sandra just hours past, Jessie's legs were feeling the stress of the day's heavy exertion. She was pushing it, and she knew it. *Should start using the horses more.* But getting the trailer hooked up and the horses loaded took precious minutes.

…Thought of her mothballed Suburban. *Maybe I should just hook it up and leave it hooked up.* Loading the horses took seconds, the animals well-accustomed and comfortable with loading, especially because they knew tasty food bribes awaited them inside. Of course, they'd never had a negative experience riding in one which was the big plus. "Tom, how hard would it be for you to keep your dad's mare ready to roll at a moment's notice?" Jessie asked.

He gave her a glance that told her the answer to *that* one.

"Okay. So, how do you feel about riding one of my horses?"

He shrugged. "Fine with me. Why?"

"Just thinking."

"Uh-oh. Danger, danger. Howie, come save me."

"You are such a brat, Tom!"

And that made him grin. ...And grab and pull her down—forcibly—him clamping a hand over her mouth for a second as he laid them over into the cover of the brush at the side of the trail. Then he let her go and pointed.

There, ahead, just seeable around the final curve in the trail before the trailhead parking area, the men from the van were standing very near Landon's Rhino.

"They're filming the interior and exterior, and, look, now they're trying to get shots of underneath it," Tom whispered.

Yeah, Jessie saw that. Crawled around the curve enough to get some pictures with her phone, then started recording video of the men's snooping.

Satisfied with the captures, Jessie listened as Tom outlined a plan. They'd approach obliquely from the woods.

Signaling the dogs and picking up Duchess, Jessie followed Tom off-trail into the trees to approach the nosey sneaks from behind.

Tom re-outlined his strategy and Jessie grinned. Then she added in the dogs, which made Tom really grin. "Okay. Let's go make them sweat, Jessie."

*

A NOTICE BEEPED as it lit up and pulsed on Landon's phone. He frowned seeing it. Touched it live—Jessie's cam. Another lit from Tom's, and he touched that one on, too, turning his phone sideways to play them side-by-side as Sol and Martin went over the spot where Linda Allen had 'toppled'. Then he heard the yells—faint from down the hill, louder on the cam feeds—as both Tom and Jessie, dogs bristling around them, surprised the two pesky Actuator Studios creeps. The men's faces went scared ...with reason. Both Tom and Jessie had called out their sudden appearance from the brush, and his two deputies were surrounded by bristling teeth and rippling fur.

"What are you doing?" Landon heard Tom demand.

"Sorry. Sorry. Just wanted footage of the sheriff's vehicle," the twerpy one said.

"Why?"

"For ...for our documentary."—cameraman.

"*What* documentary?" Jessie asked.

"Cou–could you call off your dogs ...please?"—again the cameraman.

"Answer the question."

"Ah...."

"We're contrasting and comparing how two different sheriffs in two different counties handle similar investigations."—that was the creepy guy speaking again.

Same thing they told me, Landon thought.

"Move away from the vehicle," Jessie said. Landon knew that Jessie knew that she had no authority to demand that. Being around the vicinity of and even filming a unit was fair game so long as it was on public property. They couldn't touch it, but they could photograph and film it. Landon groaned, watching. Jessie had no legal grounds for the demand.

Amazingly, though, Jessie got her way. Her command was obeyed …probably because of Milo, Mitch, Sumi, and Acer—especially Milo because of his menacing, deep growl, a very audible rumble on the cam's audio. And Acer looked ready to launch himself. The big shepherd had his head low, ears stiff, the dog slowly easing forward, one small, slow-motion step by slow-motion, creeping step.

The men shuffled away, then, almost as if cued, bolted for their van.

Doors opened. Doors slammed, and they drove away, tires spitting gravel.

"Done and dusted," Landon heard Tom say with a laugh.

"Done and dusted," Landon repeated softly, and they'd done it all with bluff and guile—legal.

He saw Jessie grin at Tom, the two clapping hands in a high five. Then Jessie begin cooing praise to her dogs, squatting down to rub their ruffs and give them hugs, them wiggling and wagging and licking her face, every one of them wagging like crazy.

The skinny man who seemed to be the boss of the two had said they were 'contrasting and comparing how sheriffs from two different counties handled similar cases'.

What cases? …And who, Landon wondered, was the other victim of their snooping? Another Idaho sheriff, maybe?

He'd call around and ask.

The bigger question was 'why'? What was the point of such a documentary and comparison? What was the endgame?

***

18 – One Shooter

JESSIE LAUNCHED her drones from the parking lot, one headed toward the spot she'd marked on her phone's tracking app of the bank, sending another up to the location of the Allen rescue where she surmised Sol, Martin, and Landon would still be poking around. Using the auto-pilot feature, she let the drones all but fly themselves, keeping hands ready in case something like a gust wobbled one or a nosy hawk or eagle tried to snatch one. "Darned birds."

"That happen?" Tom asked.

"Yeah. Lost one a couple of weeks back to a Golden that decided that it must look like lunch, I guess."

Tom laughed. "Or else he just didn't like you invading his privacy."

"Right. I'm waiting for the replacement to come in."

"That could get expensive at five grand a pop," Tom said.

"Cameras were okay. Just got them to send a new unit so I can remount them. Only a grand for that. It's the cameras that are the big, spendy stuff. ...Well, a grand after the insurance pays up."

"That's a lot of money, though."

"Yeah, but the bennies are worth it. We can cover a lot of territory so the dogs don't have to, especially when we're in bad country."

"Like those cliffs where that guy fell?"

"Yep." Jessie brought one drone to hover at about five feet over where Sol had pointed out the disturbed bank, Scanned 360°, checked the recording—good visibility of the surrounding country—then, nosing around lower, Jessie dropped it down to about two feet from the steep downslope. She slowly lowered it along that bank where it showed that somebody had definitely climbed up, using exposed tree roots as handholds, the telltale scrapes in the soil around those roots giving sign.

Brought the drone back up, rescanning the disturbances, then, on top, found solid footprints. Hovering, she saw something that resembled a yellow bottle cap or small compressed propane cylinder cap—plastic. "Tom?"

He looked as she hit magnify. "Yep. That's a CO2 canister cap, I'd bet."

"You want to advise the guys?"

"Yeah."

*

LANDON WAS always happy when he was allowed to actually *do* something. Right now, he was photographing what appeared to be a series of wedge-shaped, shallow divots in the forest floor that led away from where a rotting log had been scraped by something, probably the same foot that made the divots. Britta leading, she was padding along beside him, nose to the ground and pausing at each divot until he got done there, then moving on to the next. "Thanks for the help, Britta."

The tail gave a wag.

His phone went off. *Of course.* Snapped a last picture, then dug his phone out and answered, "Reid."

"Found what we think is a CO2 tank cap," Tom's voice said in his ear.

"All right. I think we're about done here. Should be coming your way in a few minutes." Rung off.

The buzz of a large insect, and he jerked back as the 'bug' came near him, the thing hovering—one of Jessie's drones. It waggled.

He forced a smile, touched his hat brim. *Darned flying cockroaches.*

Of course, cockroaches weren't pale blue. The thing rose straight up, then took off to somewhere else. Grumbled about Jessie hazing him on purpose as he made his way along to the next spot where Britta sat, paused.

*

JESSIE BROUGHT back the drone that had scoped out the bank and caught a look at the tank cap, landed it, stowed it, then concentrated on manually flying the drone she'd buzzed by Landon with. She kept assist on, but purposely was angling from where Homer Garrison's attack had happened, taking it backwards to where they'd found Linda Allen. The bank Sol had seen was almost in line with the same direction of travel, with just a slight deviation. And it made sense. The trail circled around the mountainside, making the three points, the bank, Linda Allen's position, and the site of the Garrison attack, almost in a straight line from one another as a crow …or drone would fly.

Jessie slowed the drone down to snoop along on the other side of the trail from Allen's fall. She was looking for sign of foot travel …and found it after scanning back and forth for long minutes.

Keeping within five feet of the ground, she was able to pretty much follow divots in the pine needle duff along a course that pretty much went along in a single direction of travel, the actual divots zigging and zagging to avoid obstacles—trees, brush clumps, rocks, and low hanging deadfalls—but the direction was pretty much along one trajectory.

Most people tended to veer to the right or left as they traveled cross-country, depending on handedness. Not this runner …and, by the apparent length of stride, it *was* a runner. They were sticking pretty much to a north-by-north-easterly line of travel. *They had an app like I do, I bet*, Jessie guessed.

Marking location, she headed the drone skyward up through the trees. Hovered and scanned full circle—nothing apparent except the bank—then dropped back down to continue to follow the divots.

Why was the shooter running? Was the attacker running *from* something or *to* something?

Jessie guessed it was toward Garrison, and on purpose. *He'd heard the shot of Garrison getting his deer. He went after Garrison on purpose*—that was her guess. *This was intentional.*

***

19 – Drone Sighting

IT WAS JUST a flash of color—bright color—but Jessie hovered, then reversed. Probably fall leaves. …But it wasn't.

Speeding toward, Jessie gasped, then, hovering the drone, eased down and around—an older man, skin white and pasty. He was prone, his face turned aside, the eyes closed.

No lividity. He's alive maybe.

Jessie nosed the drone closer.

The eyes opened, and she yelped, the drone wobbling as her fingers jerked. Grounded the drone, turned on the mic and told him, "Special Deputy and Paramedic here. I'm on my way to you. Hold on."

The eyes slowly blinked.

"Hold on," she repeated, and, grabbing her med pack, Jessie swung it on, buckling into it as she took off, dogs with her, Tom scrambling after.

*

"Medivac en route came the chatter as Landon, Britta with him, headed at a run for Jessie's target, the coordinates from the drone having hit his phone the same time Jessie transmitted it to Dispatch.

He got there before Jessie did by long minutes, the man—a man he recognized—aware as he ran up. "Mr. Parker," Landon huffed. Moved the drone, then jerked his jacket off and put it over the man who was cold to the touch.

He turned to the dog. "Britta? Can you *Platz* next to him here, please?" he asked, motioning where he wanted her—next to Parker's belly, as he himself laid down next to the man's back to share his body heat, his heart warming as Britta laid down, snuggling in on the other side.

The man moaned.

"It's okay, Cornie. Help is on the way."

*

JESSIE WAS running hard, Tom right with her, dogs trotting and easy-loping along beside and around. She took the shortest way possible—up the trail, then cutting through the brush, trees, and bramble on as straight a line toward the victim as she could manage.

She went down once, jarring her shin and knee, but rolling right back up. Now kept her eyes on the ground she traveled, setting her app to beep like radar if she strayed too far off the line toward her target.

And her brain clocked time traveled—four minutes, five …six.

Suddenly, the dogs bounded forward, heads coming up, noses high, ears alert. They smelled the quarry. They smelled human. "My good, good dogs."

The terrain got easier as her dogs started leading, choosing the path. She touched the app silent. Her dogs *had* this. They'd get her there. *My wonder dogs.* Scooped up Duchess who was flagging and tucked her close under her arm.

*

…PANTING BODIES—Jessie's dogs. Then the fresh air and sunshine smell of Jessie herself as she crouched down by Britta, the dog scooting back to give her room.

"Good job, Landon," Jessie huffed out, her hands doing things—fingers to Cornie's neck, fingers at his eyes. "Turning him," she said. "Help me by rolling with him, Landon, then you can clear the field."

He did as told. Watched as Tom pulled what Landon recognized as heat packs, rolling them in his hands to catalyze the chemicals inside, as Jessie got through to the hospital on her phone. Tom stuffed them inside the man's paint-covered jacket and shirt, both of which Jessie had undone with quick fingers. "Put them on top of his thermals, Tom. Don't want to chance burning him."

"Yes'm," Hudson responded.

"His name is Cornelius Parker, Jessie," Landon said. "Late seventies. Friends with Sam Hull and my dad, too."

Heard her relay name and age as approximate to the doctor on the other end of her call. Heard the doctor indicate she had his medical history up. Heard the same voice chatter something about one BP med, no known heart complications, then okay warm normal saline IV. "IV push," the voice said. "Get me BP, pulse, respirations, and temp again. Can you give me oxygen?"

…Watched Jessie cut Cornie's jacket and shirt arm, stick and get blood, tape the catheter. She pulled an IV bag out of her pack.

Jessie's eyes reached up to his. "Landon, could you put this in your armpit inside your shirt to keep it warm? And get your jacket back on, please?"

"Yes, Ma'am," he said, taking the IV bag, warm to the touch, and did as asked.

Jessie plugged the end of it into the catheter's hub, opened up the flow, then ran up the BP cuff again as Tom put a clip on the man's finger—oxygen sensor. "There's a battery pack on his hip. Dead. Pulling it," Tom said.

"That and the fact it didn't rain kept him going," Jessie said back.

Saw Jessie stick a thermometer in Cornie's ear, then, when it beeped, take it out and read it. Report it and the oxygen numbers to the woman doctor she spoke to—no oxygen necessary.

Landon felt relief surge. Cornie was going to make it. He just knew it. The man was doing well, in fact—temp low, but BP, heart rate, and respirations within good ranges from his first aid knowledge.

Now Jessie started to check the man over. She cut the thermal underwear he wore, right through the wires running back and forth through it. And there was the cause of Cornie's mishap …which they already knew from the paint covering him. Jessie outlined it for the ER doc. "Blunt force trauma to the torso, lower thoracic, starting around the 6th rib continuing down upper and perineal abdomen, traveling laterally from left to right across to the illiac crest, right side. High velocity paintball strikes suspected. Significant bruising in bulls eye patterns."

Overhead, the sound of the rescue helicopter.

"They say they're going to try landing in a clearing west of us," Tom said.

"Good," Jessie responded. ...Relayed more numbers. Stuck hot packs down Cornie's pants, the man shifting uncomfortably, his eyes rolling and a frown coming to his brow.

"It's okay, Cornie," Landon said. "She's just putting on more heat packs. Not getting fresh with you. Okay?" he told him, then squatted down by the man opposite of Jessie.

Cornie reached a hand toward him. He took hold of it, the grip of that old hand strong, but the skin icy cold.

*

JESSIE SAT on the ground, her dogs downed around her, them watching as she repacked her gear. She knew what they wanted. Had been remiss. Pulled out a baggie and gave them each a goody, cuddling and praising each. Felt Landon walk up, Britta with him, of course. Kept mum and acted like she wasn't aware of him …which, if he was dog aware, he'd know was a lie.

"You're bleeding, Jessie," he said, pointing.

She looked where he pointed, saw her jeans below the knee, right leg—the fall she'd taken getting here. Stood and dropped her pants, pulling the knee compression sleeve down, too, which ripped the already coagulated blood and started the wound bleeding in earnest again.

Landon abruptly stepped back, then turned away.

"I'm decent," she said belatedly,. *Should have warned him.* "I have on slip shorts."

Heard him grunt.

She had to keep reminding herself to work with Landon appropriately. He just wasn't like other people. *Reward him, now.* "…But I appreciate you blocking everybody's view."

He didn't comment. Just stood with his back to her as she checked out the wound—a peeled back wedge of skin, the edges curled under. Sucked in breath, chewing lips at the bad sting as she cleaned it and uncurled the edges of the wound's skin flap. Put salve on the wound interior, not the skin, then a butterfly strip, a non-stick pad over that, then wrapped the area with a cohesive self-stick bandage. Pulled her knee compression sleeve into place, then her jeans back up. Turned to Landon's back, Britta watching her.

She smiled seeing the happy dog— ...what *used* to be her big blonde dog, and Britta wagged, decisively blinking her eyes just once in that way dogs had of giving somebody, usually somebody who was *not* their person, an 'attaboy'. Jessie smiled more. Got on with business. "Okay, Landon. It's safe, now. Sorry for making you uncomfortable."

He turned around, nodded once, eyes avoiding until, with an audible breath, he said, "You have time to talk?"

"Sure. Tom's off dropping evidence markers. He'll be awhile." She should be helping Tom, but not until 'the boss' was done.

"Your thoughts?"

She knew what Landon was asking. She didn't want to share. She had nothing but pure speculation. "That's a Sol Preston question, not a Jessie Anderson one. He's over there." She pointed.

"I'm asking Jessie Anderson, CSI."

"Ex-CSI, strong on the 'ex'."

The head tipped down and sideways, the eyes locking on hers. "I'm asking, anyway," he came back, the voice getting deeper, slower, and quieter.

Uh-oh. He's getting testy. Did she tear into him and cut him off, or give it up and share half-baked assumptions based on …nothing much. Sighed.

"Jessie?"

…Told him her impressions. "Wild guesses, Landon."

"One or two shooters?"

She shook her head. "I think one. The strides never deviated much in length, and it's a straight line between here, that bank Sol noticed, where Linda was toppled, and where Garrison was attacked …well, almost a straight line. …And that's the other thing. The line of travel was too straight—trued—like they were using a compass or trekking app."

He nodded. "Thank you. Now, see? That wasn't hard, was it?"

Baited! "Yeah, actually, it was! I don't like sharing my half-baked thoughts and outing them half-cocked."

"It won't go any further. I just needed to know if somebody else was thinking along similar lines."

So, he thought so, too.

"The perp was out hunting hunters," Landon muttered.

And that came out of the blue. Jessie frowned. "Why do you think that?"

"Because both men *are* hunters."

Jessie shook her head. "Don't assume. And that doesn't explain why Grant and Sandra were attacked. They were just out stamina training, not hunting."

A sigh. "I don't know. A mistaken assumption on the part of the assailants?"

"Uh-uh. I don't buy it. People who are anti-hunting demonstrate, petition, mostly online, make noise on social media, call their Congressional rep, donate to anti-hunting groups, like the US Humane Society and ASPCA …PETA. They don't pick up paintball guns and go out hunting hunters."

"How do you know that?"

She rolled eyes. "Just not the type. Most of them couldn't even figure out how to *load* a paintball gun, much less aim and fire one."

He chuckled. "Follow the instructions on the package?"

"Well, you do have a point there, since all of them we've caught, so far, are women. Only women read instructions."

He ignored her jibe, but Jessie smirked. She'd got him with that one, for sure.

"You think this one is a woman, too?" he asked.

"I do. The foot size and stride coming away from here and heading for Garrison gives me that impression, mostly because there's a slight, telling look to a woman's stride based on the shape of the pelvis and how the hip joints move, but, again, that's Sol's territory, not mine."

"So the assailant hit Parker first, then went for Garrison."

"That's what I think."

"How about motive?"

Now Jessie really shook her head. "I haven't a clue."

"But you dismiss my suggestion that they're hunting hunters?"

"I'm going to repeat myself, Landon. First rule in criminology—never assume."

He nodded. "Thank you." Touched the brim of his hat and walked away, leaving Jessie standing there, and that somehow irritated her.

*

LANDON PUT a call into the newspaper and the local radio and television stations for anyone who'd been shot by a paintball in the last several days to drop by and file an incident report with the S.O. He was very sure that what they had was someone or a group of someone's out hunting hunters ...or anyone they thought was a hunter. Yes, he was sure.

***

20 – Dinner Out

BEATEN AND battered again by her dad with his pushup regimen at the firing range, Jessie was prepared this time. She handily bested Landon every round. Satisfied, her dad let her go early so he could work with Landon, and, happily, she made it home in plenty of time to get ready for yet another dinner out with Jedidiah.

Her dogs watched as, freshly showered, she got on clothes, make-up, fixed her hair, and put on earrings and a necklace. "It's okay, guys and gals," she told the dogs. "We're just friends."

Was that true? She looked at herself in the mirror. Nodded. Yes. "Just friends." Jessie had no intention of falling for a guy again. Not ever. It just hurt too much, especially when they either didn't even see you or, the worst, they died right before your eyes.

*

EXHAUSTED FROM Oli's very physical workout at the shooting range, Landon headed back to the S.O. to shower, change, then collect Sol. And his brain again turned to what they had so far.

Between Jessie's drone footage, the crime scene photographs, and hard evidence collection, including both Garrison's and Cornie's paint-coated jackets, pants, and shirts, plus casts of footprints, and somebody's fingers on ice, they were pretty sure they had a solid case against whomever had attacked the men …and they suspected it was only one person. Unfortunately, no-one had surfaced via clinics and hospitals who had lost parts of the second finger plus both the third and fourth fingers of their right hand, and they had expanded the BOLO statewide, and even into Washington. The good thing was that it looked like Garrison was going to make it. Cornie was a sure survivor. He had bruising on his chest, but nowhere near as bad as Garrison. Sol posited that he'd been shot from a much greater distance. He was just being kept for observation, now that he'd rallied, his internal temperature stable, no other complications.

"You ready to go meet Mrs. Lindholme?" Landon asked, poking his head into Sol's lab.

"Almost. Take a look at this," Sol said.

Landon stepped over to where the criminologist was working with what looked like tweezers and forceps under a light-ringed magnification lens. "These are the plastic shards found up at the scene of the Garrison shooting."

Landon looked at what amounted to a puzzle of pieces carefully arranged on a slab. The doctor shifted the light to the plastic-wrapped paintball gun they'd taken off of the woman suspected of shooting Richard Orr in the throat. "See it?" Sol asked.

He didn't.

"The mold pattern on the stock...." Sol pulled the magnifier back to focus on the shards. "...Is identical. They are the same model of gun—a highly customized Charper Pro 2—which is the same model taken off the two assailants who attacked Grant Evans and Sandra Darstead. All the paintball guns we have in evidence are not only the same model, but from the same manufacturing lot."

"So the guns all came from the same purchase order."

"Or at least they were all manufactured at the same factory in the same batch."

"And the significance is that the incidents and shooters are somehow related, correct?"

"That would be one assumption, yes."

That, to Landon, was a given. They'd all been dressed almost identically. At least they had circumstantial evidence of some sort of collusion, now. And he was betting the colluding factor was targeting hunters. Got to be an organization behind this—an anti-hunting organization or affiliation. "We need to get going, Sol. We're going to be late."

Sol shifted the light and turned it off. Stuck a hard cover over his work, and took off his lab coat. Hung it up. "Ready when you are."

Landon stared. The good doctor was wearing an impeccably tailored black suit with satin lapels—not quite a tux, but almost. "I suddenly feel very underdressed," Landon said.

"I want to make a good impression."

"You definitely do that, Sol, even without the fancy threads."

*

TONIGHT, it was The Hereford again—eating out instead of at home. "Why don't you like eating dinner with my family?" Jessie asked, poking at Jedidiah with the question again. She'd asked repeatedly, every time they did this, but he always managed to avoid answering. This time, she would pursue it and get an answer. "Or invite me to your house?"

He turned in his seat, sat back, his dark, liquid eyes focusing on her in a way that flustered. "Because I like dining alone with you," he said softly. "I don't have to share you."

"Um…. Okay. Thanks for finally answering." She wasn't sure she was comfortable with the answer, but at least she had one.

"Shouldn't it be obvious?" he asked, watching her in the disconcerting way he had.

She shook her head. "Not really."

"Have you ever dated before now?"

Out of the blue! "Nope. Almost made it to the prom, but didn't go at the last minute. My twin ruined my dress. And, of course, at college, I was way too busy for that stuff."

He chuckled. "Me neither. Well, that's not quite true. But I found it lame. I've always been way too not interested. …Not anymore."

Uh-oh. "Um, Jed. We've had this discussion. Friends. *Only* friends. Remember?"

"Mm-hmm. Friends. I'm hoping *best* friends in time, Jessie. You share a love of horses and the outdoors. There are too few who *truly* hold that passion. They play, but it's not a lifestyle. With you, it is. Just like it is with me."

That was true. *Lighten it up.* "Okay. But I am not *ever* going to smear myself with rancid bear grease!"

And that brought soft, gleeful laughter from the dulcet-voiced Jedidiah. "Better than becoming a bear snack, wouldn't you agree?"

"That's what they make bear bombs, spray, and big bore rifles for."

"Rancid bear grease is less confrontational. They just think you're another bear, and no competition to their territory 'cause you're already a dead bear, at least by how you stink."

"Right! Here comes dinner, thank Providence! No more bear grease talk, please, Jedidiah."

Again the gentle laughter. He raised his wine glass toward her, eyes happy. "You brought it up."

She had. And Jessie smiled and raised her glass of seltzer in turn. Touched crystal. Jedidiah really was nice to be around. She did like him.

*

LANDON WATCHED two people he cared about touch glasses as the hostess led them through to their table. He hadn't been expecting to see them, especially not together on a weeknight. Jessie was usually in bed by this time.

"Here you go, sirs," the hostess said, and the woman sitting there already was looking at Sol like she'd seen a ghost.

"Thank you," Landon said to the hostess. He extended a hand toward Sol. "Mrs. Lindholme? I'd like to introduce Dr. Sol Preston. Sol? Mrs. Lindholme."

"You- …look the spitting image of my son," Mrs. Lindholme said, her voice cracking. Tears welled.

"He's too short," Landon said, attempting to head off an emotional crisis.

The elderly woman caught herself up. A short, sharp laugh burst out. Then, "He …is."

"But he does drive a lime green 2003 Chevy Spark."

The woman's eyes, now halfway between teary and surprised, calmed a little. "You do?"

"Yeah. I had it custom painted. People see it coming."

The woman laughed again, the sound a bit like a hiccup. "My son had his painted that for the exact same reason."

Crisis averted. "May we sit?" Landon asked.

"Oh. I'm so sorry. Of course. Please."

*

THE DINNER went well, Sol regaling Mrs. Lindholme with anecdotes from his childhood, about being the shortest guy in class, on always getting into trouble with his sense of humor. "Yeah, I've always been a troublemaker. I gave my mom fits because I love playing practical jokes."

"Does the same thing at the office," Landon muttered. "Pure jokester."

"Laughter is better than sourpuss faces, right?" Sol said.

"Definitely," Mrs. Lindholme agreed. "Most definitely."

*

OUT OF THE corner of her eye, Jessie caught sight of Landon and Sol, both of them dressed up. *What are they doing here?!*

She kept her eyes on Jed. Kept up her end of the conversation with him as their plates were set down by the waiter.

Enjoyed her meal, enjoyed the young man she dined with. Fretted.

*

"WELL, THAT was a success," Sol said as they headed home.

Landon nodded. It *had* gone well. "Putting ghosts to rest," he said.

"Is that why you're so quiet?"

"Mmm. Didn't know I was."

"You are."

He processed that. Finally said what was on his mind: "Jessie looks happy with Jedidiah."

There was a long pause to that. Then, Sol quietly agreed. "She does."

***

21 – Evidence & Witnesses

WEDNESDAY

'WAS TOPPLED'—that phrase was stuck in Landon's head. They needed to speak to Linda Allen. Had she seen something? Had she, in fact, seen the assailant? …But how to approach the woman?

That was the first question in Landon's mind when he woke at 4AM after a night of bad dreams he didn't remember except as vague flashes that made no sense.

The question stayed on his mind as he let Britta out to potty, brushed his teeth and got dressed in running gear. It pestered him as he fed Britta and the cats, nuked the last of yesterday's coffee, then started more so it would be ready when he got back. It persisted as he and Britta headed for the Andersons.

He'd spent last night after getting home from dinner at the Hereford searching for, then reading through Linda Allen's blog—eleven years of weekly posts, all of them rather bland, but all of them dressed up with beautiful pictures taken of nature in the

Bitterroots—leaves, 'shooms, birds, slugs, salamanders and newts, pine squirrels, even the occasional burl or shelf fungi. There was even a five-point buck in one. The woman had a good eye and was a reasonable photographer with her phone. She had a noticeable affinity for pools of water—from rain puddles to woodland ponds and quiet lakes. Not for her were their more dramatic rushing waters of the Bitterroot lands. She liked the quiet things.

Thinking about it as he joined Oli and Jessie for their every weekday morning run, it was the pictures that gave him best insight into the Linda Allen. What it didn't give him was help in figuring out how to interview her without her being on guard.

Use Tank? It was a possibility, but Tank was an intimidating-looking man, and, with insights from her blogging, Linda seemed woman-friendly, only.

Jessie? She was female.

He chuckled. *Obviously*.

Jessie didn't act like a woman cop. More importantly, Jessie had established a high level of trust with Allen simply because she had been the one who'd found the woman and managed Linda's injury.

A glance her way as Jessie flew past him and Oli on her long-sprint training iced it for him. Yeah. Jessie. "Oli, next time Jessie comes by, I'm going to match her speed. I need to ask her permission on something."

"Go for it."

So he did and was rewarded by her agreeing.

"Where? At the S.O.?" he asked, his words coming in bursts with his breathing.

"Her home would be better," Jessie answered, and that's when Landon realized that Jessie wasn't breathing the way he'd been taught to by his high school track coach. Shortened his stride to match hers and paid attention. Caught her inhale—hard, quick, and deep through her nose for four full strides, a pause for four strides—then her exhale—long and measured through her mouth for another four strides. Matched it and ...after a few minutes, felt the strain and, returning to his own breathing pattern, he lengthened his stride back out to normal and slowed, Jessie disappearing around the bend in the trail ahead and Oli catching up with him.

"And?" the man asked.

"And she's willing to help with the witness interview."

"That's my Jessie."

It didn't work out that way, though. Landon put the call into Linda Allen, asking if Jessie and he could come out to ask a few questions about the toppling incident and the woman volunteered to come into the S.O. after her doctor's appointment this very morning. "I think I have something you might want to see," she said.

And she did. It was picture of leaves, water, a very strange shadow, and an obvious piece of a shoe tread.

Sol's magic to the rescue as he got a program to extrapolate multiple versions of what the image might be, and, finally, with Terri sticking her brains and fingers into the mix, they got something meaningful. It was the shadow of legs and, yes, the sole of a treaded boot …and, more computer magic, the tread of that shoe sole matched the castings taken at both the Parker and Garrison scenes.

"Same shooter," Sol said.

"Same shooter," Martin agreed, knocking then appearing through Landon's door on his 'come'.

So Jessie and he had been right. Same assailant. The boot tread iced it—identical tread, identical details of small imperfections in that tread to those exhibited on two castings Sol had taken. Whether the assailant was a woman or a man was still up for grabs. *Maybe both?* Landon mused, thinking of their problem human in lock-up. Sighed. Still no bed in the psych ward at the hospital. Still none down in any of the psychiatric hospitals run by the state, the ones capable of handling problem prisoners. He was stuck with her/him, and the job was a time- and personnel-consuming task. "Oh, the joys."

Martin's portable phone rang, and he answered. Grunted. Hung up. "More news," Martin said. "Kins just found our suspect in the Garrison case, a woman passed out in her car, her right hand bandaged and bloody."

Of *course* it was Deputy Dave Kins who'd found her, called an ambulance, and followed that ambulance into the hospital. Kins, like Jessie, was one of those 'lucky' individuals who always seemed at the right (or was it wrong?) place at the right (or wrong) time ...depending on how you looked at it. Both of them had a tendency to be on scene where trouble happened.

"Garrison is allowed visitors today, too," Martin said. "Thought you might go talk to him, instead of me or one of the deputies."

Landon eyed his undersheriff. Noted the still face and eye gleam. "Why?"

"Isn't that obvious?"

"No."

"The hat."

Scowled.

Martin raised a warding hand. "Just kidding." He watched Landon, then said, "...But, also, not kidding. People recognize and trust you, Reid. Garrison will talk to you, especially since you field dressed his deer and took care of his horses."

Landon pulled a deep breath. Let it out. "All right. I'll do it." But he hated hospitals—now he did. Got the jitters every time he walked into one. It was his duty and obligation to step in to see the victims of crimes that happened on his watch as sheriff. It was his duty and desire to check on his own people. But to have to stay longer than friendly chit-chat and commiserations was all but intolerable. Hospitals were, in essence, nothing but prisons where the inmates were guinea pigs at the mercy of the medical

216

establishment—his take, and he admitted the prejudice of experience. *Never again.*

*

JESSIE PICKED up Grant Evans from the hospital as soon as they released him at 8 AM. "Thanks for doing this," Grant said, getting in, his dogs, which Jessie had loaded up, too, crowding in with joyful slurps of tongue and happy barks—all five. "All right, all right. Settle down, please." But he was laughing. Sockmo, the Beagle, Grant's 'first dog', jumped over the back to the center console and crawled onto Grant's lap. "I guess they missed me."

"Yeah. I'd say so. It's all those dog cookies you slip them that does it."

And, again, the man laughed, rubbing ears, ruffs, and then, surprising to Jessie, burying his face in Sockmo's fur. "I missed them, just that short time. These guys are my life, now."

"Yeah. My dogs are mine, too. Dogs are best."

"They are."

"Home?"

"Car?"

"I had my dad drive it to your place." She held out his keys. "Here ya go."

"Thanks, Jessie."

"You're very welcome. But let's not do that again, okay?"

"Let's hope. Saw Sandra. She's in a cast up to her hip. She says the doctors say she'll be out of commission they figure for six to seven weeks, but she should be able to get the cast off just in time for her daughter's wedding. Just. Barely."

Jessie didn't tell Grant she'd already stopped by and spoken to Sandy. Just said, "I'm glad."

"So am I."

*

LANDON STEPPED out to the front, and, once again, his curiosity was roused as the deputy manning the counter quickly slid something big underneath. *What gives?*

He'd have to take a look for himself …when he got back.

He looked around the lobby. He counted sixteen heads. As he stood there, a deputy came through to collect one of them. He frowned. "You all here answering my call for people who have been attacked by paintballs?" he asked.

Heads nodded.

"I thank you for coming forward. We're going to catch these people." Then, before he got snagged by questions or grousing he didn't have answers for, he turned back to the counter. "I'm heading over to the hospital, Red," he called to his third in command.

"Checking on our fingerless suspect?" Red asked.

"Yes. And on Grant Evans, Sandra Darstead, Homer Garrison, and Cornie Parker," Landon answered.

"Five birds, one stone."

"Something like that."

"Kins is over there."

"I heard."

"You should be able to see Garrison, but both Grant Evans and Cornelius Parker are being released today. Maybe have already gone home."

"And the suspect?"

"Kins already sent in the preliminaries. Car in tow for Sinclair and Preston to process, wallet found identifies the suspect as one Caucasian female, Calista

Sabrine Roegerson, twenty-three, single, U.S. citizen, no record, resident of Phoenix, Arizona. Sending Kin's photo of the woman plus her DMV photo to your phone now in case you want to see if Garrison can ID her."

"All right." Landon's phone pinged, and he looked. Photos as promised. "Thanks, Red." Tapped the counter, paused to study the desk deputy's face …which instantly flushed up, then went toward the back.

*

JESSIE HAD just gotten parked when her dad stepped up. "Jessie?"

"Yeah, Dad?" she said, grinning as she let the troops out, Sandra's Border Collies with them. …Lifted Duchess down.

"Are you getting serious about Jed Blackthorne?"

That question about knocked her over. "N—no. We're just friends. Get along."

He stood there watching her, his eyes bright and hard. "What gives, Dad?" she asked cautiously. "You know something about Jedidiah that I don't?"

"No. He's a good man. I'm just worried."

Relief. And she knew about what. "No worries. I'm not falling head-over-heels in love, if that's what's stressing you. Not hardly. I like Jed, but, no. Been there, done that. Never again." She gave Oli square eyes. "I promise. I'm yours for life, Dad."

"You mean Anderson Working Dogs."

"That, too," she said with a grin. *Take his mind off it. And mine.* "Snack? I baked cinnamon coffee cake this morning, one of your favs."

He relaxed. Gave a little thin-lipped smile. "I thought I smelled it in the air."

"Yep. Put it in just before breakfast. Pulled it out just after. It's been cooling since before I picked up Grant from the hospital. It should be perfect about now."

"Is there enough for everybody?" and, of course, he meant their employees.

"Yep. Call 'em in."

*

HEADING OUT, the pesky TV van followed him. It followed Landon all the way to the hospital, Britta grumbling under her breath as she kept jumping all the way to the back, then coming up front again to cast looks out the back of The Rhino, then do it all over again.

He parked in a shady spot, even though it was a cool day. Rolled the windows down. Turned on the security—audible warnings and outside shocks both, thank you. Put cones around the rig, too, then strung tape. That should do it. "Britta, stay. Um... *bleib*.

And, there, filming him do it all were the guys from the van. And then they followed him to the side entrance door. Well, they couldn't follow him into the hospital—against the privacy laws. Through the glazed sliders, and he was out-of-reach once out of sight. "Pests."

A check in Emergency found Kins there. "You are one of my best, my very best," Landon said, and watched the young man flush. "...But, just like a certain 'dog girl', you have a knack for finding trouble."

"Sorry, sir."

He chuckled. "Just don't ever get hurt doing it, or I'll have to read you the riot act."

"Yes, sir."

"Joking, Kins."

The young man smiled. "I know. I'm getting used to you not being like your dad."

He nodded.

A check at the desk got him the knowledge that, yes, Parker had been released and so had Grant, but netted floors, wings, and room numbers for Darstead and Garrison.

Darstead was asleep. He left a card and some flowers he'd snagged from the hospital gift shop, then went to find Garrison who was still in CCU. "Can he have visitors?"

Once Landon had cleared a visit to Garrison with the floor's head nurse, he found Garrison looking good. "Mr. Garrison," Landon said, touching on his cam and stepping in.

"Sheriff."

"How are you feeling?"

"Like I've been put through my wife's food processor. ...Thanks for takin' care of my deer and my horses."

"Can't waste good meat, and horses need to be home in their own pasture."

The man eyed him. "You did that personally, I was told."

"No. I just brought them down to the parking area. One of my deputies took it from there, and it's all part of the job, Mr. Garrison. Just part of the job."

"And part of the job is you bein' here to tell me I'm under arrest for murder, too, isn't it?" The man raised a hand up—the one without the IV, offering it.

Landon shook his head. "No. You didn't kill anybody. Blew off some fingers, but that's all. And it was self-defense."

A frown met that. Then, "I killed somebody. Shot them almost point blank, me on my back, them standin' over me."

"Your clothes demonstrate they had a muzzle of a gun on your chest, one that matches a specific model of paintball gun."

Garrison swallowed. Tears welled, and he dropped his face away. "Thought I was a gone'r. Didn't know it only shot paint," he muttered.

"Paintballs that about killed you. Paintball guns are capable of killing, and the person shooting it is then guilty of felony assault with intent."

Again the man's eyes raised to Landon's and some of the worry had gone out of them. "How did you figure that all out?" Garrison asked, his voice almost a whisper.

"The magic of modern forensics."

"Yeah, well, she put that gun right on my chest, me having a devil's time tryin' to breathe," Garrison said, and his voice shook saying it.

"She...." Landon said, keeping his voice oh so soft.

"Yeah. She had boobs."

"Good to know," he said even more softly. "If we bring her to trial, would you be willing to testify in court?"

The man's face went hopeful. "You bet!"

Landon smiled. Held up his phone, a picture of the woman missing her fingers on it. "Is this her?"

The man's eyes looked astounded. "Tha– that's *her!*" he said, and his voice shook with emotion.

Garrison's eyes grabbed Landon's. "Who *is* she? Why did she *shoot* me?! What did I ever do to *her?!*"

Landon had no answers.

Now to talk to the woman who was presently still downstairs in emergency.

But, when he got there, a lawyer was in speaking with her. He recognized the man, one of their most potent criminal defense lawyers, the same man Jessie had employed. Obviously the woman had wherewithal …or somebody footing the bill did.

Turned away and headed to the courthouse …and, of course, the van guys followed. They followed him all the way into Judge Laird's office where her clerk manned the desk, technically still public space. They couldn't follow him further, though. They could not come into chambers.

*

IT WAS RARE for Sol to ask her for help except at crime scenes. Very rare. "Okay. I'll be there in thirty."

"Thank you, Jessie."

When she got there, she saw why.

"This one took souvenirs," Sol said.

She had—chunks of hair, all of them neatly and cryptically labeled with unorthodox symbols, and no decryption key that they had found in her belongings or on her laptop to translate the woman's code into comprehendible.

"A puzzle right up your alley, Jessie."

"Well, not quite, but I'll see what I can figure out," she said, sitting down at one of Sol's computers, pulling up the pictures, and getting to work.

An hour later, she thought she'd figured it out. "It's a cipher of a cipher created for a deprecated video game," she told Sol. "Each one backwards, last swapped to first, middle to last to meet in the middle. Here you go."

Jessie hit the enter key and the redrawn symbols she'd taken from the images, swapping them into vectors, translated into comprehensible—date, place, and a number. "I'm guessing the number is the victim number in order of takedown from the sequential order as per date."

"Awesome, Jessie. Thank you sooo much!"

"You're welcome."

*

"I'VE BEEN summoned," Landon told Judge Laird's clerk. Saw the man smirk. Nod. "She's in chambers and will see you," the man said, then looked up at the camera people. "See that line on the floor?" he asked them, pointing to it. The camera man was behind it. The squirrely guy wasn't, but was nosing around near Judge Laird's inner office door.

The camera man nodded. The squirrel came back and got behind it, too. "Stay behind it," the clerk said.

Landon touched the brim of his hat to the clerk, eyed the van guys, then went to face whatever music awaited him with Judge Laird.

Tapped on the door.

"Enter."

Eased the door open as he took his hat off.

"Hat *on*. I do *not* want to see that scar, and it is still much too visible."

Slid his hat back in place. His hair was grown out, but, yes, the scar was still apparent. Shook his head and grinned to himself—Judge Laird, middle-aged and auburn-haired with a temperament to match— *Can you say red hot? And don't forget punctilious and adamant about it.*

He stepped in and closed the door. Stood there. "Your Honor. You wanted to see me?"

"I did. I expected you yesterday, but word has it that you're busy chasing tails, your own and other people's." She smirked saying it.

"It– ...it's been busy the last couple of days. I'm sorry I couldn't get here sooner, Your Honor."

The smile disappeared. "Well, you're here now." The eyes went to a folder on her desk.

One blood-red fingernail picked at a corner, but left it closed. She looked back up, eyes studying him, and he felt an almost irrepressible urge to squirm. Then, she smiled, again, eyelids dropping enough to make her look sinister. "I've issued a bench warrant for Nicholson."

He nodded. He'd gotten a copy of it. Is that why she wanted to see him?

"I think he's fled to somewhere he thinks we can't find him," she said.

He probably had. He had the money. Landon didn't respond, though Judge Laird seemed to be waiting for it. He'd wait till she prompted, though— safest.

"Enough of that," she said finally, waving a hand. She opened a drawer on her desk. Pulled out an odd-looking pen. Touched her phone. "David, bring the box, please."

Moments later, the door opened, Laird's clerk pushing through with a box suspiciously familiar. Landon frowned. Watched.

Laird got up and lifted a desk extension, pulling out some wooden slides for it. The clerk put the box down and left, the door closing with a snick.

She gave him a look. "Sit." She pointed to a chair.

He sat.

Laird opened the lid. Reached in and pulled out a very weird-looking …bronze object. Set it down in front of him. Then another. And another. And another. Two were bronze. Two were steel.

"Ah…."

Laird held out the pen. "Sign, please." Pointed, blood-red fingernail, explicit as to where.

"That's my…."

"Sign, please."

"…Fist."

"Sign."

He did as bid.

"Keep the laser engraving pen," Laird said once he'd finished signing all four. "You'll need it."

***

22 – The Fist

JESSIE'S XV was in the parking lot when he got back from the courthouse, him trailed, of course, by the camera van. His anger threatening to blow its lid, he managed, just, to make it to his office without something tripping the detonator, this despite the irritating presence of the Actuator Studio boys, now back in the lobby, camera rolling. Hit the intercom. "Deputies Jessica Anderson and Doctor Sol Preston, my office *now!* On the double."

Threw his hat down on the desk and slammed butt into chair. Anger brimmed.

*

"UH-OH," Sol said, grinning up at her.

Jessie rolled eyes. "Laird spilled the beans," Jessie groaned.

"She warned us. Besides, he was bound to find out sooner or later. We actually got more time and more done than we thought we would."

"We did."

"Let's go face the music, shall we? He did say 'on the double'."

"Yeah. Let's mosey. Come on, guys," Jessie called, her dogs picking up their chews and flooding out into the hallway.

"Ooo. Look at that," Sol said pointing. "Nice job."

And it was. Maintenance had done a perfect job with mounting the statuary of Landon's fist slamming into the wall in the very place it had happened. The sculpt was perfectly fitted into the hole Landon had punched there. A clear, plexiglass cover fitted over it and the brass protective bars to either side didn't ruin the effect …maybe enhanced it. "It is," Jessie agreed. She read the dated brass plaque:

'Be It Known: The damage preserved here is credible evidence, the result of Sheriff Landon Reid being informed of criminal motive for malevolence, whereupon he loosed the full weight and authority of his office to capture the offenders who are, at the time of this installation, now awaiting trial. Therefore, To Whom It May Concern—that would be you, the criminally inclined—Do NOT tick off Sheriff Landon, or this may result.'

"Yep. Perfect."

Martin poked his head out. "Need reinforcements?"

"Naw. We'll be okay," Jessie said. "He signed the model release form. He's not got a leg to stand on."

"Good luck, anyway. You're braver than I'll ever be to face an angry Reid."

"Thanks, but, like I said, he's not got any grounds. He signed away that right. Besides, it funds his new foundation and its charity."

"Does he know that yet?"

"He will soon, won't he?" Jessie said with a laugh and waved adieu as the undersheriff began humming a recognizable doom tune.

"What's that?" Jessie whispered to Sol. "I've heard it before somewhere."

"Chopin's *Funeral March*," he replied.

"Oh."

*

LANDON WATCHED them come on his surveillance monitors. The two of them, Sol and Jessie, were chattering away, Jessie's dogs surrounding them, as they navigated around the Actuator Studios guys. Laughing and grinning, their nonchalance and leisurely pace demonstrated complete disregard for his fiat, 'on the double'.

Keep calm. Temper never accomplishes— He broke that thought off as a bolt of laughter came through his speakers—Jessie's laughter.

Turned up the volume to hear Sol say, "He has no idea."

"*You* have no idea," Landon growled, Britta's ears flattening.

The dog laid her head down and gave a big sigh. Rolled her eyes up to him, then closed them and sighed again.

A tap at the door.

"Come."

*

JESSIE EYED Sol. He roll-eyed back. "Sounds ominous, doesn't he?" Sol said, grinning up at her.

"He does. Worst that can happen is that he fires us, though."

"That's true." Sol levered the handle, then gave the door a shove so it swung open. Grinned. "Hi."

"Get in here, the two of you, and close the door."

"Yes, sir," Sol answered, and Jessie had the hardest time not breaking out in giggles. The situation was totally off-the-wall, Landon looking like he was ready to commit murder over something completely beneficial to him and to Bitterroot County, and, of course, Sol was taking on the role of a naughty tormenter. *This will not end well for Landon.* And now she did lose it, a grin breaking her carefully composed face. Then she laughed outright—couldn't help herself. Lost it completely, laughing so hard, the fit bent her almost double.

Hands on knees, she couldn't stop, her dogs all wagging around her. It was so perfect. The look on his face.... *Worth all the work!*

*

LANDON WATCHED the impudent dwarf and the audacious 'Dog Girl', both. Sol unabashedly was grinning at him, glee blatant. Jessie was doubled over, her laughter a scald to his ears. "Sit down, both of you," he growled.

Sol complied, the smirk on his face getting even broader. Jessie put a hand over her mouth, her laughter blowing raspberries through the fingers as she practically staggered forward. She didn't make it to a chair, collapsing in giggles and just plopping her butt on the floor, hands grabbing stomach, dogs—more dogs than usual—nosing all around her, tails wagging.

"You tricked me, Sol," he said, Jessie's laughter burning as he focused on the only one of the two people capable of listening at the moment. "This was your idea, and you enlisted Jessie to help you!"

The man he considered a friend …who he had just asked to consider the ranch his home, nodded. "Yeah. We kinda did. Only way to make it all happen. You provided the perfect opportunity to get some really, really productive balls rolling! Findlingham then went to town for you and got the paperwork drawn up, got you to sign it all, then filed it, all neat and tidy."

Findlingham! His own lawyer had also been party to it!

He shifted his attention to Jessie who had finally gotten over her paralyzing paroxysms of hilarity. He pointed to the empty chair next to Sol's. "Sit."

She chuckled. Didn't move. "I am sitting," she said, her voice choking up with laughter again.

"Jessie?!"

Rolling eyes, she got herself to her feet and sat down like a human being.

"Thank you."

"You're *not* welcome. I'm more comfy on the floor. You know that."

Exactly why he wanted her in a chair, thank you! "You tricked me, Jessie! That was no poultice you put on me the night that happened."

"It was. It was soft and moist and it relieved the inflammation. That's the definition of a poultice."

"That was casting material. That's why it got so hot!"

She just smirked at him.

"You violated my rights, both of you. I could sue—"

"No, we didn't," Jessie broke in. "You signed a comprehensive model release."

"No, I didn't—"

"Yes, you did. Check the foundation's paperwork."

He got up. Went to his big, ugly, physical filing cabinet. Got out the copy he kept in the office. Thumbed through it. Unclipped the top. Thumbed through it, again …and found the pages in question. Jerked them out. Sat down. Read them through, word by word …and there it was.

He looked up to see two smug faces watching him. Checked the signature and the date of signing. He *had* them.

"After the fact. I signed after the fact of you taking that casting of my fist."

"The mold, yes. But it wasn't sent to the foundry until after you signed, and, legally, Graham and Findlingham both agree that, so long as I didn't do anything with the casting until after they got you to sign, I was …in …the …clear! So was Sol."

"You tricked me!"

"Stop being such a fuddy-duddy, Landon …oops, Sheriff, *sir*."

She got up. Grabbed his laptop. "May I?"

A bit disconcerted by her forwardness and, as usual, by the fresh air and sunshine smell of her, he sat back. "Sure. Why *not?!*"

That got him another smirk.

She brought up an interface to his bank. Typed in a user name and password, and up came an account and its balance. "There," she said. "That's what the fist sculpt has made you for your foundation in just a couple of days, all proceeds from the sales."

He stared, unbelieving. Stammered, "Ho– how?!"

"Everybody wants one," Sol chirped.

"Of course, the first few days of a release are usually always the best, but it's a good start," Jessie said. "And the website is selling them to outsiders, too."

"Website?" he asked, his voice to his own ears sounding like a croak.

She flipped to a new tab and typed in a URL. "See?"

He swallowed. There he was, the stupid picture somebody had snapped of him, hat on, head down, white suit, after the even stupider Meet the Candidates fiasco before the election.

Then his brain caught up. He turned to Jessie and caught her eye. "How come you have all this access?"

"I'm one of the officers of your foundation."

"Oh." Blinked. Blinked again. He hadn't known about any of this.

"Didn't you read any of the paperwork?"

He swallowed guilt. He'd left it all in Findlingham's hands. Had trusted the man.

He frowned. Stood. "Dismissed."

Grabbed his hat.

***

23 – Not a Robot

"I'D BETTER call Findlingham," Jessie said as she and Sol, plus the dogs, Sandra's Border Collies, too, split off toward the hall leading to Sol's lab and office.

"Look, Jessie," Sol said, stopping to turn around and watch something.

Jessie turned to see the two van guys track Landon with their eyes and camera as he headed down to the back exit he always used. Then they made a beeline for the front door and were gone.

"I bet they follow him," Sol said. "They've been pests every morning, now, the last few days out at the ranch."

"Hmm. Okay. I'm on it. You call Findlingham for me, will you? Warn him Landon is headed his way and on the war path."

"Will do."

And, with that assurance, Jessie sprinted for the exit, too, dogs right with her. Turned on her XV's cameras and hit record as she tore off once Landon turned the corner and disappeared in The Rhino.

Coming out right after, she saw the van glue itself to The Rhino's bumper as Landon pulled out on the county road. "Those snoops!" she muttered, and followed, the cameras recording.

*

HE WAS LUCKY. There were two open parking spaces side-by-side in the back lot behind Graham and Findlingham Law Offices, perfect fit for The Rhino. Of course, the Actuator Studio van followed him in. "Private parking lot," he muttered, but there wasn't any law that said they couldn't be there. They could have an appointment, after all …though he really doubted it. If they didn't, the van would get towed …maybe.

Getting out, Britta with him, he set security and locked up. Took the back way in. Nodded to the front receptionist as he passed through, ignoring her as she called out that Findlingham and Graham were both with clients.

Heard her footsteps by the time he hit Findlingham's door, Findlingham's secretary yelping, "He's busy, Sheriff!" Then she tried following him, too.

Burst in, Gilbert Findlingham looking up, startled. The man rose. So did the man sitting opposite him.

"Sheriff," Findlingham said, the short, middle-aged lawyer immediately going smirky, the almost rodent-like eyes behind his wire-rimmed glasses smug.

Yeah, you know! What? Did Jessie call to warn you? "You tricked me, Findlingham!"

"If you'll excuse us, Mr. Kline? I'll have my secretary reschedule."

*

JESSIE CAME IN the alley. Snuggled into a loading zone, dropped a couple of cones, and got the dogs out, all except Duchess and Sandy Darstead's two Border Collies. She asked her dogs for stealth. Wicked gleams to eyes, doggy grins, tails faintly wagged. They knew this game.

Jessie, dogs surrounding, Milo and Mitch at lead, Acer and Sumi to either side, and Oso and Queenie bringing up the rear, as usual, they crept along the building edge till they came out into the law office's hidden, private lot. There, bright and bold, was The Rhino. And there was the Actuator Studios van.

Jessie headed for it, but there was nobody inside by a careful check around it. The dogs sniffed pavement, then heads coming up, they all looked in one direction. "My good, good dogs," she whispered. "Find it, *such*."

The dogs led, Oso and Queenie now taking lead and showing Jessie the where. The two circled around to behind her when both Milo and Mitch, second in the lead, stopped as they reached the office wing, ears quivering and alert. Acer grumbled. So did Sumi. *Gotcha.*

*

"DID I OR did I not leave you with the paperwork to read through at leisure? Did you not indicate your willingness to sign, whereupon Ms. Sherman, one of our notaries, and I joined you for the signing of that filing?"

Never argue with lawyer. Especially never try to accuse them of wrongdoing. It just didn't work. Especially with one like Findlingham.

"We have the recording of that meeting, if memory fails," Findlingham said, voice so discreet. "I do realize that there still may be some memory compromised by your—"

"Cut it out," Landon groused, cutting him off.

A smile. "Did you fail due diligence in your reading?"

He had. He'd skimmed. But, yes, he had seen the model release form. And, yes, he hadn't objected to the language …because he hadn't read it until just a few minutes ago. Now he knew, though. Every portion of him, including his voice, was covered by its stipulations …so long as they didn't jeopardize his reputation or refer to the Bitterroot County Sheriff's Office. Sighed. It had been …was for a good cause, after all. "I admit it. I skimmed."

"Have you seen the results for just the first offering?" Findlingham asked nicely. "Quite tidy for only three and a half days, I'd say."

Landon dropped his face. It was.

"Just think how well things will improve once these are released," the man said, placing a small statue of him on the desk—the same darned 'semblance' as the photo everybody loved, but, this time, done in a piece of 3D porcelain.

Landon closed his eyes. "Oh, no." Rubbed his brow. Opened them again to see Gilbert Findlingham watching him closely. Swallowed gall.

"And this." Gilbert brought out both a backpack and a lunchbox, his image on it, a Hummer similar to The Rhino in the background, no discernible official insignia apparent.

"And, of course, this."—the poster of him, same one as the statue, head down in his hat, white suit blown open a bit as he had been walking out of Meet the Candidate night.

He groaned.

"Jessie's getting all this ready for launch on the website as soon as you approve them."

A wedge! A gotcha! Finally! "I didn't approve the fist!"

"No. Jessie and I did, and it only takes two officers of the foundation." And again the smile. "We knew better than to ask."

Landon got up. Put his hat on.

Findlingham nodded toward the items. "Approve?" he asked.

What was the point of arguing …of fighting their program. "Approved."

"Good. ....Oh, and, while you're here, would you sign, please?" Findlingham said, bringing out one of the fist sculpts, carefully hefting it with two hands.

Landon frowned. Double-took. "Gold?"

"I like the best. Special order."

"Right."

*

JESSIE CUED the dogs, and, together they eased up behind the snoopy weirdos who had their noses to an office window, their legs and feet stepping on and breaking the foundation plantings.

"Recording people without their consent when you're not a participant is a felony in Idaho, subject to a maximum $5,000 fine plus five years in prison, boys," Jessie said softly, holding her badge out.

The two men jerked, their heads swiveling around, eyes going wide at seeing the dogs, all still and on alert, giant Milo beginning to rumble as soon as the men turned. Acer stood stock still, attention riveted. So did Mitch and Sumi.

And the fools ran, Jessie signaling to the dogs not to pursue. "Oh, and criminal damage to private property, the bushes you destroyed? That's a misdemeanor, fine of a grand, plus time," she called after. And she laughed.

*

LANDON STEPPED out the door just as the Actuator Studio guys ran past, them scrambling to get in their van, then, moments later, starting it and gunning it out of the parking lot. He watched the van bounce hard, the rear tire jolting off the curb. It yawed as it turned onto the street too fast. Frowned. *What in the world?*

"There you are!"—Jessie's voice, her dogs appearing around the entry shield in a 'dog flock' as she rounded the corner, too. The dogs were all wagging, happy to see him ...and to see Britta who bounced forward to wag hello and do the dog sniff thing with them.

He frowned. *Two and two.* "What did you do to the Actuator Studio pests, Jessie?"

"Me?"

Way too innocently spoken. He watched her. She grinned. "Yes, you, Jessie."

"Oh, just enlightened them about Idaho law and the penalties therein. It was more the dogs that worried them, I think." And her eyes did that wicked slow blink she used when 'being bad', as her dad called it.

Hands brushing across one and all of her wonder dogs, she cooed, "My good, good dogs."

And, for sure, he knew she'd done something wicked of which she was extraordinarily proud. "Right."

She glanced at him, eyes merry, grin going even wider. "Did you get the answer you wanted with Findlingham?"

"You warned him I was coming, didn't you?"

"Me?" She shook her head. "That was Sol. I was busy following the Actuator van by that time. But you didn't answer my question."

No, he hadn't answered it. And didn't plan to.

Her face changed. "What's wrong, Landon? You look devastated. Findlingham fire you as a client?"

He shook his head. Swallowed. Bit down discomfort.

"Come on. Talk to me."—soft-voiced.

Again, he shook his head.

Her mien changed that fast. "I'll sic the dogs on you. 'Lick Landon, lick Landon'!" she told him, her voice gone to a tease, her eyes gone sparkling. Then she laughed.

That broke him, and he laughed, too. Couldn't not. Brushed his nose as if to rid himself of his humiliations. Jessie had a way of penetrating his self-pity, usually by haranguing him, but, sometimes, like now, with humor.

"Then you'd smell like a dog for the rest of the day."

Pulled breath. Blurted, "I just feel …exposed."

Again, the mien changed. To serious. "What? …Like …naked?"

He ducked his head. Muttered, "Yeah."

*

JESSIE KNEW exactly what he meant. It wouldn't do, though. Better to play dumb and happy. "You've got it easy, Landon. I'm the one who they made into a dolly that kids can dress and undress. Now *that's* exposed."

The look on his face was priceless. Oh to chance a picture, but she didn't dare. "Why do you look like

you just swallowed a live frog, Landon?" she teased
...on purpose.

"Uhhh...."

"Anyway, so, until and unless we have a dolly of
you made, don't talk to me about feeling naked."
Purposely, she now put super 'bright' into her voice.
"But there's an idea. I'll bring it up with Findlingham
at the next meeting—"

The head raised. The eyes got stormy. "Don't
you dare! No dolly!"

There he was. She didn't grin success. Went
completely solemn-faced, or tried to. "Why not?"

"You just don't understand! It's bad enough
having to go perform, doing public speaking
engagements, doing press conferences. You're ready
for that. Have a persona you put on. Brain has a
script. But to have your moments of pain, the private
moments of frustration, of anger ...of losing control,
exposed for the world to see and laugh at.... Like
that fist."

The fist.... He felt exposed because the world
could see he cared. *Got it.* "Oh, they might see that
the 'oh, great Sheriff Landon Reid' is human, not
always restrained, contained, and perfect, always

saying and doing the right thing, never a feather ruffled, always in absolute control. Oh, dear. It bleeds. It feels. It's *real*, and here we thought it was at least part android."

That brought more storm clouds. His face hardened. "I'm not a robot."

She laughed out loud. His objection was adamant. He was coming out of it—good. "No, you're not a robot, Landon. Thank God. Or you'd beat me at the range, night after night. Now, come on. Let's go get ice cream at The Soda Shop! Meet you there."

A grumble.

"Come on. I'm parked illegally in a loading zone."

And Jessie was proud of herself. She'd managed to manipulate Landon out of his funk. He was back to being Landon, in control, arrogant, and aloof.

***

24 – Jessie's Heart

LANDON INSISTED on getting lunch, not just ice cream. He also insisted on paying for it.

Jessie let him, but drew the line on hamburgers for all the dogs. "They've got their dog jerky."

Eyebrows twitched. Landon groaned. "I'm glad I left Britta in the unit. She'd feel so deprived."

Perfect opportunity. "And about that—"

"Don't start on me, Jessie. Oli told me it was okay, except for grapes, potatoes, chocolate …stuff that's toxic to them, especially anything containing xylitol. I've got a huge list of forbidden foods. I've got a printout on the wall and a copy on my phone and on my laptop, plus I've pretty much committed it to memory."

"Yeah, well, how about Britta getting fat?"

"She's not. She runs with me, does chores with me, comes to work with me.…"

"Yeah. And lays around on the floor while you sit around on your butt." She watched him flinch. *Shouldn't have said that …again.* She was not doing her 'treat Landon like a very sensitive dog' handling very well since Britta abandoned her. *I'm so angry at him!* And had no reason to be. The dog herself had decided whose dog she wanted to be, and Britta was really happy, now.

Lucky for Jessie, despite her barb, Landon fought back. "She does not. She has a nice dog bed, plus she's allowed on the couch."

And Jessie couldn't resist the temptation. "You mean your *day* bed."

Another groan met that. "I needed it when I first got back. I thought it was nice of Martin to donate it to my cause."

She chuckled, remembering the hassle of getting it in and situated. She'd helped. "He just didn't want to be acting sheriff anymore. You never heard so much grousing!"

Now, though, she *was* baiting him. Again on purpose. Like she had her brother when he got all moody. Of course, Landon wasn't her brother, and he was not at all like Erik. But he was a man, and men, when they got down in the dumps, got destructive. In Landon's case, by all the research she could find on brainiacs, he could get very *self-destructive*. The Bitterroot did not need that. She didn't need that. Mental health and well-being were as important as the physical. She felt responsible. *We should have asked and explained the fist sculpt.* But it would have never happened. And it *was* perfect. It was making money to fund Landon's charity projects. It was for the Bitterroot and its needy, the ones that slipped through the cracks—Landon's self-appointed crusade.

"I'll meet you at The Soda Shop," he grumbled.

"Done."

*

"SO, YOU AND Jedidiah are …an item, now?" Landon asked, trying to move the discussion to something safe once Jessie finally quit picking on him, which only happened once their sandwiches and ice cream sodas came.

She gave him a look like he'd just slapped her, and that confused him. "What? What did I say?"

"No. We're *not* in a relationship, Landon. Just friends."

He wondered if she'd made that clear to Jed. Sighed. Another touchy subject …but, then, what wasn't a touchy subject when it came to Jessie, unless she chose it. Asked the needed: "You've made that perfectly clear to Jed?"

"Yeah."

"Good. Don't hurt him, Jessie. Jedidiah is a good guy."

"I know that. Or I wouldn't be friends with him. And it's none of your business, Landon."

It wasn't, in one sense, but, in another, it was. He felt responsible …to Jedidiah. He'd taught the kid to read. Protected him. Felt obligated to continue to protect him. Jed's adoptive mom, Annie, was a friend. So was Jedidiah. "Don't lead him on, Jessie."

Indignation met that. "I'm not. I've never led any guy on. You're thinking of Jennifer."

He dropped his face. No, he wasn't thinking of her twin. He also wasn't thinking of Jessie. But it was a female thing, to lead men on.

"The fact is, I'm not interested in even *thinking* about a guy like that ever again. I'm too busy, and it's way, way too painful when either you're not even on their radar or they do something *stu*pid like *die*."

Ouch. She was talking about James Kingston. "Sorry for your loss," was all he could come up with, a stupid, scripted answer.

"*Stop* it, then. I don't talk about it. Not even with Dad."

"How about Tank?" he ventured.

A heavy sigh, her eyes avoiding as she spun her soda glass around and around.

And he repeated himself, despite knowing he shouldn't: "Don't hurt Jedidiah, Jessie."

The head raised, the eyes angry. "*Got* it, *Lan*don!"

Move on. "Do you have time to take a drive with me?"

Her eyes, bright now, but cooling, went slantwise and watched him without looking at him. "Where to and why?" she asked, after a long moment.

"Nearby."

"And, a*gain*, where to and why?!" she repeated.

She was really miffed at him. He'd hit too many sore spots with the mention of Jed. He should have waited for another time. But the opening ceremony and official ribbon cutting was next week. "I'm not willing to share that till we get there."

She twisted on the stool to face him. Watched him for a long moment, eyes gone calculating and half 'bright'. "I'll follow you in the XV."

"No. Ride with me in The Rhino, please, but the dogs can come, too."

She tipped her head aside, eyes on her soda, again. Finally, he got an "Okay."

"I've got to make a phone call," he said, getting up.

Now her face went suspicious all over again. "You can't make it here?" she demanded.

"It's private."

"Right. And, now I'm going to say 'no'."

"You already said 'yes'."

*

SHE KNEW as soon as he slowed and put his blinker on. It got her over her mad at him and his impertinence about Jedidiah.

She didn't ruin Landon's attempt to surprise her, even as he turned in and honked.

The gates opened, and he drove in. He stopped. Turned to her. "I know you recognize it," he said.

"Yep."

"It's almost ready, so I thought we'd take a tour."

"Okay."

He got out, so she did, too. Left the dogs in The Rhino.

Landon gave a sharp blast of a whistle, fingers to mouth. It was so penetrating that it hurt her ears. Moments later, a huge tarp dropped, and she saw it— the sign and the mural.

She felt …proud …and shy …and happy …and….

*

HE WASN'T expecting her to break down—not at all. He wasn't prepared for that kind of reaction. Anger, indignation, disapproval, yes. He'd been ready for that. Or, if they were lucky, joy, laughter, maybe happiness. But not tears. Tears is what he got, though.

She turned to him, her blue eyes gone their darkest. Tears rolled down her cheeks. Then she grabbed him and hugged which really caught him off guard. "You *brat!*" she muffled into his shirt.

Stiffened. He didn't know how to take that.

"Thank you!"—still muffled.

Lightly, uncomfortably, he put an arm around her and carefully patted her on the back, the smell of her sunshine and fresh air wafting up strong in his nostrils. Felt more discomfort. Spoke what was needed. "You made this happen, Jessie. It's only right." Then, he asked what he needed to know. "So it's all right with you?"

"I'm honored."—sobbed.

Relief: The official designation, 'Bitterroot County No-Kill Animal Shelter & Sanctuary', to be known to all as its alias, 'Jessie's Haven of Heart & Hope', had stood the test of its biggest benefactor. So had the mural painted of her and her dogs that graced the right side of the front wall. Oli had been right. Jessie would allow it. Raised his face Heavenward. *Thank you, God.*

*

JESSIE HAD a lot to think about as Landon drove her and the dogs back to town. She'd hugged Landon, a completely spontaneous thing. *Wrong. Shouldn't have done that.* Landon did not like any form of public displays of appreciation, much less affection. He always tried to keep things to handshakes, not that her dad let him—the man hug thing.

And she'd felt something of her old puppy infatuation stir about him that she'd had in high school ...an infatuation shared by all the rest of the girls. *Definitely wrong. Got over that.* And why had he done that with the shelter when it was just as much his doing? Sighed, again.

"Something wrong, Jessie?" came a grumble.

"Just thinking."

Heard him suck breath in. Turned her face to the window.

Today had been a day of firsts for her—the surprise of the shelter naming and the mural, her dad turning a quarter of their dog operation over to training SAR and HRD dogs, all hers to guide. Her dad confronting her about Jed, about her commitment to Anderson Working Dogs. And Landon himself. ...Another sigh.

Last was what Landon had said about Jedidiah. None of his business, but, yeah, she knew he was right. As usual.

She watched out the window, the autumn landscape beautiful, and sighed again. All her dreams, all her plans had done a turn-about on her. Six years spent struggling at college, all for nothing.

No. Not true. If she hadn't gotten the degrees, she'd have never become a deputy in Blaine and have never rescued that kid, never gotten Queenie, Oso, Milo, and Mitch ...or had her dad give her and her mom Acer and Britta—Britta who had become hers, rejected by her mom, but now a dog that was no longer Jessie's. But becoming a rooky deputy in Blaine, one who ran SAR as a hobby with a crack two-dog team, had put her in the national spotlight and made her foundation 'happen', the toy company approaching her, all without her turning a hand ...except to sign the paperwork Marge Seaton and her mom had had drawn up. They'd done all the work. They ran the thing, day-to-day. Along with a lawyer. And that foundation funded no-kill shelters in poor and rural communities nationwide.

More, if she hadn't been in that horrible firefight, she'd have never turned in her badge and, on Christmas Eve morning, driven home to her family and the Bitterroot, fleeing like a whipped puppy running back to where it knew it was safe. And she was safe here. She knew that. Not only that, but her dreams were happening, again without her having to do anything but what she loved …mostly. And that was due to the man sitting next to her.

Landon pulled up beside the XV. Jessie thanked him, forced herself to smile and got out. Opened The Rhino's back passenger door and the XV's back driver's side door, got the dogs to jump from one to the other, her scooping up Duchess to put her in, too.

She paused her hand. Took the small dog with her and got in the driver's seat, The Rhino pulling away, Landon giving a nod and raising a palm to her …and she to him. "Time for you to become my dog, not just the pack mascot, Duchess." She didn't need another Britta to happen. It hurt too much.

The tail wagged just a little. Little Duchess was unsure. For Duchess, this was a big change. She always rode in the back with the pack.

Acer jumped in front from the back, and Jessie smiled, then glanced in the rearview, all eyes there on her. "My good, good, good, good, *great* dogs." Even Sandra's Border Collies wagged.

So Life was giving her a ride where it decided she should go. …And she laughed. "Bring it on, God. I'll take it." She didn't always have to be in control. Not always. Maybe letting go and just riding the waves might be a better way of dealing with it all. …Including Jedidiah and Landon.

Dog tails thumped, practically in unison. Beside her, Acer gave her his wise dog glance. Milo stuck his nose in her ear. Another glance in the rearview showed Mitch looking pleased. So did Sumi. Queenie blew cheeks. Oso, the Independent, gave a little yip, tightly curled tail wiggling. Even he was dog smiling. The Border Collies looked confused.

"What are you dogs doing? Listening to my thoughts?"

More thumps and doggy grins.

She started the rig, checked her mirrors, and pulled out into traffic, heading for home, one hand on Duchess, the warm body settling in, head on her thigh.

∗∗∗

25 – Reported Body

"JESSIE?"

Nelson Remmers' voice. "Go ahead," she said.

"Where are you?"

"Headed home."

"From?"

"Northridge."

"How would you feel about lending a hand with an HRD search down south, here?"

She'd seen the call come through on her phone early this morning. She hadn't been called out, though. "Having problems?"

"Cain't find the body. Hunter swears it was there, but four teams of dogs are giving it a no-go …includin' mine and Madeleine Browne's."

That didn't sound right.

"Thought maybe you could turn your crew loose an' see if they catch a whiff."

She looked around at her crew, plus two. Tipped her head. Slowed and took the next emergency cross-median access to make a U-ey. "On my way."

*

THE ACTUATOR GUYS were parked in the public lot again as he pulled in. They were in the lobby, the camera man with his camera on his shoulder, recording light on, when he walked through, headed for his office. He paused his step. Calculated. Decided no.

The lobby door opened, deputies coming alert.

"Quit struggling. You ain't gettin' loose o' me. Git in there!"

Landon turned and stood slack-jawed at what and who entered.

*

TOM HUDSON'S unit blew past her as she passed Benton Slough Road. He was hauling a horse trailer. He flashed his lights and, moments later, her phone rang.

She answered. "A horse trailer, Tom?"

"Hey, I took you seriously. Thought that, just in case, I'd set up Dad's and park it ready to roll. We're rolling. Brought both Sass and Buster, your choice on which you want to ride."

She laughed. "Thanks, Tom."

"See ya there."

*

BIG WES BRIGGINS was coated with splotches of paint, front, side, and back. In his ham-fisted grip was a disheveled young woman—a girl, really—dressed in dirt-covered black pants and a padded jacket. Coming in behind was Wes's oldest son, Glen, just as big a guy. He held a paintball gun.

"Pressin' charges against *this,*" Wes snarled, shoving the girl forward into a deputy.

"Want to tell me what *'this'* is about?" Landon asked ...as if he couldn't guess.

"She shot me and Glen, both."

Wes nodded toward the gun his son held. "That's an automatic. Felt like bein' pelted with rocks. *Hard!* Ruined my morning hunt, and I don't take kindly to being shot at, even if it *is* only paintballs. It *hurts,* plus it ruined my deer stalkin'. I was homin' in on a nice five-point. He's long gone now, thanks to her, and I got me sore spots that won't quit!"

The man pulled his shirt and jacket wide, splattering paintball goop as he displayed bull's eye types of welts.

Battery and aggravated assault.

The deputy running desk was cuffing the woman and reciting her rights to her. The woman was grinning at Landon with a sly smirk. Then she actually laughed right at him. "I want a lawyer, Lonnie."

Of course. They were too obviously well-drilled on this end of things. Shook his head. *At least she got my name wrong!* "How'd you catch her?" Landon asked, eyes back on Wes and his kid.

"*I* tackled her, Sheriff," Glen said, and the young man was also coated in splotches. "She started to take off, tripped and went down, and I got there before she could find her feet, again. The other one ran off. Figured you guys could round up the likes of her. She had purple and orange hair, all in, like, stripes. Can't be many of those around. Not that I've seen, anyway."

Landon nodded. So, now, they had another one in custody and knew a sort of description of another one still on the loose. These people were definitely hunting hunters. Question was, how many paintball gun-wielding hunters were there and who was behind it—which organization?

Got to his office and touched a call through to Martin's.

"Yeah?"

"We got another one."

"Yeah, I just heard. There's got to be somebody running the show."

"That's what I figure."

"I've got deputies out checking the local motels, hotels, B&Bs, or AirBNBs. So far, dead ends, all."

"That's not good."

"We're still canvassing. Only gotten to about half of them. There's still a lot to go."

"All right. Keep me in the loop?"

"Always."

"Thanks."

*

TOM HAD the horses unloaded by the time Jessie rolled in and got Mitch and Milo vested up.

Acer went nuts. "Okay, okay. You can come, too," she said.

The rest of the dogs looked hopeful. Sighed. "Well, come on. All of you. Let's get your protection on."

Looked at Duchess. "You want to try to keep up, too?" She didn't have a vest for Duchess, but, well....

The tail wagged, nose up, eyes happy on Jessie's.

"Okay. I'll take the dog sling just in case, though." Got the pup down.

"You want Sass or Buster?" Tom asked.

Sass was Tom's go-to mount. "I'll take Buster."

"He bucks some, sometimes."

Hence the name. "Thanks for the warning."

"He doesn't mean anything by it. Just spirit."

Buster, a bright red sorrel, didn't look like much, but Jessie more than knew that looks were deceiving. Her Chesterton didn't look like much, either, and he was a go-er.

Going over to talk to Nelson Remmers, she gave him a hug. "Haven't seen you for a few days."

"Got that bug that's goin' around," he said. "Been layin' low so's not to give it to nobody."

"Appreciated."

He smirked a grin at her. "Hunter, a Jim Grover, said he found a chunk of human body here," Nelson said, bringing up a map. "We've gone and searched that whole area. Come up with nothin'. Moved out from there and cleared this, this, this," he said, pointing. "Been at this since ten-ish'."

"When and where did he see the corpse and was he sure it was a dead human body?"

"He called early this mornin'. And he said he was *darned* sure. Said he 'bout fell into it—chunk of a chest. I'm pretty sure he didn't look close, though. You hear the call in?"

"Mmm. I didn't hear it. I saw it come up on my texts."

"By the sounds of it, body had been dead for a bit."

"Right."

"Probably ate on is my guess why he only saw what he claims he saw. But Jim Grover ain't one to go flakey or get strange 'bout these things. You wanna listen to the call?"

"Not necessary. Your thoughts?"

"I'm wonderin' if maybe Jim got confused as to exactly where he was."

"That's what I'm wondering, too."

Jessie called Terri. Sent the location identified by Jim Grover. "Can you locate similar terrain …like places in the area close that might look comparable, especially to somebody on foot."

"You want magic," Terri came back.

Jessie laughed. "No, just a bit of Terri genius."

"Give me ten."

"You got it."

Terri found three somewhat similar locations within a ten mile radius using a combination of satellite and AI enhanced prediction formulas. "I'm voting for these two," Jessie said, showing Nelson and the other HRD teams. "How about Tom and I head for this one. It's farthest. You guys willing to cover the other? I know you've been at this for hours already, so don't feel obligated."

Murmurs of assent.

"Great. If we don't find something, we'll try the last possibility."

"Aren't you going to go over what we covered?" Madeleine asked.

Jessie shook her head. "No. You guys cleared it. Good enough for me."

Tucking Buster's get-down rope under her belt, she gathered the reins and put her foot in the stirrup. Felt the gelding tense, a gleam coming to his eye. She paused. Took hold of his bridle's cheek strap and turned his head to her. "You don't want to do that. Honest." Let go.

The horse tucked his head and rubbed his face against his knee, raised his head, and gave a soft overblow, then settled.

"Thank you."

She stepped up, swung on. He didn't tense again.

"Now I know for sure you're an animal whisperer," Tom said.

"No. Just wise to their wickedness, and they know it. My granddad taught me. He's the expert." She gave Buster a scratch on the withers. Smiled. She liked him. He had feistiness. Luckily, Buster seemed like he was okay with dogs. He had no problem with hers and Sandy's running along beside and in front of him. She worried on Duchess, though. Got back down. Scooped her up, then remounted.

Pup slipped into dog sling, Jessie asked Milo and Mitch to lead out on the search for 'human, dead, all', the other dogs to heel to horse, the Border Collies mimicking, and they were off toward one of the locations Terri and her computers suggested as having high potential. They had five hours till dark.

***

26 – Fits and Starts

"They know each other," Martin said, coming into Landon's office.

Deep in the throes of deciphering a cryptic email from the psychiatrist who had evaluated their problem prisoner, Landon welcomed the intrusion. "Who knows each other?"

"Terri got a hit on facial recognition on something she calls Mastodon® which finally lead to DMV photos."

Landon sat back. "Finally! Who are they?"

Martin rattled off names. "They're all tournament level paintballers …from Phoenix, Arizona, Las Vegas, Nevada, and Los Angeles, California."

Landon frowned. "Are they part of an anti-hunting group?"

"Not from what Terri could ferret out."

"What are they doing up here, and why are they targeting our hunters?"

"Well, now, there's the question, isn't it?"

"Recruited by an anti-hunting group?"

"Maybe. Now that we know who they are, we're requesting access to phone records, text data, and checking financials. As soon as we get that, we may get some answers."

"Right."

Landon blew out a long breath. "All right. Keep—"

"'Keep you in the loop', and I will." Martin didn't get up.

Landon eyed him. "And?"

"Harvey's patrol officers are being targeted, too," Martin said. "Four of them have had their cars hit by paintballs. Didn't get hurt and didn't hurt the units."

"Catch any of them?"

"No. All happened at night and came out of nowhere—surprise assaults. Twerps disappeared. In unrelated news, I had lunch with Harvey today. He's got a camera van following him, too, so don't feel picked on."

"Not the same one, then?"

"Nope. Got RealTake on the side. Harvey confronted them, same as you, and they claimed they were doing a documentary on Idaho law enforcement."

...Which reminded Landon. He needed to call around to other county sheriffs in the state to see who else was being camera stalked.

*

THE WIND WAS from the southwest today, so Jessie started her dogs from the northeast. At first, they got nothing. Then both Mitch and Milo stopped dead, heads up, noses sifting air currents.

Pulling up, Jessie watched, Tom coming up to stop beside her. The young man was quiet.

The dogs sat, then suddenly downed. Jessie frowned, seeing it. Beside and around her, the rest of her dogs did likewise.

Moments later the distinct sound of huffing. *Uh-oh.* Now she knew why the dogs had downed.

Tom pulled his rifle from his saddle scabbard. "Buster is fine with bear, Jess. Just keep the dogs quiet, please."

"Done," she told him as, though not needing to, she signaled 'silence' and 'still'. She pulled a bear bomb from her front saddlebag. Put that hand on Duchess, bear bomb palmed, thumb stroking the pup's head. Heard another huff, this one closer. Drew a long breath and twitched the reins when Buster shifted.

The horse settled.

Ahead of Milo and Mitch about twenty-five yards, the approaching animal crossed—yes, a grizzly. It was a sow, and two half-grown cubs gamboled by. Stopped. Looked. Then followed mom into deep cover.

"She's not interested in us," Tom said softly. "And she knew we were here."

"How do you know that?"

"Those huffs? That was her warning us and her cubs, both, telling us that she was coming through and telling her cubs to stay close."

"And how do you know that, too?"

He grinned. "Hunting out with my dad and granddad since I was a kid. They usually will leave you alone, unless they feel threatened."

"Oh."

"You don't hunt?"

She shook her head. "No. Dad and Granddad hunt, but I don't see the point. We raise most of our food."

"Right. No elk steak for you."

She grinned. "I've had it, and, yes, it's very good."

"There's some hope for you, then," he said, grinning.

"Some."

*

CALLS AROUND the state got Landon assurances that no other sheriff was being targeted by camera vans. No other county was having problems with paintballers hunting hunters, either.

"There have been a few assaults happen over in Spokane over the years, but nothing targeting hunters. Mostly property damage and some squabbles between kids, as I understand it," the chief deputy of Kootenai County told him, "but nothing here ...yet."

"Thank you."

Heading down to Martin's office with the news, Landon stopped and stared at the wall. Walked up. Looked. Read. Swallowed. Rolled eyes Heavenward and only saw ceiling. Turned back to Martin's door and tapped.

"Well? What do you think?" Martin asked as he stepped in on his undersheriff's 'come'.

"About?"

"The installation. I saw you coming. Watched."

"You knew?"

"Yeah, I did," Martin admitted, a grin playing across his face.

Sighed. Shrugged. Sat down. He had nothing good to say about his fist mounted as a permanent fixture right where he'd had his meltdown ...but he also knew when he was beaten. Somehow, his deputies ...even his undersheriff were proud of it ...maybe because it showed just how much of a dufus he was when it came his job. Compared to people like Martin, Red, and Howie, he was a two-bit bush leaguer.

*

THEY WAITED till Mitch and Milo gave the all clear by getting up, then looking back and wagging. "My good, good dogs," Jessie called. "My very good, good dogs."

Back on the job, Milo just strode along, Mitch, the Marvelous jog-walking beside, nose high and working. "They're getting nothing," Jessie said.

Jessie's phone vibrated, then auto-answered Nelson Remmers. "What's up?"

"Found it, Jessie. It's scattered parts of a body, all right. Ugly, stinky pieces scattered all over the place."

"We'll head back you're way and help."

"If you could." There was a pause. "Jessie, this looks like another one of them fallen bodies. The ones thrown out of planes or somethin'," Remmers said.

A chill ran the length of her. "Okay. On our way."

It took them the rest of the afternoon, Mitch and Milo pitching in to help find the pieces of body. And, to Jessie, yes, it did look like another of Nicholson's victims …except, when they found pieces of the pelvis, Jessie knew this body was a man's. She called Sol. Sol patched in Martin …who patched in Landon.

Then Andy Newsome came in on the call, too. "Your best guess on approximate date of death?" Newsome asked. "Just a rough estimate is good."

"At least a month, but, actually, I have no idea. Found a piece of mandible with teeth still in it. I hope it's enough for a good ID."

"Any other evidence?"

"Not that we found. We can come back out tomorrow, if you need, but we did a pretty thorough search—six teams of dogs that know their stuff."

"No. If you say it's done, it's done."

"Thanks."

Jessie called her dad next. "Just heading into town. I'll be about fifteen minutes late."

"See you when you get here, Jessie."

And, when she got there, dogs parking themselves in the observation area, Jessie watched her dad working with Landon for awhile before stepping up. The two men really *were* friends. They got along. *Get over it*, she told herself. *Landon's no threat.*

In her head, she knew that. Her dad loved her. In her heart, she resented it, though. It had been bad enough with Erik, who'd she'd bested over and over, outperforming him at every turn, only to have her dad keep treating Erik as his number one kid. Now here was Landon moving into Erik's spot, a man who was more than her equal in just about everything except dogs, running, and marksmanship, the last two seeing them racing neck and neck, no matter how hard she worked. And, yes, she did resent it ...and knew she shouldn't. Landon was no threat to her with her dad. At all. *Then why do I care that they're friends?* But she did. And, unlike Erik, there was no beating Landon, not in the long run.

*

LANDON SAW Sol's car come in, the security now warning him of all traffic, even knowns, Terri having reprogrammed it once Landon pointed out the security flaws—the possibility of somebody else driving, the possibility of somebody holding the driver at gunpoint.... He pulled their dinners out of the warmer and set the plates on the table as the door opened.

Nobody came in. He frowned. Glanced at Britta who wasn't concerned. Looked back at the open door. "Sol?"

A kid's cheap cowboy hat—black—flew in and skidded across the floor towards him. He stared at it. *What in the world?* Looked back at the still empty, open door. "Sol?"

The man's head poked itself around the door frame. "Just seeing if the hat came back out all mangled," he said, a grin on his face, but a strange look in his eyes.

"Why would it?"

"So, I'm still welcome here?" Sol said, finally coming in to then stand in the open doorway.

What was going on?! "Why wouldn't you be?"

"Um …because of the fist casting?"

Landon shook his head. "Does that somehow change our friendship, Sol?"

"I don't know. It would for some."

"I'm not some. I don't go back on my offers or on my word, either one, especially to friends. I'm surprised you would think so." And, yes, he was hurt by the mere suggestion. Picked up the hat. Stepped forward and handed it to the man.

Sol's face had gone all serious now. "Sorry."

Landon stepped to and grabbed the door. Stood aside and pointed to the table. "Would you just get in here?! Dinner's getting cold, and the chess board is gathering dust waiting for you."

"Okay."

***

27 – Lonnie Tuunz

JESSIE AND HER gram were cleaning up the kitchen after dinner when a high emergency alert came through on audio on Jessie's phone. Running for her gear, she bumped headfirst into her dad. "You coming?"

"I am. Howie says its bad."

"Meet you at the XV."

"Hurry, Jessie."

*

LANDON HAD just finished evening barn chores when his phone went off. Answered. Listened. There would be no chess game tonight.

Ran to the house, Britta with him. Found Sol redressed and running around like a madman. Grabbed his hat, gun, badge, and keys and, not bothering to change, made for the door. Sol was right behind him. Britta led out. "Set the security, Sol," he yelled back over his shoulder.

"Doing it," Sol yelled back.

289

Starting The Rhino, he watched his computer come alive, feeds flooded with traffic. Howie and the tactical team was en route. "He stayed late again," Landon muttered.

The passenger-side door opened, Sol climbing in. "Seat belt," Landon said and put it in gear as the doctor complied. Beat it out the drive, lights alive and strobing.

Fidgeted as the gates finished opening. Aimed at the van guys who were, as usual, parked there. Turned just in time to miss them, the driver's eyes going big. Put the hammer down and tore off down the county road.

In the rear view, here came Jessie, for once using her lights, too.

"Why would somebody hit the Northridge Police Department?" Sol asked. "That's *stupid.*"

"I have no idea, Sol."

Behind him, behind Jessie, there came another set of lights, lights he too well recognized—the Actuator Studios boys were tailing. And the question hit him: *Are they connected?!* The paintball attacks and the van surfacing started almost simultaneously.

And, of course, his brain jumped to conclusions from there, none of it grounded in fact or evidence. *Tilting at conspiracy windmills.*

*

"*PUSH* IT, LANDON!" Jessie fumed as she ate his dust down the county road. The lights from the van on her tail, bright in her rearview and side mirrors, didn't help her mood or ability to see. The van had on its high beams. Behind her, several dogs—the prowlers, she guessed—rumbled low and soft. That matched Jessie's take on things perfectly.

"I ought to blow out one of that van's front tires," her dad muttered as she turned onto the highway and accelerated.

"Don't."

"I didn't say I was going to, Jessie."

"Yeah, I know." And she *did* know. *You wouldn't have said anything, just done it.*

The onboard chattered through an update. Her dad turned the screen to look. "Some of your ten codes here, but the rest is legible. 'Eleven injured, one dead, four suspects apprehended, ISP, P.D., and S.O. units giving chase to suspect vehicles southbound 95. Air One lift off. Traffic cams down'.'"

"What?" Jessie asked. "Say that last again?"

"'Traffic cams down'.'"

"How can that be?!"

"Jammers?" Oli suggested.

"To take down the whole *system?!*"

Her dad didn't answer, and that was an answer all in itself.

*

SECURITY CAMERAS were down at Northridge P.D. They had no visual of what was going down …except through Howie's team's cams, and that was a mess to try to decipher. And not only were security cameras down, but traffic cams were, too—all of them around Northridge proper, then up and down the 95, north and south, for over five miles both ways. *What happened?!*

On the horn, again, he asked that, but nobody had an answer, not the ISP, not the Highway Department, not the contractor employed by the state to maintain them—he called them all. Then he called Terri.

"I'll look into it, sir. Off the top of my head, I'd say jammers. Wifi is easy to jam. But that's just a guess. It could be something else. I'm almost to base. I'll get you an answer if I can as soon as I can."

"Thank you." Closed the call. Then, "Sol?"

"Yes?"

"Jammers are illegal, right?"

"That is correct."

"Right."

*

IT WAS mayhem. There were cop cars and ambulances scattered helter-skelter. Weaving through them, Jessie left her dogs even as her dad got his and pounded off toward the S.O.'s APC where Howie was working.

Jessie grabbed her med pack and ran. She ran straight inside and faced seriously injured, plus one copse—a man Jessie knew. She'd gone to high school with him. Another paramedic pointed. "Him next," he yelled.

"On it."

*

ONE DEAD—broken neck from falling backward into the edge of a desk after being hit with a barrage of paintballs—thirty-six years old, married with kids. Eleven injured, EMTs and paramedics, including Jessie, working on those who were still awaiting transport, the most in need having gone first.

"Blew in here and just opened fire," Harvey said, the chief of the P.D. dressed casual in slacks and a polo shirt, a light jacket over that—not the usual Harvey Mueller look. A paint-coated P.D. officer stood beside him, the woman silent. Captain Dirk Compton, now the P.D.'s second-in-command, was helping document evidence.

It had been all over by the time Landon had arrived, crime scene tape being strung, P.D. officers and his own investigators and crime scene specialists beginning the process of collecting and documenting evidence. Sol joined them.

Howie's team had apprehended two suspects, the P.D. had gotten three more, one by an officer running straight at the paintball attacker, right into the blast of her automatic, and tackling her. That officer was now in Emergency, the woman perp, too—damaged ribs and extensive bruising on both of them. Both had been wearing Kevlar®, the woman perp the cheapest, the officer standard issue.

The APC had aided in corralling one of the getaway vehicles by ramming it. The ISP, P.D. units, and one of the S.O.'s, too, had run down two others, and Air One had pulled a daredevil move to make another getaway vehicle crash. Some of the occupants of those vehicles had fled the scene, and Oli and his prowlers along with Remmers attack dogs were out on search, more of Howie's team with them.

Traffic cams on the 95 were still down. *What gives with that?*

So much for modern tech. There was always more under development, rendering anything they did inoperative in a matter of months. *We can't keep ahead of them!* And Landon guessed that a lot of somebodies were making a lot of money on developing and selling the technology and armaments to all sides.

*

JESSIE TOOK note. Every one of those incapacitated by the attack had not been wearing body armor. Every one. The Northridge Chief of Police didn't require his personnel to wear it unless out in the field, and, even then, it seemed, the policy wasn't strictly enforced. *A minute of effort and some personal discomfort to save your own life*, though nothing would have saved the deceased, not the way he'd fallen.

Helping to lift another of the injured onto a dual operator stretcher, the woman's injuries were a lot less dire than the others because she'd been hit in the back with, luckily, only one hit to the right kidney. She was bruised and that bruising was nasty, but survival instinct had kicked in and she'd crawled under a nearby desk. *Glad the shooter didn't come around and blast her where she'd cornered herself.*

Wheeling her out, a P.D. officer armed with a rifle ran by just as Jessie was lifting the stretcher's undercarriage, the other paramedic pushing it into the waiting ambulance.

From the corner of her eye, Jessie saw it happen—Landon coming out the door talking with the chief of police, Britta at heel beside, the P.D. officer opening fire, point blank.

*

"SCORE! I GET LONNIE TUUNZ! BOTH OF THEM FOR THE WIN!"—he heard that as he recognized the face screaming it …as he felt his chest collapse as she opened fire on him. *How'd she get out of my jail?*

He saw Britta launch. Felt himself falling backwards. He heard his heart hammer in his ears. He felt pain—bad pain. He knew he couldn't breathe.

Hands grabbed. Arms held. Blue eyes, eyes he knew, eyes he trusted. Something covering his face. Where was his dog?

"Easy, easy. Shallow breaths. Little puffs. Little puffs."

He heard her say that. He couldn't breathe. Panicked. *Suffocating.*

"Your diaphragm is stunned. Just quick, shallow breaths. Pure oxygen, full pressure. Just puff. In, in, in, relax. Quick, tiny puffs. The machine will help you. Just tiny puffs."

He tried.

"Tiny puffs. Use your upper chest muscles. …Good. Good. Keep going. Give the O2 a chance to work. Tiny puffs, tiny puffs."

Heard her yell. "Oxygen meter. Get it on for me."

"Intubate," he heard someone say.

No!

"No. Not yet," he heard Jessie snap.

Thank you.

Her blue eyes—bright—came back to his. "Good, good. Tiny puffs. Slow your heart rate down, Landon. Remember Dad? Slow your heart rate. Pretend you're at the range. Now, tiny puffs. Just tiny puffs."

The other voice—"seventy-four. Heart rate coming down. Pulse one-thirty-eight. Seventy-five O2."

"Tiny puffs. Slow your heart rate. Think it. ...No. Don't try sucking air to do it. *Think* it slower, Landon. Tiny puffs. For me. Tiny puffs."

It was hard, but he got the system. He wanted more air. Tried for more. The world jolted. He jolted. Pain! He was suffocating again.

"No, no. Tiny, tiny puffs. In, in, in, relax. In, in, in, relax. One, two, three, one. One, two, three, one," a finger tapping where her hand held him leaned across her. The other held something—the thing pressing on his face. "Tiny puffs," she said again.

"Pulse and O2, one-twenty-two, seventy-eight. O2 now seventy-nine ...eighty."

"Good job, Landon! Tiny puffs. Quick, tiny puffs. You're doing soooo good. Keep it up."

"Eighty-two. O2's coming up. Got the ER finally."

"There you go, Landon. Nice and easy. Tiny puffs. You can do it. I've got ya, and I'm not letting go."

...Obeyed the tap of her finger. Obeyed her orders. Watched her eyes. Saw Britta come close. Felt her lick his face. Britta was okay.

"Pulse one-oh-one, O2 eighty-six ...eighty-eight."

He fumbled. Wanted. Managed. Grabbed her arm, grabbed for Britta. Hung on to both of them—hung on for dear life.

***

28 – Don't Let Go

JESSIE RODE IN the ambulance with Landon. She would have, anyway, but, because of his death grip on her, there was no other option. He wouldn't let go ...or couldn't. She didn't know which.

She managed to undue Britta's collar with one hand, that collar crushed in Landon's other hand, just like her left arm was crushed in his vice-like grip. "I'm right here. I'm staying with you. Tiny puffs," she kept repeating. Watched his eyes blink. Told Tom who finally showed up to load Britta in the XV, her commanding the dog to go with Tom and to obey.

Britta's training held ...barely. The dog loved Landon. *Oh, boy. We're going to have to work with both of them.*

These thoughts and happenings seemed to swirl around her as she realized something else—she ...loved ...Landon.

Don't think about it.   Just do your job.   You're his lifeline.   Do your job.

*

'TINY PUFFS' was his mantra.   He had to keep in time with Jessie's tapping.   He couldn't fight.   He had to keep control, keep calm—tiny puffs.

Jessie was his lifeline.   Britta was okay.   ...*And I love her.*

Who did he love?

Britta?

Yeah.

Jessie, his brain supplied.

No.   Not possible.   Not happening.

"Landon, tiny puffs."

Bright lights.   Voices.   *Keep her with you.   You lose hold, you die.*

He didn't want to die.

...And I love her.

No!   Not acceptable.

*

THE WORRY was the diaphragm. The heart and lungs, too. But the diaphragm refusing to reengage was the present biggest worry, especially when rushed blood work showed no abnormalities except a slightly reduced oxygen level. Was the muscle ruptured? Blunt force trauma could cause that. Depending on severity, it was life-threatening.

Again, they wanted to intubate. Again, Jessie fought them. "His O2 is holding. Not unless absolutely necessary."

"Give me a number," Dr. Bill Moynahan demanded—Bill, her friend.

"Seventy-nine."

"Done. Spiral CT Scan, *stat*," he snapped to his ER team.

Landon's eyes begged hers. She saw it. "I'm here," she told him. "I won't let you go."

Jessie felt herself shake inside. Blessed her training. She was steady on the outside, her mind calm as still water, despite the earthquake rattling her soul.

His eyes blinked.

"I'm here. You're okay, Landon. Tiny puffs."

She was proud of him. He was obeying her, taking quick little sips of oxygen, not fighting it, not failing it, not trying to breathe like normal. He obeyed her every finger tap—quick puffs about three per second, relax, then again. And it was working. His O2 saturation was holding steady at ninety-one and ninety-two, just three to four points below minimum optimum. He was doing great.

Of course, there were other worries aside from a ruptured diaphragm—bruising to the heart, to the lungs, to the liver, spleen…. His chest, when they cut his clothes off, the look of it was a shock. It was turning dark red and purple, the skin pulpy, seeping blood and serum.

They ran a strip. "No arrhythmia," the on-call cardiologist declared. "Normal sinus rhythm. Pulse significantly elevated from his previous recorded normals."

Jessie breathed relief, despite that. The elevated pulse was normal for his present condition.

"Can you let Jessie go?" Dr. Moynahan asked Landon.

The head shook 'no'. Jessie saw Landon's face go hard. The head shook 'no', again. The eyes sought hers. Eyes pleaded. The heart rate increased. A lot. BP blipped hard up. Oxygen levels started going down.

"It's okay. I'm right here with you, Landon. I'm not going anywhere."

Another team came, Jessie quick-walking alongside as they wheeled him out, her arm aching where he gripped her. They headed for the radiology department, her talking to him all the way. She felt his pulse come down a little. "Good job, Landon."

They got Landon on the table, quick and easy. Set the IV. Used his left arm because he would not let go of her. "Okay, Landon. Move with me. You have to put your hands up over your head."

A violent head shake. Jessie knew why. That's what they'd done to him in the nuclear stress test. "Trust me. This is not going to be like the stress test. I promise. They need to scan your chest. Please, Landon. I won't let anything bad happen. I promise. I'm here for you, okay?"

Jessie put her free hand over his where it gripped her arm. "Trust me. Move with me, please."

He obeyed.

He's being so good. "Okay. Here we go," she told him.

Then, suddenly, he sat up, his arms coming down, Jessie dragged along, her scrambling to move fast enough. His face read instant shock. The two nurses standing by reached in and helped support his back and head, bracing him. Somebody rolled a crash cart near. Everybody was expecting the worst.

Jessie's eyes were riveted on Landon's face. Paid attention to his chest and breathing. He wasn't puffing air. He wasn't breathing, at all.

"Heart rate one-thirty. O2 eighty-five …eighty-four.

Jessie held her breath. Prayed. "Come on, Landon. Breathe. Tiny puffs."

Landon's eyes were focused straight ahead and centered. It was like he wasn't looking, like he couldn't see or hear …was focused somewhere else.

Please, God. Don't take him, Jessie prayed.

He crushed his eyelids shut. His body spasmed, shuddering. And then he breathed, the sound harsh, tortured.

"Oh, my God!" Jessie whispered. Then, "Thank you, God."

"I think his diaphragm just reengaged."—some doctor Jessie didn't know. A resident. It had.

They waited till Landon's body finally relaxed. Waited till he came aware of them again. He was breathing—not real deep, but his diaphragm was working. They kept the oxygen mask on. He needed it.

"Thank you, God," Jessie whispered, again.

They waited till his pulse came down and his oxygen stabilized up. "O2 Ninety-three, ninety-four …ninety-five," someone called.

"Let's get this scan,"—the head radiologist on duty.

Once Landon was stable, again, Jessie got him to cooperate and put his arms back over his head.

The table rolled him through the gantry of the scanner, Landon gripping her, her inching forward, staying with him, as the machine did its position scan tests, then its scan.

Then they wheeled him back to the ER, her with him, talking him calm. "I'm right here with you. Not going to let anything bad happen. I promise you."

Felt him squeeze her arm, then relax the grip just a little bit, but not let go.

"No rupture, no myocardial contusion," was the good news. "Mild pulmonary contusion here and here," was the worst of it, that and the bruising to his diaphragm and all the muscles of his anterior upper torso, some bruising to his back. And, of course, there was his skin—potential staph infection in the making without proper care.

Jessie's relief about made her knees give out. She managed not to fall. "You're going to be okay, Landon,"—whispered.

"His heavy pectoral and abdominal muscle development saved him worse injury," Dr. Moynahan pronounced. "He must have braced against the impacts."

Moynahan turned to her once they waited out the worst of his numbers. Got his torso bandaged. Gave him IV fluids to counteract the serum loss. "He's got barely three percent body fat, Jessie." It was a warning. "If he's going to body build like this, he needs to feed his body better."

Jessie took the admonition seriously. She'd had no idea. But then all she ever saw was his head, neck, and hands, all of them showing him thin, but no

longer quite as dangerously so. He was gaining
weight. She had to cheat at their contest to keep
ahead of his strong weight gains to keep him working
at it. "I'll see that he feeds up more."

"Do that."

She would. She'd engage Sol to help.

"We're keeping him overnight for observation."

Landon, still under an oxygen mask, shook his
head—violently. "No," he muffle-spoke.

Jessie looked at him. "They need to, Landon. I'll
stay with you."

"No. No admission."

Dr. Moynahan leaned toward her. Pointed to the
heart monitor. Whispered, "He's stressing, again.
How about if we keep him in Emergency. Ask him."

She did.

It took cajoling, but, in the end, with his eyes
narrowed, watching her, he finally gave assent with
one short nod and a whispered, "All right. On your
honor, Jessie."

"On my honor. So help me God, I swear I won't
let them admit you, Landon. You have my solemn
word. I'll obey your wishes." He was *so* difficult, so

distrustful of the medical system ever since his brain injury.

***

29 – Her Say Goes

LANDON WOKE just before midnight, Jessie sitting beside his bed. She was leaned forward in a chair, her head down, cradled on one curled arm, that arm laying on the mattress beside him.

He still had a death grip on her other arm. *How does that happen? You're supposed to relax when you sleep.*

He loosened his grip a little, but didn't let go. He thought about it, but the idea made him wary. She was his lifeline to freedom from this prison. If he let her go, she'd flee, abandoning him.

He paid attention to his breathing …which hurt. But it was hugely better than 'tiny puffs'. *Yeah, I'll take the pain, thanks.* Tiny puffs had been better than suffocating, but breathing like a human being was better than everything. *Yeah. I'll take the pain.*

"How are you feeling?"—Oli's voice.

He started. That hurt, too. Just about everything hurt, right now. Turned his head. Swallowed. Tried to speak. Had no saliva, his mouth stuck, skin on skin, tongue glued to roof of mouth. Nodded instead.

Oli got up from the chair and came over. Held out a plastic water glass with a straw. "Here you go."

Landon managed a couple of swallows. "Did you get them?" he asked, his voice sounding like a croak to him.

"My dogs got two. Remmers' pair flushed out another one. That's it."

He nodded.

"You know better than to go out without a full kit of body armor on, Landon." Oli's voice growled. The eyes were icy.

He nodded, again. He *did* know.

"Four minutes, and you would have spared yourself this misery." Oli gave a nod toward the sleeping Jessie. "And her. As it is, you're going to be okay. Mild lung bruising, heart okay. Diaphragm is really bruised. That's what they tell me. And the only reason you're not a lot worse off is due to our workouts. Congratulations. You're getting there ...becoming one of my steel warriors like Howie. Now, let's get you dressed. I brought clothes. I used my POA to get you signed out."

"My badge? Keys...."

"Jessie's got your property—keys, guns, badge, hat, boots. Your clothes are in the trash. They cut them off you. So, come on. Get yourself up. We're leaving as soon as the nurse comes in to take that IV port out of you. You're going home—"

"Thank you."

"...Before Britta tears up your house. And you're welcome."

Britta. "Is Britta okay?"

"She's just fine."

Huge relief.

"Harvey Mueller is almost as bad as you."

"She hit him, too?"

"She did, but not as bad. He took cover. He's got broken ribs, a broken arm, and other damage from you falling backwards on him."

"I did?"

Oli laughed. "He hid behind you, using you for a shield. Deserves everything he got."

Landon didn't remember that.

Oli touched his daughter's shoulder. "Jessie? Time to wake up."

*

THERE WAS no way Jessie was okay with Landon driving, not with the bruising to his upper torso. Even putting on his clothes made him wince. Her dad had to help him get dressed. Getting out of the wheelchair after the mandatory ride out of the Emergency, then walking to her Dad's car was difficult for him he hurt so much. It was obvious. Putting on a seatbelt when he got in was also no joy. She pointed that out. He, of course, groused.

"You can pick your unit up some other day. Nobody is going to steal The Rhino," she said as her dad pulled out of the ER parking lot, the Caddie devoid of its usual fur brigade. The world felt empty without dogs around her. Her dad had taken them all home and left them—his, hers, Sandra's, and Landon's Britta.

"I'd rather drive it home," Landon told her.

Men rationalized with men better than women who they just argued with. "Dad?"

"We'll do as he asks, Jessie."

She rolled eyes. No help there. "Okay."

Oli headed toward the police station where, floodlights bathing it, people were still working on cleanup and evidence. She flashed her badge as Oli pulled in, then parked next to Landon's Hummer. "There you go," she said, not bothering to get out to help. If he was going to be contrary, let him suffer the full effects of his stupidity. "You riding with him, Dad?"

Her dad gave her the hairy eyeball.

She gave it right back.

Oli audibly inhaled, turned his face back to front and center. Gripped the wheel. Didn't answer.

"Jessie, I need you to drive The Rhino for me. I don't think I'm ready to do that, yet,"—Landon from the back.

She turned around to face him. "Nobody can drive it, Landon. Just you."

"Not true. I can authorize someone. I've got the special code I need to do that from the security software company. I'm picking you."

"Do the powers that be at the S.O. know this is happening?"

"I *am* the 'powers that be', Jessie," he said, his low grumble almost indulgent.

Right! And there was his arrogance, again, even when injured. *Officious man!*

*

"COME HERE, please," he said to her, her all stiff and prickly. "Don't fight me on this, I beg you, Jessie. There are very few people I trust. You and your dad are top on the list, and Oli's not a deputy." *Yet,* reminded himself. He needed to get Oli formally sworn in for criminal apprehension, and his dogs exempted from liability. As soon as possible. Then, "Computer? Authorize Deputy Jessica Anderson to drive this vehicle in my stead, at will, my authorization. Held his thumb on the sensor and spoke out his authorization code.

The computer acknowledged, then demanded Jessie do the same.

She hesitated, then, him waiting, staring down at her, she finally put her thumb to the pad. *Seven inches on her five-nine has its advantages.*

"Authorization complete," the computer acknowledged.

SHE WAS SILENT on the trip home, her dad driving on ahead, his white Escalade practically glowing in the dark in the waxing gibbous moonlight. Landon watched Jessie's handling of The Rhino. He watched as she used things he wouldn't, the security beacons live, the computer warning of possible hazards, reporting license plates belonging to previous or suspected criminal offenders, continually updating whereabouts of the nearest potential escape routes. Landon wanted to ask her to turn it off. Didn't.

Her dad was like this—always an eye out for potential danger, brewing trouble, for the means of securing advantage in case of danger. This was not a way to live. It was, he realized, an extension of Oli's time in the SEALs. Probably her granddad Darby's time in service, too. Between the mob attack on her and with the training he knew Oli was putting Jessie through, training that seemed completely contrary to her personality type, Oli was making her into a female version of himself.

Whatever happened to the real Jessie—the quiet, demure, reserved, even shy girl she'd been in high school when he'd first become aware of her? He missed that Jessie, a Jessie he'd never come to know because her brother Erik had warned him off …in no uncertain terms.

He chuckled at the memory—"I'll pound your face in if you even look her way!" And Erik had meant it.

Yeah. Landon had had a reputation—not a fair one, but it had stuck.

"What's funny?" Jessie asked, her eyes glued to the road, the glow of the dash lights giving her face a strange pallor.

"Nothing."

"That wasn't nothing."

"Just memories."

"Of?"

"High school."

A groan met that. "I hated high school."

He'd loved it. It had provided every opportunity and excuse to avoid having to be home. His silence must have cued her, because her next words nailed that truth: "You loved it, didn't you?"

"I did," he admitted.

"Figures that you would. Where brainiacs and sports heroes shine, and you were both! Couldn't see the rest of us lowly also-rans for dust."

He turned to look out the side window. That wasn't true. He'd even tutored kids who'd asked for his help, his dad giving him high grief about not charging them.

He frowned. Jessie was usually patient, maybe even kind, with him, now. Set her off, though, don't do what she said, and she became rock hard, her tongue a lash. She was borderlining that at the moment. She was angry with him.

He smiled. That was okay. She'd flip once she got over it, go into her wicked, happy side.

She turned into his drive, the gates opening. Drove up, parked, shut down.

She opened the door the same time he did, the four guard dogs all wags, two on his side, two on hers, the dome lights not coming on until Jessie touched them. "Come on. Inside."

"Just drive The Rhino home, Jessie. I'll have Sol drive me over in the morning to pick it up."

"I'm staying the night."

"What?!"

She gave him a 'Jessie look'. "We need to keep an eye on you in case of a setback since you wouldn't stay at the hospital for observation. You had a choice of Dad or me. You've got me since I'm a paramedic. You have bruised lungs. ...Well, the bottoms of them, anyway, a bruised diaphragm, bruised whole upper torso, and your skin is a mess."

No, he did not want this. "Sol's here. Besides, it's almost time for you to run in a couple of hours."

"I'm taking the morning off. Believe it or not, Landon, I do get tired, just like you do."

He could not resist the comeback. "Never know it. I was beginning to think you were a robot."

She grinned. "Not hardly. Dibs on the couch."

"The bedroom upstairs you used last time, the one next to Sol's, is still open."

"Nope. I need to be able to hear in case of trouble. You'll keep your bedroom door open so I *can* hear."

"No."

"Then I'll take the door off its hinges."

"It's *my* house!"

"You want me to call Dad and have him explain it to you? We hold POA, remember? You were released into our care. Right now, that means *my* care, and my say goes."

Right. Her undying officiousness. *Overbearing, bossy woman!*

***

D. L. Keur

30 – Unknown Motive

THURSDAY

LANDON GROUSING the whole time, Jessie took his morning vitals, then got his chest cleaned, treated, and re-bandaged. Then, him begging, she cut holes for his arms and head in a contractor bag and eased it over his upper torso, sealing it to good skin with transpore polyethylene tape. "Okay. You can take your shower, now. Do *not* get that bandage job wet, or I'll have to do it all over again. That's a breathable non-stick pad—very expensive at that size."

A huffed out sigh, a groan of pain accompanying it, then he finally said, "I won't, and thank you."

"You're welcome."

She looked at Britta who was glued to him. "*Kommen Sie*, Britta. You can't take a shower with him."

His hand touched the dog. Did some sort of weird turn and finger twitch, and Britta came away. Jessie frowned. *They're developing their own language. ...Okay.* Went out to do chores, Sol helping, her teaching him how. Then, she helped Sol with breakfast.

Landon was still in the bedroom when Sol called, "Breakfast."

After a minute of no show, Jessie tapped on his door. "Chores done. Breakfast is ready."

No answer.

"Landon?"

Finally, a "Come."

She opened the door. He was dressed, but sitting there on a chair, boots akimbo, socks in his hand. He was breathing funny. "What's happening, Landon?"

A moan. A groan. A roll-eye. Finally, "I can't get my socks and boots on."

"Okay. Let me help."

"I hate this."

"Then don't get injured. ...Or at least try not to."

He frowned up at her. "Are you always this bossy?"

"Only with uncooperative morons."

Silence.

Okay. She was back to treating him like she did regular guys like her brother and her dad. "I'm sorry. Didn't mean to be a harpy."

"Forgiven."

Always. There he was trying to be Saint Landon all over again. She got his socks on, then, with a struggle, his boots pulled on for him. "There you go."

"Thank you."

Straightening up, she brushed his torso with light fingers. Yes, he was wearing protection under his uniform. *Good.*

*

JESSIE INSISTED she was staying with him. "All day. I'm responsible, Landon. You've had an unknown cardiac event in your recent history and just had your chest pummeled." And, again, she enumerated his injuries …like he couldn't feel them all by himself. "Whether you realize it or not, skin is also a life-critical organ, one of the largest in the body, its health very important to your survival."

It was a repeat of what she'd lectured him on last night, and, yes, he knew all that, thank you very much.

What he didn't want was yet another babysitter, especially not Jessie.

"Give me fifteen minutes," she told him as he pulled in to park in front of the Anderson's front walkway, desperately glad to finally shut down. It hurt to turn the wheel, it hurt to shift gears, it hurt to clutch and brake. "I've just got to shower and change, then get the dogs," she said, opening the door.

The dogs! She always had to have the dogs with her. Always.

Thought of her out with Jed. Well, almost always.

He glanced at Britta. One dog was one thing. A whole passel of them was quite another ...not that he minded—the wonder dogs. "Are you taking the XV?" he asked before she shut the door.

"No. I can't monitor you if I'm not present. Be back in a flash."

Right. Flinched as she hip-slammed the door shut. Started to blow out a sigh of exasperation and caught himself before he hurt himself. Got out, carefully straightening, Britta with him, and went to find Oli.

Found the man in the biggest dog barn, but, of course, Oli was geared up, lined up with three others, one a black woman, dogs launching themselves to grab hold and take them down to the sand and wood shavings mix that floored the place. Oli always seemed to get up laughing. *Of course he would.*

Easing back out, Landon went back to The Rhino and found a wet-haired Jessie along with all her dogs, less the two Border Collies who belonged to somebody else. They were all waiting for him, the second row seats folded down, dog tails wagging.

He glanced at his phone. True to her word, Jessie was back …in under fifteen minutes. *No woman is that fast.* He eased opened the driver's side door, no pulling it open as usual . Britta jumped up, then over the center console. Then he poked his face in. "I thought you'd drive since you consider me an invalid," he said, getting in when she just sat there.

She shook her head. "I don't consider you an invalid, Landon. Just injured. Let's see how you do."

She handed him a bubble pack of pills. "Ibuprofen and oxycodone at a dose that allows you to operate a motor vehicle. One, only, every six to eight hours at most."

"Is a painkiller advised?"

"Dr. Moynahan wouldn't have prescribed it if not."

He blessed the man for his forethought. Gulped one down, Jessie handing him a bottle of water. Put The Rhino in gear once he managed the seat belt, being careful not to flinch or moan as he did it, and, thankfully, he didn't hear another medical caution or instructional lecture out of Jessie all the way into the S.O. In fact, she didn't talk at all. Just texted messages back and forth to somebody—Jed. Landon caught the name on a sideways glance. *Yeah. They're an item.*

*

SOL WAS HARD at work in his lab when Jessie stuck her head in. "Sheriff's in huddling with Martin, and it was too obvious he didn't want me there. Need a hand?"

"No, but I'll take a brain."

She sidled up to what he was working on—a paintball gun taken from one of the latest arrestees. He pointed to something. "See this?"

"Yeah."

"The gun is identical to all the rest we've collected in the last three days. Like the others, it has been customized to increase the velocity well beyond the safety limits and has a much higher psi, too. This thing has an unusual regulator, a customized barrel, special canisters …lots of tweaks." He looked up at her. "This is meant to incapacitate the opponent."

"I'm not familiar with high-velocity paintball guns. We just use low-impact ones with the dogs."

"It makes no sense to me why, if they're committing crimes, they're using paintball guns."

She shrugged. "Less legal liability, less criminal penalty?"

"Yeah. I get that, and I get Landon's theory that they're hunting hunters. If he's right, it would make sense …in a way. Plaster the game hunters and let them feel how it feels to be shot like they're shooting an animal. And it *does* make sense. The theft from the sporting goods store even makes sense, considering what was taken—paintballs, paintball gun helmets, jackets, plus small caliber rounds for the Stingers®, which I thought they were carrying in case of being attacked by a dog or some other animal, like Matthew Orr's dog, Brown. But these people just blatantly attacked the P.D., so our good sheriff's theory gets thrown right out the window."

Again Sol's eyes reached for hers. "Any ideas?"

She sighed. "I didn't have my cam on last night. Forgot to turn it on in the flurry and hurry. But the woman who was dressed up in a fake cop uniform yelled something. She said, 'Score.' Um…. 'I get lonnie tunes!'"

Sol grabbed a notepad and pen. "Say again?"

She repeated herself.

"Lonnie Tunes. …Like *Loon*ey Tunes®, only 'lonnie' with an 'ah', not an 'uu'."

"I don't know."

"Huh…." Sol frowned. "I wish you had that on cam."

"Sorry."

"Anybody else hear it?"

"I'm sure the other paramedic I was working with heard it, too."

"You remember his or her name?"

"Nolan Price."

"Thank you."

"Jessie?"—Landon's voice.

She turned. "Yeah?"

"Heading back to my office."

Surprised he had actually notified her, she said, "Okay. Be right with you." Looked back at Sol. "Later, Big Guy?"

"Later, Fast Girl."

Grinned.

They no sooner got to Landon's office when in trooped Martin and Sol, both. "Tell me about this Lonnie Tunes thing, Deputy Anderson," Martin demanded.

Landon frowned. "...Yeah," he said softly. He gave Jessie a weird look. "I remember that. As she was pelting me, she said, "'Score. I get Lonnie Tunes. Both of them for the win.' I remember it."

"'Both of them....'" Martin muttered, glancing down at Sol. "'Both.' And 'win'"

"The sheriff and the chief of police?" Sol suggested, his own frown curling his brows.

"I think so," Martin said. "They're gunning for law enforcement.... Maybe heads of law enforcement in particular?"

"And the 'for the win' means it's a contest of some sort," Sol said.

"That makes *no* sense with their attacks on the hunters," Landon pointed out. He turned a disturbed look Jessie's way, but he wasn't seeing her. His eyes had gone distant. "I had a thought while I was driving into that incident last night. Are the camera vans connected to this?"

A Martin frown-down met that.

"The whole thing is set up for the documentary they claim they're doing?" Landon pursued. "…Making exciting things happen for the camera?"

Jessie pondered. She'd never thought about the persistent van guys. But it struck a chord.

Dare she say her unsubstantiated thoughts? Went for it. "Research required, but what if this is for some weird movie or TV show?"

"That doesn't explain the attacks on the hunters,"—Sol.

"Let's bring them in for questioning," Martin said. "From both vans."

"On what pretext?"—Landon.

"That they were there."

"You can ask them, but they're not obligated, and I bet they won't cooperate."

And Landon's take proved right.

***

D. L. Keur

31 – High

"TERRI?" LANDON called softly, poking his head into her tech domain, the ranks and rows of computer screens on the walls doing rapid-fire switches that, were he to watch them, would make him dizzy.

The other two deputies on shift with her kept their faces glued to their work, ignoring him. Terri held up a finger, her face watching a big screen right in front of her that looked, from where Landon stood at the doorway, like it had varied colors and lengths of lines quickly scrolling up to disappear on a pitched black background.

The screen stopped abruptly, then went completely black. She swiveled around to face. "Come on in. I don't bite."

No. She hugged.

With her foot, she nudged a rolling chair free from the counter that ran the length of the wall. "Sit. Take a load off. You, too, Jessie …and, Jessie, I could use your quick fingers and savvy for a Sol project since you're here."

"Sure!"

Landon watched his platinum-haired guard leaning back against the hallway wall bounce upright, then dodge past him to a station, her dogs trooping in, too. She slid into a swivel chair, and Terri handed her a printout. That fast and easy, his babysitter problem was solved. *Escape while you can.* But he couldn't. He needed to talk to Terri, and he needed to do it right now.

*

SOL'S RESEARCH request was predictable. Seven variations in the spelling of 'Lonnie'—'lonnie', 'lonny', 'lonnee', 'lonnei', 'lonneigh', 'lonney', and 'lonni'— coupled with six variations of the spelling of 'Tunes'—'toons', 'tunes', 'tuuns', 'toonz', 'tunz', and 'tuunz'—forty-two possible combinations. Jessie went to work, setting up her parameters, then sending out the queries on the Web—the consumer web, sometimes called the surface web, the deep web, the dark web, and the dirty web, all.

Done, she turned to find Landon watching her, him sitting in the chair Terri had originally offered him. "Oh. I didn't know you were done."

"Obviously. How long before you're done here?"

"It just has to run. I don't have to babysit it."

"But you do me."

"No. Not you. Your body."

He dropped his face and chuckled. Stopped immediately. Took a slow breath and shakily sighed it out very carefully. "I hurt."

"Yeah."

"I can't even have a laugh at something where it doesn't hurt."

"Yeah." But she wondered what he'd found funny in her answer.

"When will you have results?" he asked.

"I have no idea when it will ping my phone that it's done and I can come back to sort and sift. From there, it depends on the volume and quality of the results."

He got up. "I've got to go see Judge Laird. Are you coming or staying?"

"Coming."

"Well then, let's roll, please."

He was being so good. He'd waited for her, when he could have just slipped out. She was proud of him. She signaled. "Dogs? Time to go."

*

"WILL YOU drive?" he asked her. "I'm feeling tired and hurting a lot."

Watched her nod and head for the driver's side. Started to toss her the keys and caught himself at the first twinge.

She walked back and held her hand out. "Each day will get better. Most people would be flat on their back, still in the hospital."

She smiled, and it deepened the color of her eyes. He'd just noticed that. Genuine smile meant calmer eyes. *That was an odd thought*, he thought, watching himself …and realized he was 'high'.

Watched her go to the touch pad, get acknowledged, the locks opening. She opened the back and urged the dogs in, his Britta jumping in with them. "Dad doesn't believe in that, of course," she continued. "Hence him strong-arming you out of there last night."

"I'm glad he did."

"Yeah. I know. Hospitals are Hades in your book, right?" she said climbing into the driver's seat, him getting in the passenger side.

"Worse," he said. "Prisons."

"Same thing by the descriptions of torment suffered in both."

"Truth there."

She put the key in, turned it over, put it in gear, and headed for the exit. "Well, I don't find hospitals that bad." She glanced left. "And here comes the van, right on cue."

He ignored the van comment. He was hoping what he'd ask Terri to do would get them the 'in' they needed for probable cause for a search warrant. "The hospital and that miserable recovery facility treated me like I had no rights, Jessie."

"You're what is labeled 'noncompliant'. Once you get that stamp on your records, they move to different protocols."

He felt his anger stir. "I have the right to determine what will and what will not be done to my body."

He watched her watch the rearview. Then the camera feeds. "They are right on our tail," she said. "And, if you're considered of sound mind, yes."

He caught the shift back and forth of subjects. Felt more anger come up. "Jessie? You're angering me."

"Oops."—sarcasm.

She is such a minx! And just that fast, his anger was replaced with an urge to laugh out loud, again— the painkiller ...the oxycodone. He was definitely stoned. Wouldn't take more of the drug, not unless he absolutely needed it, and he, for sure, wasn't going to drive. "You sound so convincingly remorseful, Jessie—*not!*"

She laughed. "Okay, okay. I know. But you aren't the most model patient."

"I don't care." He watched his side mirror. Watched the van maneuver itself so it could see him riding shotgun. *Irritating pests. I wonder if they are part of it?* Sighed ...gently. Got back to the conversation. "I have inalienable rights—human rights. I have the right to refuse treatment. I have the right to decide what I will ingest, what I will allow, and what I will not."

He heard her blow out a huge breath. Finally, she said, "Medically-speaking, it's tricky. But I get your position, and I do my best to support it." She flashed him a glance. "Really, I do. And I don't always ...or even *often* agree with what you have codified in your living will and Durable Power of Attorney, but I do my very best to honor it. Honest."

He knew she did. She'd proved it last night, not allowing the intubation. "And I thank you for it."

"You're *not* welcome. It puts me against my own morals, my own training."

"Sorry about that." Of course, he *wasn't*.

"You should have been intubated immediately. Normally, I would have done it, but didn't, and I had to fight myself the whole time. You were dying, Landon." She glanced a sideways scowl.

He said 'sorry' again, and, again, didn't mean it.

"You sound so convincingly remorseful—not!—your words coming right back at ya," she snapped. Her eyes were quick back and forth—windshield to mirrors to security feeds and back. "I really want to let loose on that van, Landon. It's taking a lot of willpower not to."

"Patience. We'll get them if they're guilty."

"If you say so."

She turned down a side street, the van missing the turn because they were in the wrong lane, and took the shortest distance to the courthouse. Parked in the restricted area so the van couldn't follow. "Here we are," she said, shutting down. Rolled the windows down for the dogs. "I don't know how to engage security in this rig."

"I'll do it, you watch."

"Okay."

"Thanks for accepting this responsibility."

"You're...." She eyed him, her face stiff. Just as suddenly, he saw her relent, the rigid jaw softening, the bright eyes darkening. "You're welcome."

***

32 – Numbed

JESSIE WAS irritated. The Actuator Studios people were already through courthouse security, camera rolling when she and Landon were being processed through. Her having to learn how to activate The Rhino's defenses had given the snoops the opportunity to get inside first. *How did they know we were headed for the courthouse? We could have been going to the P.D. or to one of the prosecutor's offices. Who or what tipped them off?* If they had tried to attach tracking to The Rhino, it's security would have immediately alerted to anyone tampering with it. *Drones? Or they're tapped into the traffic cams? Maybe tracking Landon's phone's IMEI signal?* It was possible. She'd have to see if Terri and Sol could help figure it out.

"What have they got, a fast track pass?" she asked the deputy running the wand over her, nodding toward the camera guy and his sidekick.

He just grimaced, his eyes flicking in the direction of the subjects in question.

And they followed her and Landon to Judge Laird's office, camera rolling all the while, even up the stairs. "Snoops," she muttered. "It's too bad the courthouse is public space."

"My sentiments," Landon grumbled.

"We heard that," came the scrawny guy's voice from below them.

"Good," Landon called down, bulling his voice, which made it reverberate in the concrete safety stairwell. Of course, he paid for it, him gasping, his arm wrapping around to grasp his middle as his diaphragm objected.

'Scrawny guy' scrambled to lower the volume on something, and Jessie realized they were recording audio, as well. Yeah, if Landon could get probable cause, they'd likely find enough evidence to easily convict these guys, condemning them to at least a couple of years in jail. *You're thinking like a cop, an embittered, retaliatory one*, she scolded herself. But, then, she *was* a cop, again, wasn't she?

Sighed. *Not by choice.* That was all Landon's doing. *The sneak.*

Through the door and into the hallway. ...And there was a line. "Wow."

As they approached, the Actuator Studios jerks pacing them, Judge Laird herself walked out, decked out in her robes. She handed out a piece of paper to each individual in the line, then turned to hold out one to Landon and Jessie. Stopped. Arched her eyebrows. Turned back to the people queued up and said, "You have what you need in that printout. Fill it out, following the instructions, and return it to the city prosecutor's office. Action will be taken. Have a gentle day."

*

"WHO WERE they, Your Honor?" Landon asked following Judge Laird back into her front office once the line of folks were happy and gone.

She didn't even glance his way. Just said, "Citizens who claim they've been assaulted, resulting in property damage and even injuries, and want criminal prosecution against their assailants. Law enforcement and the prosecutor fobbed them all off."

"Not my office!"

"Not yours, Sheriff. No. Not the County Prosecutor's office, either. You have Mr. Dutfeld well in hand." Now she turned and smirked, then went serious, again. "No. It's the Northridge Police and the City Prosecutor, too," she said, handing the remaining stack of printouts to her clerk. "They refused to arrest and charge vandals, thieves, assailants, and, worst of all, batterers."

The camera man eased in, recording. So did the scrawny guy who Landon swore was in charge.

Judge Laird turned. "This is a one party consent state, and you are not part of this conversation," she told them.

They retreated.

Again, she smirked at Landon. "They don't want to go to jail, and I *will* put them there if they persist in breaking the law."

She motioned and walked to her chamber door. "Come." Then, "David, make sure we're not disturbed …and the city attorney is sure to show up at any moment. Remember what I told you to tell him, exactly as I instructed you to say it."

"Yes, Your Honor."

"Excellent."

Landon frowned. *What's going on?!*

*

JESSIE WAS SURPRISED that Landon didn't remove his hat. She frowned. Waggled eyebrows at him, touching her head with a finger, but he just shook his head.

"Sit. Both of you," Judge Laird said, Landon closing the door behind them as the judge went to her desk, the fist sculpt sitting front edge, center, right next to her statue of 'Blind Lady Justice'. Laird stripped off her robe, and hung it up. Finally, she sat down.

Landon touched the back of a chair, his eyes on Jessie. Cued, Jessie took a seat. Only then did he follow suit.

"To what may I attribute this visit, Sheriff?"

Landon pulled a piece of paper from his pocket. Unfolded it. Handed it to the judge. Then he dug out his phone. Did something, then turned it to face Judge Laird.

"Oh, Saints preserve us. Who is that?!" Laird demanded.

"Me, Your Honor. And the names on that list and the charges listed against them should have short-circuited any instant get-out-of-jail-on-bail card …which is why I'm here. The woman who shot me and did the damage I just showed you was one of those released. I recognized her as she opened fire. Your magistrates let her …let all of them loose."

"Article 1, Section 6, Idaho Constitution…."

Thus began a back and forth, tit for tat exchange between the judge and Landon, him firing chapter, title, and section references from what he referenced as either state or federal legal code, and Judge Laird returning with more. And, devoid of a cheat sheet, Jessie had only a vague idea of what they were talking about and hadn't a clue who was winning.

An hour later, they both finally ran out of steam. By that time, Jessie's ears had gone numb and dumb. "Lunch?" she heard Judge Laird ask. She was all smiles. So was Landon.

"With pleasure, Your Honor." And, to Jessie, the tone in both Landon's and the judge's voices seemed to indicate that they'd come to some mutual agreement.

Thank you, God. Otherwise, Jessie was pretty sure they'd have gone at it for even longer. Not only were her ears and brain numb, even her butt was asleep. So this was what Landon did for 'fun'?

Spare me.

*

LUNCH WAS an absolutely stimulating experience, Judge Regina Laird going into detail about some case law concerning the right to release until convicted that Landon hadn't yet gotten to in his research. It explained why they'd had to let Nicholson out. It also made him doubly conscious of how important was completely compelling hard evidence of criminal action, including premeditated …which Nicholson's had been, but which neither his office, nor the FBI investigation had been able to directly attribute to Nicholson's hand. Nicholson's release had been a shock. And Nicholson was so slippery that nailing him for his malfeasance was mostly by circumstantial evidence and association, not direct involvement …except for his attack on Jessie …which was completely solid. "And that should have been enough," he said, frowning.

"It was. Hence the steep bail that was set."

"Steep by whose standards? He was easily able to meet it."

Laird nodded. "By normal standards, Sheriff."

"Call me Landon, please, Your Honor."

"Only if you stop constantly calling me 'Your Honor'. Reggie is fine when we're not on public display." Laird took a sip of water. "Will your office try to locate him?"

"Special Agent-in-Charge Andy Newsome is actually handling that, now. I have to defer to him because it's FBI territory. Them and the Federal Marshals."

Laird smiled, her eyes going almost predatory. "You didn't answer my question, Landon."

Landon returned the smile. He knew the game and so did Laird. "My deputies are on the lookout." Then he added, "So am I."

"Good."

The judge then turned her attention on Jessie. "You raise and train protection dogs, do you not?"

Jessie started. Looked up from her phone. "Ah …yes, Your Honor."

"I'm interested in the purchase of one. Can you arrange it?"

"Ah …yes. I'll have my dad call you if you give me your contact information."

Landon watched as Regina Laird handed across a card. "My old-fashioned card," she said, and Jessie nodded, pocketing it.

Judge Laird looked toward Landon. "Shall we?"

Landon stood, trying his best not to wince, pulled Judge Laird's chair out, would have done the same for Jessie, but she was already on her feet. Then he walked the two ladies in his care out to their vehicles. The visit to Judge Laird's chambers, then a continuation of stimulating conversation over lunch had been the first real pleasant moments of his day.

Jessie obviously didn't share his viewpoint, he discovered minutes later. "That was exhausting," she said, climbing into The Rhino's driver's seat.

"It was necessary," Landon responded, a certain sadness coming down over his good mood. Nobody liked what *he* liked.

"I'm so glad it's your job, not mine, dealing with all that legal stuff."

She had just struck a solid point, her comment hitting him where he lived. Since he hadn't been able to become a lawyer like he'd wanted, maybe being sheriff, much as he hated the job, was the next best avenue to doing exactly *what* he wanted—law—public law—the Constitution of the United States of America.

"Next stop?" Jessie asked, bored blue eyes watching him.

"To the hospital to talk to Harvey Mueller."

She groaned. "Should have guessed."

***

33 – A Watershed Moment

CHIEF-OF-POLICE Harvey Mueller was allowed visitors. Landon, Jessie with him, walked right in, but not until Landon got the scoop from Dispatch on what calls from the city had been logged in the last week to week-and-a-half, which ones had resulted in responses, which had been ignored, and which had had arrests. "Harvey, how are you doing?"

"I feel like I got crushed by an elephant."

Landon started to laugh, almost buckled at the knees with the pain, and barely breathed through it. "Please don't make me laugh, Harvey, but I think...." He turned to Jessie and she nodded. "Yeah, I think that was me who landed on you."

"I know. And I don't hold it against you. Not at all." The man looked him up and down. "How is it you aren't still hospitalized? You got the worst of it. I just got a broken arm, a few cracked ribs, and a handful of nasty, ringed, red-purple bruises on my chest, stomach, arm, and shoulder. She must have hit you point blank."

"She did," Jessie put in.

Landon scowled at her. "Private information, Jessie," he muttered.

"Sorry …sir," she whispered back.

Harvey was watching them, eyes shifting from Jessie to Landon and back again, but Landon pretended he didn't notice. "So, I'm wondering, Harvey, if any of the incidents of vandalism, theft, and/or assault and/or battery in your jurisdiction that have happened in the last couple of weeks are related to our paintball assailants of last night?"

The man scowled. "When it comes to crime, Reid, hindsight, as you know, is twenty-twenty."

Landon waited for more, and finally got something.

"The answer is yes …in hindsight. And to your next question about why didn't we do something, we thought it was pre-Halloween pranksters. That's all. And, honestly, the city prosecutor just lets them go. Why waste my officers' time and effort?! It's not good for morale."

"Understand. Thanks for the candor. It goes no further." He glanced at Jessie, and she nodded. "Guaranteed."

"Thank you."

*

"SORRY ABOUT that slip-up in there," Jessie said. "I didn't mean to share private information or to seem so cavalier by not saying 'sir'. I'm too used to us just being friends."

"We're friends?"

She felt as if she'd taken a cheap shot to her solar plexus. Managed to hide it. "I thought we were …sir."

"Stop with the 'sir', please, Jessie, and never mind my poor stab at being funny. I said it tongue-in-cheek, but, as usual, failed to effectively deliver. Comedian I'm obviously not. And, yeah, I'd count you at the very top of people I could put on my friend list, which includes your dad, Sol, and you …maybe a couple of others, all mostly old timers …and, of course, your new beau, Jed, who I've known since I was twelve or thirteen."

"He's not my beau!"

"And, honestly, I'm not sure about Sol. I don't think he shares the trust in me that I do in him. Or the genuine appreciation. I think, to him, I'm a subject to be studied. …In fact I know I am. He's said as much."

Landon's words made Jessie feel a little better, but she was warned, now, about something else. Last night's incident had put him right back into that spot where he was feeling unsure of both himself and others. "Um…. Landon, Sol studies everyone. He studied me for years. *Why* did he study me?" She shrugged. "I don't know."

"Because you think differently than the rest of us. He told me so, but I already knew that about you."

"Like you don't?"

He didn't answer. What he'd said, though, he'd said with such authority. Like he *knew*. That was what she called his 'arrogance'. *He's always so sure.* So, why wasn't he sure about himself and his relationships with others? She nixed pursuing that. There was no way to figure that one out. That was a Tank job.

"What do you like to do for fun, Landon …um …and I don't know if I'm supposed to say 'sir' or not, right now, since you're technically on duty?"

A sigh. A catch of his breath as pain from deeper breathing hit him, then a pause. "Only around people who expect you to say it. Please not to me in private or around people with whom we're both on familiar terms …like Sol, like Martin, like …oh, don't make me have to enumerate a list."

"And there's the Greek speak."

His brows went wonky. "What?"

"'With whom', 'enumerate'—phrases and words like that. You never speak …or, more truthfully, rarely speak 'normal' with me—the relaxed way you do with Dad, but rarely me. And, no, don't bother to make up some excuse why. I've already figured it out."

"You have *no* idea."

And that made her mad, because, yes, she did about that, but, no, she didn't, not about important things.

She braked and pulled over in a wide spot. Turned off The Rhino. Turned sideways, the dogs coming up to poke noses in her face, all concern. She gave them her hands. "It's okay guys and gals. I just need to straighten a few things out with the boss, here. Go back to your chewies."

And they did. Even Britta.

Landon had dropped his head, his eyes staring at the glove box, seeing nothing, she knew. He was trying to hide under his hat. He was waiting for what her gram called 'the other shoe to drop'. So she dropped it.

"I need to figure out who you are and how to deal with all your gi-normous number of eccentricities, Landon Reid, especially since I hold POA, Health Care. For me, it's a *huge* responsibility. I need to know you better, so please answer some questions for me, right now, right here, or I'm going to have to resign the commitment."

He was absolutely still. His head didn't move. His eyes didn't shift. He just stared in the direction of the glove box.

She pressed on. "Okay, first question, honest answer, please. Do you believe in God, the father, the son, and the Holy Spirit, that Jesus, son of God, born of Mary, died for our sins?"

Softly—"Yes."

"Do you believe in Heaven?"

Again softly—"Yes."

"Do you believe in Hell?"

Firmly, but just as softly—"No."

That answer made her pause. She took stock, took a breath, then came up with the only next possible question after that. "Do you believe in Life after Death?"

"Maybe."

Blinked. Her brain just stopped at that surprise. Regrouped. Or tried to.

…Failed.

He turned in the seat as was his way, but very slowly and carefully, him easing to lean a shoulder to the door window, lifting a knee up onto the corner of the seat, the other leg, foot flat on the floor. One hand he propped on the dash; the other arm draped over and around the seat. "Jessie, why are you asking me these questions?"

Wasn't it obvious?!

Obviously not! "Because I hold POA, and, if you're incapacitated, I don't know you well enough— not *you* you—to be able to make an informed decision about what *you* would actually want to happen, *that's* why!" And she felt like she practically screamed it at him. She felt like she did. The dogs didn't react, though; her ears didn't ring, so she must have kept her cool, her voice under control. She breathed out stress. She breathed out frustration. She felt more brim up even worse.

He picked up the mic. Keyed it. Called in their twenty, and told Dispatch not to disturb them except in the case of emergency. "We're brainstorming."

She heard Dispatch acknowledge. Then he put the mic down. Spoke slowly, his deep voice enunciating very clearly and precisely. "All right, Jessie. I want you as my chief POA. And that, by the way, I notified Findlingham about this morning. Your dad is second. Your grandmother, third in line. I trust you—abso*lute*ly trust you—and that's not something I do easily. So, whatever you need to know, whatever you need to ask, ask, and I'll answer."

*

THEY TALKED, sitting in The Rhino, walking the dogs, going back and sitting in The Rhino again, walking the dogs again, until it was near time to meet Oli. Then they talked some more once they were done at the firing range, eating take-out from the Chinese place. It was a candid talk, Jessie baring her fears and her moral conflicts to him, him answering her very pointed questions, sharing things that made him cringe, some of which he'd never even thought through until she asked, then explained consequences. In the end, they wound up sitting on the steps of his porch as the moon rose steadily to its meridian, having finally and completely talked through all the things she felt she needed to understand in order to feel safe, to feel comfortable, making the life-and-death decisions that he needed of her if the worst came. And, in the end, tears glistening, she said, "Thank you," and so did he ...and he meant it.

***

D. L. Keur

34 – No Motive

FRIDAY

JESSIE GOT UP feeling better. Yesterday's heart-to-heart and mind-to-mind with Landon had cleared up a lot of her stress and moral predicaments.

Her dad picked her up at four, and they went running, just the two of them. They talked as they ran. She told him what had happened—her breakdown and Landon's answers to very serious questions. "Some of this stuff he was never informed about. Some of it he'd never even considered."

"What did you expect, Jessie? Nobody but medical people know the significance of some of these procedures or these decisions. Informed consent isn't really informed. They keep it hazy, and I think they do it on purpose."

Her dad could have a point. Jessie didn't know. What she did know was that, now, she had a better handle on what Landon would and would not agree to, and, with consideration to any end-of-life care, what he wanted. Shared that with her dad, too.

"Can you write it down for me?"

"I can. I will."

"Thanks. Want help with chores over there?"

"No. I can handle it. I should be able to turn him loose on his own recognizance by, maybe, Monday."

"Good. He hates intrusions on his privacy."

"I know. He made that pretty clear. Even somebody taking his temperature and BP, or listening to his heart and lungs is like some sort of violation of his right to privacy and autonomy."

"Well, think about it, Jessie? It's true. Whose business is it? Our bodies do not belong to the medical profession, the insurance companies, or to the government."

"I actually agree with you about that, pretty much."

"What? No nanny-state argument this morning?"

"Not from me. His positions made *me* think, too."

Oli stopped, pulled her in for a big hug and a hair tousle, then took off at a run again, making her chase after him.

*

"IT'S FRIDAY!" came Jessie's voice, her tapping on his door. "Breakfast is on the table. Need help with your socks and boots?"

He did. It embarrassed him. He'd tried every maneuver he could think of. Getting on his underwear he'd mastered yesterday, a trial in itself. But, just like yesterday, he could not manage the socks and boots. He'd tried propping his ankle on his other knee, but it was bending forward at the waist, even a little, that sent screaming pain through him, never mind making him feel like he was suffocating all over again.. *Give it up.* Would let her. "Yes, please," he answered, trying his best not to sound surly ...but he *was* surly. He hated being hobbled and beholden. "Come."

The door opened. Britta wagged as Jessie slipped in.

She gave the dog a quick pat, didn't look at him, just grabbed the sock he still held, knelt down, and, bundling it up, thumbs inside, fingers crawling the cloth into a wrinkled clump, she slipped it over his toes, foot, then heel, and up. Then the other one, him wanting to groan with humiliation.

Then came his boots, a bit of a struggle for both of them. "You know, you could wear TRs, instead, at least until you're well."

"No, I can*not.*"

"Okay." She stood up. "Well, there you go. Let me check that bandage on your chest, just to make sure it's not trying to unstick because of your shower and dressing yourself antics."

Stifling another groan, he let her. Stared somewhere off into nowhere as she did. This is what he didn't like about medicos of any kind. They were always invading his personal space, wanting to check on things in places ...which was *any* place, thank you very much, that was nobody's business but his. It was like blood pressure. It was like weight. Nobody's business. It was like *toes.* Toes belonged under cover of socks and shoes ...unless you were at the beach or something. And here she was checking the huge bandage that she reapplied twice a day on his chest, a complete invasion of his person!

"I need to restick one corner. Hang tight," she said, bounding out the door. Back moments later, she squeezed some goop on him. Rubbed. "There ya go. All done. That's not going to come off for sure, now," she said with a grin. She was watching him, blue eyes alight with laughter.

"Thank you," he said, but didn't mean it.

She stood there looking down at him where he sat. He dropped his head away. Muttered, "What now, Jessie?"

"I'm sorry nursing and medical care in general makes you uncomfortable. We do our best to try to protect personal dignity. We really do—all of us— EMTs, nurses, physicians—everybody. It's no fun being exposed, I know. But we do get that. Bodies are just bodies to us, though. There's a life to help. It's what we do, just like you don't think twice about doing a pat down. You're not trying to get fresh. You're checking for weaponry and illicit paraphernalia."

He didn't dare look at her. He was too mortified, and her words just made it worse.

"Okay. Breakfast is getting cold, and I like my waffles hot." And, thankfully, she left.

His stomach rumbled at the thought of waffles. Got up and headed for the table, Britta with him, already begging him with her eyes. "We'll see what I can get away with for you with Jessie watching, all right?"

The tail wagged.

"There he is," Sol said. Plopped a plate down in front of him, steam and good smells coming off of it.

Landon plied butter and scooped some raspberries on the pile, Britta begging all the while. Forked some breakfast sausages onto his plate. Managed to drop one which Britta immediately snagged ...and Jessie didn't notice. *Success!* Poured maple syrup.

"Sausage is sort of okay, but no waffles for dogs, Britta," Jessie scolded when, sausage downed, Britta looked for more. "Here. Here's a chewy."

Landon quashed a groan. Jessie *had* seen it. *Of course!* Couldn't get away with anything.

Landon watched his golden girl look an ask to him, and he smiled. Nodded. She wagged and accepted the treat from Jessie.

"Britta, go join the wonder dogs," Jessie urged.

Landon lifted, then waggled a finger toward Jessie's pack, and Britta swapped ends and went over to squeeze in next to Acer.

Landon couldn't help himself. He smiled even more. *She really* is *my dog.* He would have to send in the transfer of ownership paperwork. Finally he felt safe doing it.

"So, this case," Sol said. "I cannot figure out a solid motive for this. Nothing adds up without it being anti-hunters targeting hunters. The assault on the P.D. threw everything out of whack. Jessie? Have you processed that data yet?"

"I've got it almost done. Probably another hour or two, then I'll get it over to you."

"What's this?" Landon asked.

"A search for homophones of 'Lonnie Tunes'," Sol said.

"Instead of that, how about working through connections between those perps we've managed to identify. We're finally getting somewhere with that. Where does *that* lead us?"

"Yeah, well, they're all tournament level paintballers. That was pretty much a given with the markers they're using," Sol said.

"Those are not 'markers', Sol. 'Markers' are something I use to write on boxes, on labels, and on whiteboards, alcohol to wipe it off if I use permanent marker instead of dry erase. What they're using are rifles."

"Manufacturers also make realistic-looking paintball markers that look very realistically like handguns," Sol said ...unhelpfully. "They shoot smaller caliber paintballs, but—"

"Sol?"

The man grinned at him, all perk, and it hit Landon just how much Sol and Jessie had similar tendencies toward wickedness, the criminologist's sagacious, Jessie's just naughty. *No wonder they're good friends.*

"Yes?" Sol came back.

Landon picked up his phone. Touched open the picture of his chest. "Those are not *markers* they're using. They're *weapons!*"

And, by the look on Sol's face, that made his point. *Finally!*

***

35 – Epiphany

FOR JESSIE, it was going to be another torturously boring day. Landon's job wasn't about *doing* something. It was about monitoring everything S.O. and, basically, running interference with the press, the commissioners, and anybody else who was bucking about one thing or another.

Jessie got that, now. Landon kept his finger on the pulse ...on everything. If a deputy came under fire from some muckety-muck who thought they should be exempt from the law, Landon to the rescue. He took the welfare of both the public and his deputies as top priority, even when one conflicted with the other. And he was good at smoothing ruffled feathers. *He is* so *PC!* ...But only when he had to be, she admitted. "Geez. And what did you say you do for fun in your leisure time?" she asked, heading into the S.O., the Actuator van following as ever. "Read Idaho Code?"

He looked away out the window to the question. Finally said, "I used to hike, fish, hunt, ride rodeo broncs, rope cows, and horseback ride."

"And now?"

"No time."

"Hmm. Don't forget drinking and smoking."

That brought his face around to her, and it was stormy. "No fair, Jessie."

No, it wasn't. "Okay. Apologies."

He looked away. "Accepted."

Arrogance!

She took advantage of his meetings to get the Special Thanksgiving invitations distributed when he was tied up with someone …which was a constant thing. Howie and Red were two of the first she hit, then Tom Hudson. "Plus ones," she said. Got nods. Hudson was the only one a bit confused. "Are you sure? I'm nobody."

"Not hardly. You're somebody. Just like anybody and everybody else. I had to limit the guest list because, well, Landon doesn't own a mansion. Just not enough room. I know a bunch of the deputies will be upset, but I found out that Landon convinced the commissioners to foot the bill for a big, all-day catered thing here for Thanksgiving since we all have to work that four-day weekend."

"Well, if you're sure…."

"I am, Tom."

He grinned.

Martin was a go. So was Tank, his plus-one to be his mom, of course. Hitting up Dave Kins was where Landon caught up with her, her barely able to slip Dave the invitation before Landon stuck his head in the break room door and said, "What are you up to, Jessie?!"

"Nothing." She gave him her best 'I'm innocent of wrongdoing' look. Raised her coffee cup to show him. "Just getting some coffee."

The eyes narrowed. "Uh-uh. I don't buy it. You both look like you've been caught in the act. Of doing what, I don't know, but I know who the instigator is…." He glared at her. "…*Jessie!*"

She blew an indignant huff and scooted past him out the door, coffee cup in hand, her dogs, heads dropped and skulking out with guilty looks, wagging the giveaway the whole time. *He's as bad as Dad. Can't get away with anything, even when it's for him!* But, by the time Remmers called with the find of yet another injured hunter—paintballs, again—and she and Landon were galloping The Rhino over to the hospital, she'd gotten every invitation out and confirmed …except the one for Judge Regina Laird.

373

*

SOMEHOW, YESTERDAY'S hours-long talk had shifted something in Jessie's and his relationship. Something had relaxed between them, and Landon was immensely grateful. The strain between them seemed to have vanished. He didn't have to be so wary, on guard about everything he did and said around her. He could even sort of joke with her …like finding her up to no good in the break room, in cahoots with Deputy Kins.

Heading to the hospital to interview the latest victim of a paintball assault, he had Jessie drive again, sparing him the pain of every turn of the wheel and shift of gear. "I'm glad it wasn't near lethal with this hunter," Landon said as Jessie maneuvered through lunchtime traffic snarls, the Actuator Studios boys on their bumper as usual.

"Mind if I do a cross-country run to lose our shadow?" Jessie asked.

"Be my guest."

Jessie put The Rhino in 4-wheel drive low, then told the dogs to down-stay with an added, "Dig in your claws and hang on, guys." That warned Landon he was in for it.

*

GRATEFUL FOR permission, Jessie dodged to the 'wrong' side of the start of the guardrail barrier on the bridge off ramp and drove straight down toward the river. Turned—gently—and paralleled the water, running aslant, the big rig holding even when they wound up over forty-five. "Good Hummer," Jessie cooed. "Howie didn't lie when he said it could do this."

She dodged a grin Landon's way, but he was dead silent and stone faced—not one peep—and he had a death grip on the grab handles. His brows were a little bit crinkled, too. She almost laughed, but didn't. Still, he was trusting both her and the rig. She grinned more.

Aimed toward higher ground and got them back up on an access road that ran up beside the back way to the hospital. Then, spying what she wanted, the jersey barriers, she eased up to one, put the bull bar on it, and nudged it wide enough to ease on through.

"You going to put it back?" Landon asked oh so expectantly, as if, of course, she would …which she hadn't planned to.

"You want me to?"

"Yes, please."

Sighed. Did as requested. Got out to take a look at her handiwork and waved at the van boys who were parked way back on the other roadway, still in the traffic snarl, the man with the camera always on his shoulder out of the vehicle, the camera aimed at them.

Landon walked up to stand and watch, too. "They don't look happy."

She glanced his way. "You do."

He smiled down at her, and she raised her arm and snapped a photo—a perfect photo of the iconic Landon Reid who was their sheriff …and got away with it. It would be perfect for the charity project. It was so rare that Landon genuinely smiled. And he didn't buck and grouse, either. Just nodded. "I think I'll keep you as my driver, Jessie. I like this."

"Okay. When I'm not out on search and rescue or training dogs and handlers with Dad or Nelson."

"Yeah, right," and his grumble was back that fast, but Jessie saw humor in his eyes. Yeah. Things were better, now. The talk they'd had, despite the depressing reason for it, had been good for both of them. He was better for it, and so was she.

"Back to it," she said, grabbing the door handle and climbing up and in.

*

"SO WHAT happened, Mr. Heppert?" Landon asked.

"Got chased," the thirty-seven-year-old man whose first name was John said shortly. "There were four of them, and they would *not* stop coming after me. Cut me off over and over again. Kept shooting at me. Didn't hit me, except once in the foot, but they weren't shooting bullets. Splots of what looked like paint when it landed, so paintball guns, I guess. Got it on my boot, just one lob—your people kept that boot for evidence, and I'd really like to have it back, by the way."

Landon acknowledged the request, but didn't commit.

"They kept chasing me until I got completely turned around down in that long draw. Went the wrong way. Got steeper and steeper. I tried climbing out and fell. I'm surprised they didn't come after me there, but I guess I was pretty well hidden by the brush."

"You were hunting?"

"Yeah. It was my last few days home before I have to get back to the base. I thought I'd give another try for a buck— Ow!" he said, as the nurse cleaned one of the deeper cuts he had among the multiple cuts and abrasions on his arms and face. The man had a bandage on his head, had been pre-diagnosed with a mild concussion, and was awaiting a determination on his x-ray and scans.

"You're in the military?"

"Yes, sir. Lifer in the Army. I'm a supply specialist."

Landon nodded. He knew all that, and he knew what had been in the reports Remmers and Lynn Hansen had filed. Horse's mouth was always best, though. "Could you identify them?"

"They were wearing goggles, it looked like. I didn't let them get close enough, so I'm guessing I couldn't pick them out in a crowd ...or a line-up, if you guys still do that."

Again he nodded. "All right. Thank you. You try to take it easy."

"I signed a statement and left it with Nelson."

"You know Captain Remmers?"

"Oh, yeah. Neighbor of ours."

"All right. Well, we'll do our best to catch these assailants."

"Sheriff?"

"Yes?"

"It's scary getting hunted by people who act like they're determined to kill you. It's chilling. Then you realize it's, like, just some prank to them, just using paint, not real bullets. But they're still scary. And these people didn't say a word—not one word. No warning, no reason given." He paused. "Of course, I didn't let them get near enough, maybe …except the first one that surprised me. He was about fifty yards away. Fired. Scared me about out of life! That's the round that caught my boot. Then I realized it wasn't lethal."

Landon had an urge to rip open his shirt and demonstrate to the guy just how much damage that paint could do. Didn't. "You know it was a man?" he asked.

"No. I didn't hang around to find out. I just assumed he was."

"So, they're back to hunting hunters, right?" Jessie asked as, having finished their interview, they headed for the parking lot. "The attack on Northridge P.D. was just a distraction?"

Landon didn't answer. He had no answer.

And, there, as they walked out the emergency room slider doors, were the Actuator Studios boys, and, yes, the camera was rolling.

"I can ram their van with The Rhino," Jessie said. "Pretend I lost control."

"No."

"I know. All the security around here would blow our alibi. Even The Rhino would betray us."

He almost laughed. Caught himself before he hurt himself.

*

JESSIE FROWNED. Something was wrong. Her dogs didn't have their eyes on them. They weren't wagging. "Landon, slow down. …And stop. Act like you're talking to me."

He did as bid.

She touched her phone mic on and listened. Held it up for Landon to hear.

"What am I listening to?" he asked.

"My dogs ...and your Britta are growling real low."

"That rumble?"

"Yeah. That's Milo, too." She quick-glanced behind them. "And the van guys are following close."

"Yeah, I know that."

"Like they expect action." She said the obvious, then. "My dogs don't growl for nothing, Landon. Something's up. Maybe an ambush, hence the Actuator Studios boys being up close and personal. Maybe these folks don't think we'll shoot them. You might not, but I certainly will."

"All right. Hold on, Jessie. Let's just turn around, and head straight back, right through our pests. Act like we forgot something."

And there he was, the sheriff. Figuring out another way. "Okay."

The camera guys slipped off sideways as they approached, then followed them as they made their way back to and into the emergency room. Landon got hospital security to replay the footage from the ER parking lot for the last hour, fast forwarding until they spied something.

Sure enough. Two people, both dressed in black and with helmets on, carrying handguns, had crawled underneath the cars parked to either side of The Rhino.

"Those could be real or they could be those paintball handguns Sol was talking about this morning," Jessie said. "The quality of take isn't good enough to tell." She turned on him, caught his eyes with hers. "I'm being serious, here. They're really after you, Landon."

"Or you, now," he answered, moving aside and keeping his voice down.

"I don't think so. This is that Lonnie Tunes thing that the woman hollered when she nailed you. You are a target. So, it seems, is anyone out hunting game."

Landon thanked the security staff, then headed for the exit, again. Said, "This makes no sense, Jessie."

"Well, you *are* a hunter, in one sense. You hunt criminals, and hunters hunt— …Oh!"—epiphany!

Landon had stopped in his tracks …was looking at her in the strangest way, eyes still, head canted, hat brim casting a shadow over half his face. Then, so softly, he said, "They're the criminals, I hunt criminals, and they *want* me to hunt them!"

"That's what just hit me, too."

***

36 – Critical Knowledge

"ALL RIGHT. Listen up, people. We think we might have something. It's not motive for the assailants, but it could be critical to achieving their objective, whatever *that* is."

Jessie listened as, deputies jammed into the briefing room, Sheriff Landon Reid stepped into his own, succinctly outlining their theory. *This is where he shines most,* Jessie thought.

"Right now, I need everybody's input on this, because, if we're right—"

"Who's 'we', Sheriff, sir?" one deputy asked. Meeks was his last name.

"Deputy Anderson and I put two and three together when we had yet another potential attack on us imminent, but we short-circuited it by letting her dogs out of my unit—thank whomever programmed The Rhino to allow the back to open off the fob!"

"The two arrestees just being processed over at the jail, sir?"

"That is correct, Deputy Meeks."

Interest had been high to begin with, and now it crested. Many of the S.O.'s personnel were friends with or even related to some of those who had been attacked, one of them killed, by the paintball assailants. Everybody wanted to stop them. Fast.

"If we're right," Landon continued, "they want us—"

"*You,*" Jessie spoke up.

He glared her way. "Us …and, *maybe,* specifically me, to—and don't laugh, please" …which, of course, brought laughter—"*hunt* them."

Silence.

"That is cor*rect,*" Sol's voice announced, the criminologist marching in, Martin behind him, Sinclair and Kins in their wake, with Terri bringing up the rear. "And it now makes com*plete* sense. Terri came through with the Internet searches, and, with the Sheriff's and Deputy Anderson's dots connecting, too, we were able to finally home in on what exactly is driving this criminal activity."

*

AS LANDON'S DAD, Bitterroot County's previous sheriff, had so pointedly informed him, there were four motives for crime—love, loathing, loot, and lust. This one fell, not into loathing, which would have fit the 'hunting hunters' scenario, but rather loot. This was about money—money paid by cable networks and from streaming subscriptions by lovers of live-action, reality TV shows, money based on market share which brought in top dollar from advertisers, money from spin-off shows, never mind ancillary products and whatever else they could cash in on—money ...loot.

"This is called 'Season of the Kill'," Terri said, turning on a video on the wallscreen, "and it started out as a game in the 90s called 'Kill Score'. Morphed into an online multiplayer roll-playing game of the same name, and, from there, became a television series, the third season of which is airing right now. I suspect that what they're filming here is for next year's season."

"How do you know this, Corporal MacLeod?" somebody asked Terri from the back.

"The phrase 'Lonnie Tuunz',"—Terri put a slide up with the spelling. "'Kill Score' was the first instance we found where that was used, both in the original game and in the online, multiplayer one, and it was kept in the television show. And, by the way, there's a movie planned, too."

Muttering, and Landon seconded that grumbling.

"Moving on," Terri said. "I'm only at Level 4 so far in playing Kill Score, but I've already been taken down a couple of times by CLEO and his force, that's Chief Law Enforcement Officer Lonnie Tuunz. He represents the biggest challenge, from what I can ascertain, and, even when you kill him in one level, he comes back in the next. He never dies ...so far as I can tell. But you don't meet him until Level 3. Everything else in the game is shooter against armed adversaries, dangerous creatures, and environmental hazards, plus shooter against shooter of opposing teams and even your own team, which you also try to annihilate when going for the final win. That's pretty much the game—you team up with others until you're going for the ultimate win. The more dangerous a scenario you choose, the more points awarded for a kill. Go into a den of an armed gang alone and get out alive, killing as many as possible gets you lots more points than taking the same out with a team. You get more points for taking out a soldier, a sniper ...somebody trained, or even somebody with a concealed carry than you do any old bystander, though you get some points for every 'kill'."

"Are they using paintballs in the game versions?"

Terri shook her head. "Not in the online game, but in the TV reality show, yes. Again, I've only watched a couple of episodes of season three, which is being aired now. I *have* purchased seasons one and two for us, as well, though, to try to help us figure this thing out."

"I'm binge-watching them," Sinclair said. "Actually, they're pretty good, despite the weirdness of kind of amateur action camera and smartphone-ish footage in it. Kind of 'The Blair Witch Project®' look meets 'Naked and Afraid®', if you know what I mean."

More murmurs and some shaking heads, with which Landon could not identify. He'd never seen either. *I am completely out-of-step with my own and even the next older generation!*

"They're very realistic …and I guess that's because they are real." Sinclair added. "Who'd've thunk?!"

"So, in essence, Sheriff," Sol chimed up, "You're not playing, so they're bringing the game to you, forcing you …forcing *us* to play."

That didn't sit well. "Ah.... I'm not taking the blame for this. No, I am not," Landon said emphatically.

"Oh, it's not blame, sir," Sol said. "It's your tendency not to go off half-cocked that's frustrating them. I think you were supposed to come out guns blazing and all that."

"And who is 'them'?" Landon asked pointedly.

"We don't know. It's not the players behind it, though. What was picked up while they were in jail and commiserating with each other was that they're pretty much in the dark as to why 'the game isn't set up right', 'not enough high value targets' ...and that's a direct quote. But we know they are being paid ...and paid well, too."

"How much?" Deputy Meeks asked.

"Ten-grand apiece just for participation is what we figure, paid up front from what financial records we've seen from a few of them so far. Their chit-chat suggests that all their expenses are paid, too. And somebody is footing the bill for legal representation on the one who had her fingers blown off by Garrison. And we heard them comparing their scores. From that, we gather that there's some big pay-off based on those. We have no idea how those are calculated …yet."

"One of the biggest scores comes from taking out Lonnie Tuunz in the online game," Terri said, and she looked pointedly at Landon saying it. "In our case, from what Sheriff Reid's attacker said, I think both that Northridge Chief of Police Harvey Mueller and Sheriff Reid are labeled as 'Lonnie's."

How wonderful.

"And there's more," Martin said, and his voice had an ominous ring to it. "Continue, please, Terri?"

"Okay. Here's the game changer. In the case notes, earlier this week Sheriff Reid mentioned that the van people said something about comparing and contrasting how he handles cases against those of other heads of law enforcement."

Landon cleared his throat to gain ear. "What they actually said, verbatim, is, 'We're contrasting and comparing how two different sheriffs in two different counties handle similar investigations.'"

"Nobody can *ever* say you lost your edge with that conk on the head," Martin said, chuckles coming from around the room to that.

Landon ignored the remark, though, inside, it made him feel a bit of a rise in confidence, because, yes, he did still feel mentally compromised ...or, at least, that people perceived him that way. "I called every sheriff in Idaho, and nobody has camera vans following them around. Nor are they having paintball gun attacks. I even called some Washington people. The only thing I can make of it is they *were* talking about Northridge Chief of Police Harvey Mueller's similar cases, cases they're responsible for."

"Sheriff? There is a *very* similar case occurring," Terri came back, her voice suddenly gentle. "Eerily similar. And it's happening concurrently. Down in Georgia"

*

JESSIE FELT a chill go through her. She'd read about that in the news just two days ago. Frowning, she looked at her phone calls and realized that, yes, it had happened the same day Landon had been hit.

She'd seen a picture of one of the victims—a cowboy-hat-sporting Black sheriff. Blunt force trauma had been listed as contributing to his death, but no other details had been provided. Cable news talking heads were speculating that it was racist and a hate crime, though law enforcement had released no details to corroborate that—'investigation ongoing.'

"Can we go after the snoopy docu-camera guys?" Deputy Meeks asked.

Jessie noted his intense interest. Typed something into her phone, and, a quick search through social media brought up that his maternal granddad was Cornie Parker. *No wonder he's invested.*

"Not yet. We're still trying to establish solid probable cause to secure both search warrants and arrest warrants to be served concurrently to each of the camera vans and their occupants. We don't want to do that prematurely, because, if we don't have solid evidence and they get wind, they could destroy exactly the evidence we need to convict whoever's payroll they're on," Martin said.

*

POINTEDLY, Landon watched Terri. He kept watching her until she finally noticed. Then she gave him what he wanted—a nod.

"We might have that now," Landon said, easing away from his lean against the wall to stand square. "Terri?"

Again, she stepped up for him. "On Sheriff Reid's request," she said, "Yesterday I managed to capture traffic both into and out of the van that's following him around. They're using pretty good encryption, swapping it every few minutes, but I managed to break it in several instances and have both verbal communication, text coms, and video streams that seem pretty convincing that they are involved in some way. They aren't directing what's happening, but there are some pretty solid indicators that they are receiving foreknowledge of where the next action could be going down."

Now it was Landon's turn again. "According to the assistant prosecutor, that might give us enough probable cause. He's going over it now," Landon said. "I'm awaiting his call-back."

"On what?"—Meeks again.

"Conspiracy," Landon said.

"When are we going to be able to get them all for murder and attempted murder?! They killed Vern Mildner and almost killed my granddad, and all for a stupid game?!"

"Televised entertainment," Landon corrected.

"So, now, killing people ...or almost killing them is considered okay, so long as it makes money? That's great solace for Mildner's wife and kids, and my granddad sure won't see any of that moolah, but he's sure got the medical bills from them playing their game at his expense!"

Landon made note. Meeks needed a short leave of absence. He was way too invested, way too close to this. *Do* not *need a sudden case of vigilante justice and a good man going to prison.* But the fact was, almost everybody in the Bitterroot knew or was related to everybody else. Ties were close. This 'game' was hitting people where they lived, and it was hitting hard.

***

37 – Probable Cause

JESSIE HAD never been inside the county prosecutor's office. Dogs left in Landon's unit, windows down, security engaged, she trailed Landon in on his invite. Keeping in the background, Jessie listened to more Greek speak from both Landon and the assistant prosecutor, a quiet-voiced man who seemed to really know his stuff. Jessie was impressed with both him and Landon. The best news was that the prosecutor assured Landon that they had probable cause. Jessie, for her part, was assured that she never wanted to have to deal with this end of law enforcement—not ever.

From there it was back over to the courthouse to get a judge to sign off on what were search warrants on the two camera vans, plus four arrest warrants on the men working out of them. Landon got right in, so they got right out, the camera guys scrambling to keep up.

"This is what you call your dotting 'i's and crossing 't's, isn't it?" Jessie asked, heading The Rhino back toward the S.O., the camera guys hard in their wake.

"Due diligence, and, yes, it is. Usually, I'll send a deputy, but, in this case, if I do it, it seems to go a lot faster."

"A *lot* faster." She grinned then, and couldn't help herself. "It's the hat."

"Oh, give it a rest, Jessie."

But he did sort of smile saying it, his eyes crinkling at the sides …just, so she dared: "Never."

*

BACK AT the S.O., Landon called in Howie, Red, and Martin. "We've got our warrants. Now we need a plan, and I'm guessing it's going to involve me, since they're constantly tailing me," Landon told them, then watched faces.

"Why can't we just walk out to the parking lot and serve them. They were sitting out there just a few minutes ago," Howie said. "It's not like they're lionhearted hero types and it's going to turn into a firefight."

"Actually, yours, Bossman, are standing in the front lobby, again," his chief administrator said.

Landon nodded. "Yeah, I saw them, Red. Or at least they were there when I walked through from getting back from the courthouse, just now." And they'd, yet again, had their camera rolling, Britta grumbling about them the whole way to, then into, his office.

"You'd have known that, West, if you ever came up front," Red added.

The Tac Team commander gave the slant eye. "Not if I can help it. Back way in is just fine, thanks."

"Skulk."

A barked laugh to that.

"What about the others?" Landon asked. "Their van was parked on the street in front of the police station. Was, anyway, when Jessie drove through town. Don't know where the occupants were."

"We'll find them," Martin said. "Deputies have eyes out. So does the P.D."

"All right. For ours here, serve them right in the lobby, then," Landon said, but let's wait until we can locate the other crew in town and get on them at the same time."

"Agreed. As soon as we've got our all our targets located, we go. Howie?" Martin asked.

"It's a go as far as my teams are concerned."

*

THEY LISTENED while Dispatch deployed deputies into town after advising the P.D., then lined up the strategy around the S.O. "Do not move until given the go ahead," the sergeant said, and received acknowledgements, one after another in turn.

Red turned to Landon. "Meanwhile, why don't you go entertain ours, Bossman," he suggested.

"Why?"

"In case the other camera team gets wind and tries to warn them as deputies move in."

He sighed. Nodded.

"No need, sir," Howie said. "I doubt the ones in town are paying attention. Mueller is still in the hospital, so I think they're slacking. They're feeding their faces in The Soda Shop, one of them flirting with the waitress." Howie touched something on his tablet, and Landon's wallscreen came on, showing the interior of the café.

"How did we do that?" Landon asked.

"Terri's been going around to the shopkeepers in Northridge and around the county, too, asking for permission to tap in, that's how," Martin said. "Businesses are happy to do it, too."

"My people are now in place to cover all egress here and are ready in town, too," Howie told them. "Got some at both vans, as well, with Terri standing by and ready to access the one here as soon as we've served them."

"And Deputy Dr. Preston has made it to the van in town. Standing by," Martin said, his phone to his ear. "Anymore, with all the techno stuff, you don't know if they haven't got some sort of kill switch to wipe the data using a remote or something."

"Good thought," Landon said.

"Then it's a go?" Martin asked.

"It's a go."

Howie was on the phone. Gave the thumbs up. "One minute…. …And executing your warrants, Sheriff, sir," Howie said, eyes on Landon.

There were yells in the hallway, and, on Landon's security monitors, the bulky bodies of some of Howie's people blocked view of them serving the warrants, then securing the men.

"And all subjects secured. Vans, likewise. Warrants successfully executed without incident, 14:43."

***

38 – City Search

IT WAS RARE for a call for search to come from Northridge, especially during the day. The only time that had happened in Jessie's tenure running SAR here was when the Flemming kids had gone missing from their backyard. This call was from Captain Dirk Compton himself, direct to her phone.

"I need you and your dogs. Now," he said. "Northridge High School."

"Okay. Let me advise the sheriff, and I'll be there in ten."

"Thank you."

Searching out Landon, she found him in the observation room. "Got a call from Captain Compton, Northridge P.D. He needs a search at the high school."

Landon frowned down. "Did he say why?"

"No, sir."

He scowled at the formality, and she knew instantly why. Pointed at the red light and his eyes cleared their ill humor. "All right, Deputy."

"Thank you, sir. I'll need to borrow a unit. I don't have my XV."

That request also seemed to irritate him. Jessie staunched a sigh. He was always so difficult.

"Why? What's wrong with The Rhino?!" he demanded.

Jessie wanted to roll eyes. *Obvious?* "Ah…. It's your vehicle, sir, and you're here?"

"Use. The. Rhino!"—emphatic.

"Yes, sir. Thank you, sir."

"Get going."

"Yes, sir." And Jessie took off.

*

THEY ONLY had four interrogation rooms, one of them a 'soft' interview room. At Howie's suggestion, they put the cameraman from the Actuator Studios van in that one. "He seems noncomplicit."

"All right. Who is taking whom?" Martin asked his hand-picked choices for interrogators—only two, so far, Deputy Kins and Deputy Lieutenant Hamilton. "Personally, I want to sink my teeth into the scrawny one."

"Better you than me," Deputy Kins said. I want to pound his face in for whatever their part is in almost killing that Orr boy's dad."

"You take one of the RealTake van guys," Martin said.

"I'll go for the mouthy one, then," Kins agreed. "He speaks geek, and so do I."

"That's why I picked you,"—Martin.

That got a grin.

"Mind if I watch?" Landon asked.

Martin shook his head, stepped close. Whispered, "Reid, you're the sheriff? You can sit in on whatever you want, whenever you want to. That particular brain marble short-circuiting on you, today?"

He dropped his face. Looked at a new scuff mark on his boot. "I was trying to be considerate."

"Well, stop."

Eyes on the floor, now, he growled, "Yes, sir, Mr. Undersheriff, sir."

Martin didn't even pause. "My point, exactly, sir. But what I'd like you to do is to interrogate the Actuator Studios cameraman. I think your soft touch would get to him, and he'd spill."

Soft touch! That's why Martin only had Kins and Hamilton here. *I'm the 'soft touch'.* "All right, Martin."

"Thanks."

*

CAPTAIN DIRK COMPTON met Jessie and Deputy Tom Hudson on the athletic fields in back of the high school, Hudson still hyped up from the arrest of the van guys and all impressed that she was driving the sheriff's Hummer. "What I have," Compton told them, "are two missing kids. Both of them were caught shooting other kids and breaking windows with paintball guns. They took off, and we cannot find where they went to ground. We've got the entire area cordoned."

"Okay," Jessie said. "Do you have scent, because, otherwise, it's just going to be miss, not hit."

"We have their last known and a dropped weapon."

"Excellent. Hopefully, nobody has disturbed that?"

"No one has."

"Let's go, then."

"Deputy Anderson?"

"Yes, sir?"

"I need these kids found, but not bitten. One of them is the mayor's kid. The other is the son of one of our top defense attorneys—"

"Mr. Pearson?" Jessie asked.

Compton nodded.

"I know him well. He's my on-standby defense attorney. No biteys, I promise, sir."

"Thank you."

"Okay, boys and girls," Jessie said to the wonder mutts, putting 'lilt-in-voice' to work, then grinned when her pack bounded up, all happy dogs, ready to go.

"Ah, Jessie?" Tom said softly, sidling up to her. "Paintballs?"

"I know. Probably copycat. It's been in the paper because of the attack on the P.D."

"Hope so." But Tom looked worried, all his hyped up energy grounded and gone.

"Let's go look," Jessie said. "If it's a Charper Pro 2, it's your call, not mine."

Relief flooded Tom's face. "Thanks."

*

39 – She Who Finds Trouble

THE GUN WASN'T a Charper Pro 2. It was a Charper, though, and, according to Tom, who spoke according to Howie, it looked customized. "Here and here," he said, pointing.

One thing Jessie knew for sure was that it was powerful enough that its salvos had broken, not cracked, tempered glass windows. It was, Jessie discovered on a quick search using her phone, a Charper Pro 3. She handed the reins to Tom. Tom, in turn, called his captain. Listened. Eyeballed her, then closed the connection. "Can you do your slow search with the dogs?"

"We can," Jessie assured.

"We need to take this careful. Cams on, live feed to base."

"You got it."

"Let me check your armor?"

"Me same you," she said, as he tightened the fit on hers to uncomfortable, then let her check his— tight and right, as usual.

"Ready," Tom said. "Go ahead and send the dogs, Jessie."

"Yes, sir."

He slant-eyed her.

She grinned.

*

THE CAMERAMAN, a Gene Reasoner, married, three kids, resident of Siskiyou County, California, was one of the most quiet-voiced men Landon had ever met, and, right now, one of the most anxious, that anxiousness exhibited, not by fretting and jigging nerves, but by tragic eyes, a stiff face, and a sagging resignation.

"You've waived having a lawyer present?" Landon asked, coming and sitting down.

"I can't afford one."

"One will be provided to you at no expense. Just say the word."

The eyes—light hazel—raised to Landon's. "I'm not a criminal. If I'm not guilty of something, shouldn't that mean I'm okay?"

Landon dropped his face away. Was glad he wore his hat. "It doesn't work that way, Mr. Reasoner. Let me get you a public defender."

Again the man raised eyes. "You're the sheriff himself, aren't you?"

Landon nodded. "Yes, sir."

"I looked you up online. You're known for fairness and integrity in the law. If I can't trust you, then who can I trust? And public defenders are notorious for being worse than having no lawyer at all."

"You *need* a lawyer. Hang tight."

Landon pulled out his phone, stepped out of the room. Called Pearson. "I need you. A Mr. Reasoner needs you pro bono for what I think is a noncomplicit arrestee in a conspiracy case that includes first degree manslaughter."

And, in his ear, Pearson started dealing. That's when Landon figured out where Jessie was. Postponed the interview, put everything on hold. Got in the APC with Howie West and team, and took off for town, running code—lights and sirens.

*

THE DOGS started where a paintball rifle had been dropped, slippery goop clogging up the barrel and palm prints potentially showing the why it had been abandoned—jammed. From there, it was, for the dogs, an easy track.

Two times, Oso, her top air scenter, bounded forward. Both times, Jessie recalled him and, reluctantly, he obeyed—Oso, the Independent. "My good, good Oso."

From there, Oso and Mitch, the Marvelous, took lead on air, but kept it slow as asked. Queenie kept on ground trail, Milo, the Wonder Mutt on Stilts towering over the three of them as if their giant protector. Yet, head up, his nose was working.

Milo was resolute in his movement, and Jessie noted it. She saw the same resolve and steadfastness in her Acer and her Sumi, one dog glued to her left knee, the other to her right. The dogs knew something …smelled it.

She touched Sumi. Cued her. And, with one upwards glance at her, the GSD bounded over to Tom's left side.

He gave Jessie a glance in question, and, keying her radio mic, she said, "She'll protect you. It's just in case."

412

Turned her mic back off as she saw him nod.

*

ON THE PHONE with Mueller who was still in the hospital, Landon was adamant. "There's an op, we're coming in, and back off the politics, Harvey. I don't care that it's two seventeen-year-old kids. I don't care who their daddies are. Those are my people, called in by Compton, so ad*vise* Compton, advise your lieutenants. We're coming in. Now."

*

JESSIE'S DOGS had the line. Across the track field, across the fields for football and soccer, across the student golf course.... Then, 'target acquired' her dogs' actions told her. Jessie went live on radio, keyed signal to Tom—one long pulse.

Beside her, Acer nudged her leg, his ask. She gave him leave, and, trotting out, he lowered his head, tail brought up to level. Sumi moved out, too.

As Jessie watched, the pack took notice. Queenie circled around and dropped back, Mitch came in, too, sliding in beside Milo, and Oso bounced and stopped dead, head up, nose high, eyes sighting something, his body still, one front paw lifted.

413

And Acer took lead, head low, traveling in the direction Oso indicated at a steady ground-eating walk—just a walk, though. The pack now fanned out behind him. And that told Jessie what she needed. They were stealth hunting, and they knew exactly where their prey was.

Jessie grinned. This was a pack working, each one contributing their expertise, communicating what they knew to one another, each one obedient to the pack lead, Acer, and the second-in-command, Milo. "My good, good dogs," Jessie whispered, ready to 'out' and 'recall' the minute she saw Acer or any other dog target alert. She'd promised Compton no biteys on the kids, and, yes, Sumi, a police dog, and Acer, a trained war dog, cross-trained to protection and now SAR, neither one would hesitate to take down an attacker. But neither would do it unless explicitly directed …unless that hostile threatened Jessie, Tom probably, and, for sure, one of the other dogs in the pack.

*

TRACKING APP on, Landon stayed in the APC as Howie barked, "Go, go, go!" his personnel pounding out over the athletic fields, then disappearing into the parked out perimeter trees that lined them.

414

Watched his app. Found Jessie's marker ...and Tom's ...and those of Jessie's dogs. Saw Howie and team coming up to them fast.

They were, all of them, heading toward the school bus maintenance barn, a building on school property, but off the high school premises, fenced off from ingress and egress by a six-foot chain link fence and gated access drive.

He frowned. There would be two people there— the head mechanic and his helper. *What do the dogs know?*

He called Jessie. Used his phone, not the radio. Called Tom, too. Joined the calls, and made them wait. Got no argument from either one, especially Jessie, and that about floored him.

*

CROUCHED DOWN with her dogs, Jessie watched the building. Binoculars out, she saw what Tom mentioned—"Fence has been cut, Jessie."

"I see that."

Pounding footsteps—the tac team. They came up around her and Tom, and Jessie felt relief. She wasn't sure why.

"What have you got, Tom, Jessie?"—Howie.

She turned to him. "Dogs are acting like it's dangerous prey. They were stalking, not on search. They know their target."

He nodded. "And you're sure it's the building they're targeting?"

"Fence is cut," Tom put in.

"I'm sure it's in that vicinity. Oso, my air scenter, was sure. Acer was sure. Queenie hard trailed toward it, too, in a direct line of travel."

Again, Captain Howard West nodded. Huddled with his people, all eight of them. Motioned to Tom who joined them. Huddled some more. Turned back to her. "I want you to stand down, Anderson. I need Hudson with me."

"You got it, sir."

*

IT WAS AN ambush and Landon stared at the cam feeds from his people as Howie and company barged right into it, the kids and two mechanics the bait, tied up to chairs, their mouths duct taped, positioned in one of the bus service bays. And his people didn't fire. Just stayed behind their shields and took the barrages of hard-hitting paintballs until the barrage ran out ...or seemed to. Then Howie moved in, his people with him, and the paintball barrage started again, but not as heavy.

"Geez."

*

JESSIE SAW THEM come out the back door, four people all dressed in black. Nobody followed—not Howie, not Tom, not any of the S.O.'s Tac Team deputies. And she heard gunfire still happening inside the building. *They're getting away.*

Four people fleeing. Two trained attack dogs, plus Mitch, the Malinois, and Milo, the Wonder Mutt on Stilts, both natural to it. She shrugged off her pack, slammed her hand on her cam to pick up recording, and sent her dogs, keeping Oso and Queenie with her. And, pulling one of her SIGs, dominant hand side, she ran.

*

"NO, JESSIE. *No!*"

Landon tried the radio—no go.

He tried her phone—no go.

Watched in horror as Jessie's cam recorded two of
the perps turn fire on Acer and Sumi, the dogs
somehow avoiding the shots and launching to take
them down. The other two fugitives kept running,
the dog known as Mitch and big white and brown
Milo catching the fleeing perps from behind and
jerking them down by their legs.

…Then Jessie running up, all bristle. She went to
those downed by Mitch and Milo. Flipped them, and
stripped them of weapons, did a quick zip-tie, hands
and legs, then said something to the dogs he didn't
catch. Then she raced back to Acer and Sumi. Took
Sumi's prisoner first, then Acer's.

Shield-carrying bodies—Howie and Tom, plus the
woman Landon thought of as a Nordic berzerker,
came slamming through the back way out, dropped
their shields, and took control of the four captives.
Now Landon heard Jessie scream for her dogs, them
running toward Landon …toward Jessie, no limps, no
pause, the cam view dropping elevation, dogs close,
Jessie's hands closer as they ran over the animals,
every inch of their bodies, stripped the Kevlar® from
them, and did it again.

Howie's voice, a bellowed ask.

"They're okay, I'm okay," she yelled back, her voice quaking.

Landon collapsed back in the seat …and hurt himself doing it.

***

40 – Terri Did It

LANDON WAS RELIEVED. Everybody was okay. The perps had a few scuff marks and punctures, but, like with Oli's manhunters, again they'd mostly come out unscathed because of their padded paintball gear—no hospitalization needed. Just a little first aid, then transport for a check over at the hospital.

"You were told to stand down," Howie growled at Jessie.

They were sitting in The Rhino, Landon behind the wheel, Howie in the front passenger seat, Jessie in back with Britta, Jessie's dogs behind that.

"I did stand down, sir," Jessie said, and, surprising to Landon, she wasn't on the defensive, she didn't even seem concerned by his captain dressing her down.

"You call that standing down?!" Howie snarled.

"They were getting away ...so I sent the dogs. You didn't say anything about the dogs standing down, sir."

Howie's eyes came to Landon's. His voice went quiet, seething. "I am *so* glad she is your problem, not mine, sir." Then loud again: Outahere!" And, with that, Howie opened the door, stepped down, slammed the door, and stalked over to his tac team and the APC.

Once Howie had stepped inside the back, Deputy Tom Hudson flashed a grin and a quick thumbs up toward The Rhino. Other team members looked at Tom, then at The Rhino, and grinned, too, and Landon knew it was directed at Jessie. They were proud of her. So, he knew, was Howie, or it would have been a lot worse.

Landon pulled a long, very gentle, slow breath, and he so much now appreciated breathing like a human. Opened the door, got out, went around to the passenger side and got back in. Turned …slowly, carefully. "You're driving."

"I have to run the dogs out to Kathy to have them checked over, sir."

"Jessie? What did I say about appellations when we're in private?"

Silence, the blue eyes watching him. Then a squiggly smile, the eyebrows crinkling just a little.

"To the vet's," he said. Pointed to the driver's seat. "Let's move. We're burning daylight, and we don't have much of it this time of year."

*

DR. KATHY CALDWELL gave Acer, Milo, Sumi, and Mitch the once over, then called for x-rays. And those showed no cracked ribs or compromised innards. Relief flooded. "Just a couple of bruises, and those aren't bad," Kathy told Jessie.

"That is such great news," she said, and thankfully ran hands over her wonder dogs, every one, including little Duchess.

Dr. Caldwell turned to Landon who stood by, quiet, Britta sitting by his side. "Sheriff, would you be kind enough to autograph something for me?"

Jessie smothered a grin and watched. So did the dogs.

Eyes shifted, went wary. "Uh...."

"It will only take a moment. Please?"

That broke Landon's apprehension. "Of course," he answered finally, the voice softening. "Yes."

"Thank you." Kathy pointed. "Out at the front counter," she said, smiling as she led the way. Held up the fist sculpt, and, of course, Landon signed.

Jessie grinned. Judge Laird had come through with getting him to keep and tote the special engraver pen. They were so on the way to success with the Landon Reid charity launch, to be held concurrently with the no-kill shelter opening. It was going to be perfect. Now if the special Thanksgiving could go as well.

She could only hope.

*

LANDON GOT WORD on the way back to the S.O. "Terri did it," he said.

"Terri did what?" Jessie asked, glancing his way.

"Broke the encryption on the hard drives in the vans, plus the traffic from whomever is running this show. She also found a whole boxful of camera drones …which is probably how they've been filming action from the sky, plus tracking me and Harvey. Plus she's got us a lead …maybe a wedge. So, maybe, just maybe, if we're smart about it …and lucky, we can stop this thing before anybody else gets hurt."

"Yes! Go, Terri!"

Yeah. Go, Terri, Landon agreed. Texted Martin and Howie. Said to Jessie, "Stop by Junior Poindexter's place. Need the address?"

"I know where it is."

Fifteen minutes later, Landon had Junior on board and called the paper, the radio station, and the television stations, all on conference call. Got their promise of cooperation. "Texting copy now," he said. Hung up and did it.

"Everybody's on board," he said, plugging his phone in to charge.

"What's your plan?" Jessie asked.

"You'll see."

***

D. L. Keur

41 – Death Game

PEARSON WAS WAITING in Landon's office when Landon made it back to base. "Mr. Pearson," he said, easing himself down into his desk chair, Britta curling up in her day bed. "Thank you for taking Mr. Reasoner on as a pro bono client."

"Thanks for not arresting my son."

"I think he's scared enough."

"So is Mr. Reasoner. I honestly don't think he's got a clue what he's involved in."

"That was my take."

"I've got my client's permission to share certain details that I think will help your case."

"In exchange for?"

"Immunity from prosecution."

"Right. I'll call the prosecutor, and we can negotiate."

"I already have."

Landon waited for the rest. Hit pay dirt. They now had names of the cameraman's employers, plus a PDF, certified copy in the mail tomorrow morning, from the man's wife of the contract Reasoner had signed—names and numbers. And that fast, it turned into a case for the FBI, but, then, it already had. Landon just hadn't officially turned it over to them, yet. Terri's crack of the vans' hard drives had sealed that fate, though. It would have to be laid into Andy's hands very soon, as soon as Landon was assured his county and its people were safe and secure again, because, on those hard drives, those from the RealTake van and those from the Actuator Studios van, was footage of the 'takedown' of the sheriff in Georgia that Terri had mentioned at the briefing just this morning.

Landon called Oli and begged off going to the range. "I didn't expect you," Oli said. "Not laid up like you are. No demerits, no penalties."

"Thanks."

Jessie went, taking The Rhino, while Landon huddled up with Howie, Martin, and Sol, Terri staying late to sit in, too.

"And Poindexter's on board?" Howie asked.

"Yes. That was him on the phone just now, calling to say his members are, too," Landon said, putting down said phone.

"What about Jerome?" Martin asked.

"He's in, as well."

"Tomorrow is going to be a long day."

"I'm betting they don't hit till evening," Howie said.

"I agree."—Martin.

Landon looked toward Terri. "You said someone called the General Manager is masterminding this?"

"No, sir. I said the GM—Gamemaster."

"All right. Gamemaster. He's the brains behind this?"

"Or she. I really think this has the signature of one of two gamemasters in the online multiplayer role-playing version of this game. Both of them are women, both are game developers in their own right, but run Kill Season for a day job. The GM would be the brains behind the action happening in the games, but I doubt they're the instigator or the money. They're just employed to do a job."

"If you were playing this game—"

"I *am* playing this game. Online."

"All right." Techis could be so difficult with whom to effectively communicate, Terri no exception. "Let me try again, Corporal," Landon said. "Were you masterminding the action in this particular game, what would be your next objective?"

"In this particular iteration, my final objective would be to pit the best team against the biggest, baddest CLEO …chief law enforcement officer—you—the top scorer getting the win when he or she takes you down."

"But I'm not down and have no intention of going down."

"Hence the gamemaster's plan of action. They're not expecting you to be there, not at the onset. They think you and our deputies will come tearing in after their initial attacks. I think the school thing was a test of that …and to get timing down. It's about the same distance to the high school as it is to Jerome's. And, tomorrow, at the bash, team one, the lower scorers according to the stats on record, will initiate. You and the deputies are then supposed to show up, and that's when team two—the high scorers will enter play."

"And you know they're going for the Center Fire Club's Bonfire Bash?"

"I do. It's all scripted."

Terri touched her tablet and Landon's wallscreen lit up. "There it is in simulation, right from the GM's livetime stream captured at 15:33 today, and it makes sense. That's the biggest, baddest crowd of skilled shooters who congregate all in one place in this county, and they do it twice a year, the end of May and the end of October. Halloween coinciding with Saturday this year made it perfect. The players could run around looking like whatever they wanted and nobody would think it more than kids acting out dress-up fantasies. They had this well-planned."

"Why here?"

"Well, from computer mapping the footage from season one, two, and what's been released of three, all of them have taken place in cities—New York, LA, San Francisco, Miami, Chicago, and Atlanta. They wanted to do something different. Problem. In the city, nobody much pays any attention to people running around dressed weird. Here they do. That's why I think they chose Halloween for this one."

"But why here?" he repeated. "Why Bitterroot County?"

Silence for way too long. Then, "Because you hit national news ...and so did the now deceased sheriff in Georgia, that's why," Terri said. "It's about ratings. It's about drawing eyes to the show. You're a really high value target. So was the sheriff in Georgia."

Landon studied the young woman. "You seem unimpressed by all this."

"I am. Reality TV is for stupid arm-chair adrenalin junkies, and the whole game, Kill Season, is banal and boring, too, if you're me."

He watched her. "Boring?"

"Yes, sir. You know you're going to either win or lose, most likely lose. There's no middle ground. There's no other game world to jump to, no parallel universe where the rules change and an alternative can be achieved. That's makes it binary and boring. It's all yes or no, not yes and no and maybe simultaneously, which could then break out into exponential possibilities for game changers. So, yes, this game is boring. Like I said, it's binary …dualistic, and, honestly, quite stupid. Bang-bang, shoot-em-up one more time. Pure juvenile fantasy stuff eaten up by wannabes."

And Landon's take? It was a game of death, and death was not boring or stupid. It was just terminal.

***

42 – Just Death

HOWIE SHOWED UP midway through their fifth target set, her dad and she running neck and neck. He watched awhile, then set up in the next lane.

Her dad called a halt. "Take a break, Jessie," he told her, and that was a first.

The smile on her dad's face warned her. *Uh-oh. Trouble in play.*

In moments, Howie came back around the partition between their stalls. Sucking down some water, Jessie eyed him. Capped it. Put it down, her skin prickling. He had an AR-15 in his hands. He shoved it into her gut—hard—his eyes harder, her hands catching, wrapping, stopping.

He didn't say a word, just went back on the other side of the partition.

Jessie eyed her dad. He quirked eyebrows. Took the weapon. Looked it over. Broke it down, then reassembled it and handed it back to her. "Good luck, Jessie."

Warned. "…Thanks …I think."

Her dad blew breath. Gave her hair a tousle. "You'll do fine."

Now she knew she was in trouble, for sure, especially when her dad stepped away to lean against the back wall, crossed his arms, and shifted to one leg, the other crossed over, ankle to ankle.

*

MARTIN GAVE him a ride over to Jerome's, and he noted Howie's unit there. *Uh-oh.*

"Thanks for the ride," he told Martin, getting out, then letting Britta out of the back.

"Anytime. *Mañana*," his undersheriff said and drove away.

Pulling open the door with effort, that effort making his muscles spring and shoot pain across his ribcage and abdomen, he paused till it subsided, Britta watching him intently. Finally made it inside.

Jerome watched him. "You okay?"

"I'll live."

Gave him the eyeball. Pointed.

Landon nodded. Headed through.

*

AN IRON-SIGHTED WEAPON she'd never sighted in and one she had not fired since she'd last trained on it back in Blaine. Jessie blew a long breath, checked it over herself, then started to set up. "Standing position, Jessie," her dad said softly.

End of easier.

"Hot range," Howie called, and she heard his first shot.

Took a breath and fired.

Her shot went wide. Out in the seven ring to the right. Adjusted the windage. Fired a second round. Adjusted again. Fired a third, all the while listening to the steady discharge of Howie's weapon.

She felt her brain go to solid ice. *This is war between Howie and me,* she told herself. *So, go to war. Make every shot count.*

Fired her fourth round. Dead center target. Fired her fifth, sixth, and seventh, fifth and sixth within the ten, the seventh off a bit, clipping the line at nine. Took a long breath. Closed her eyes and took another breath. Opened them. Inhaled …started her exhale. Fired an eighth. Center target, the spread within her allowed inch. Fired a ninth and tenth.

Center target within tolerance. Took another inhale—

"Hold your fire, Jessie."—her dad.

She secured the weapon. Slung it. Pulled her ear protection down. Turned …to find both Howie and Landon watching her, her dad still leaned against the wall. He was grinning.

*

"I NEED YOU and your dogs, Oli," Howie said.

They were sitting in the cafeteria, a Friday night ritual after their shooting session. Tonight, it was Howie along with Oli, Jessie, and Landon, and Landon hadn't even participated. Still, he was glad he'd come over to witness the contest, a contest he hadn't even known was happening. He'd have to ask Howie about it later.

Jessie was too quiet, though. That bothered him. What had upset her?

"I need as many dogs as you can muster," Howie pressed. "I believe …we believe we're facing an army of these shooters."

"Howie, what are you thinking?" Landon asked. To this part of Howie's strategy he had not been privy.

"Can we talk about it later, sir?"

He'd just been told to hold his tongue. Landon sat back, watched Howie's face, then nodded. "Yes."

"Thank you, sir." Howie turned back to Oli. "Terri's counted forty-eight different IDs, Oli. We've got five in custody, two still in the hospital, one finally headed to a psych hospital down south as of this afternoon. The rest are out on bail until they break the terms. ...Which I'm sure they will. Tomorrow. And we can't use lethal force until *they* do. If they pull a real weapon—something that fires bullets, not paint, then we can return fire. Until then, we can't, except for rubber bullets. And most of us will be using rubber bullets, but they're wearing IIA protection, cheap, but effective enough for their purposes, especially knowing our limitations."

Oli raised eyes to him, and Landon knew what was coming. Sure enough, the next words out of Oli were: "Why *is* it that your rules of engagement always put you behind the eight ball, both arms tied behind your back, and in lethal danger? Ex*plain* that to me, Landon?!"

*

JESSIE DUCKED her head. There were no rules of engagement for law enforcement. Only the military. There was policy, and policy constantly changed, depending several things, like who was in office …in the law enforcement organization, in politics …all the way up the ladders of institutional government. That ruled. The other policy changer was case law, everything from local court rulings on up to U.S. Supreme Court decisions, and that could change on a day-to-day basis. There were new precedents being set all the time, usually to the detriment of law enforcement. The one basic rule was, the only time you could use lethal force was if and when your life or that of another was in imminent danger by a deadly threat, and a lot of that was guesswork decisions that had to be made in nanoseconds when trying to determine 'if' and 'when'.

"Why even bother to carry a gun?!" her dad pushed. "Why not just bend over and grab your ankles, Landon?!"

"Dad!"

"Sorry, Jessie, but it's true!"

"Dad, *please.*"

"No, *you* please.   Somebody answer me! ...Jessie?! Anyone?!"

"Excuse me," Jessie murmured, getting up.

"Sit *DOWN*, Jessie!"—her dad.

Swallowing something between hurt and outrage, she did as told. Mugged her lips before she said something she shouldn't. This was her *dad*.

*

TIME TO defuse this. "Oli," Landon said. "The reason for it is a U.S. Supreme Court ruling based on the Fourth Amendment, and, in today's climate, we have to tread with extreme caution. The courts are siding with the rights of the felon."

"Felons have *no* rights," Oli came back, his blue eyes bright and hard, his voice a snarl.

"They do."

"Not in my book!"

There was no reasoning with Oli on this in his present furor. Landon just shut up.

"Dad?"

"What, Jessie?"

"Law enforcement officers have to err on the side of caution or wind up being prosecuted as felons themselves. Even good cops—very good cops. The courts second guess their in-crisis decisions. They wind up at least losing their job, their career, and sometimes wind up convicted for use of undue force or even for murder if a suspect winds up dead, and prison for a cop …an ex-cop, more times than not, is a death sentence in itself. So Landon's and Captain West's tight rein on use of force is prudent."

Howie nodded, and Landon was blessing Jessie for her words. She was the only one here who could say them, right now …because Oli would listen to his daughter. He hoped Oli would hear them.

Oli didn't respond for a long minute. Then he said, "Do you have your badge with you, Jessie?"

Confused, Landon frowned. Watched Howie's face go still. Watched Jessie's eyes go cautious. She nodded.

"Fish it out."

"Why?"—said even more cautiously.

"Because I told you to."

She dug into what she called her day pack. Brought out one of the two issued. Held it.

"Give it to Landon. Now. You quit."

And, with only a small pause, Jessie did as bid, her hand shaking as she gave it to him.

Howie's head bowed. Landon's heart dropped. *Oh, Oli. Don't do this to me.* He didn't say it, though. The man was one spark away from detonating.

Oli stood. "We're done here. Jessie? With me."

"Ah …what about Landon?"—softly.

Oli watched her for a moment. Took a long breath. His eyes shifted to Landon's. "Take him home, then he's on his own. I'll pick you up there."

"Yes, sir."

*

IT WAS RARE that her dad got mad. It was *really* rare. It was rarer still for him to deliver ultimatums. Something had happened. *He's lost someone he cares about.* And, immediately, her brain buzzed in panic. Texted her brother. Got a reply, so, not Erik. *Thank you, God.*

Texted the one person other than Howie that she knew might know—Tank. Got the answer. A John Tandy had been killed in the line of duty down in

Arizona—'DOA yesterday, got word today', Tank re-texted.

'Xmil cop?'

'Y West knw 2. Our platoon.'

'Thks'.

Thumbs up.

*

LANDON FELT numb as Jessie headed The Rhino toward home. He'd just lost his best friend in the world. He'd just lost Jessie and her wonder mutts, too. All for what? His failure to properly respond and defuse a volatile moment. *One failure, and it all comes crashing down—my failure. I should have said the right thing at the right time. I should—*

"Landon? May I have my badge back now, please?"

He started. Dropped his face and glanced sideways just a little. Took a moment. Softly—"What?"

"May I have the badge I gave over to you back now?"

Hope rose.

He dug it out of his pocket. Put it on the center console.

Her hand took it. Stuffed it somewhere he couldn't see in the dark of The Rhino's cab.

"Dad lost someone today. That's what happened."

"Oh."

"I'll need to go home tonight after re-bandaging your chest. Dad and I have to talk."

"Understood."

"I'll be back in the morning to re-bandage you and drive. Okay?"

He nodded. Belatedly realized she wouldn't see it. Breathed out, "Thank you."

"Stop blaming yourself. It's nothing you did or didn't do. It's just death."

Just death. ...Just.

***

43 – Wounds to Lick

JESSIE'S DAD was not waiting for her at Landon's when she pulled in. *So he's already rethinking things.* That was going to make things a lot easier.

She cleaned and re-bandaged Landon's chest, Sol helping, then headed for home, hoping. Pulled in. Parked. Got out, the dogs reserved in their dismount from the rig. They knew.

Picked up Duchess and headed for the house.

"Jessie?"—his voice.

She turned to, and he stepped out of the shadows. Walked up—her dad, big, tough, precious. "Hi," she said gently, softly.

He reached and pulled her into him in a smothering hug, Duchess whining as she got crushed between them.

Jessie eased the dog down, dropped the pup when she was inches from the ground, then wrapped her arms around the man she most loved in all the world—her dad, the very best of the best.

*

SECURITY ANNOUNCED him. So did lights in the drive. Landon braced himself. *Here it comes.*

A tap on the door.

"Come."

Landon kept grilling the steaks. Put another one on, hoping. …Despaired.

"Landon?"—Oli's voice.

"Be right with you," he said, his tension peaking.

Landon felt the man come near. A hand reached. Plucked the meat fork out of his hand. Grabbed his shoulder, turned him around …which hurt, but he quelled a yelp. Oli handed him a bottle. "Get the glasses and the ice. We've got wounds to lick. I'll finish the steaks. I'm better at it than you."

Breathed relief. It wasn't an end to a friendship. Did as bid.

***

44 – Leave Tac to Tac

SATURDAY

TENSIONS WERE running high at the S.O.
Armored up, her weapons cleaned and checked, Jessie
had left the wonder mutts home, all but Sumi and
Acer, plus a Malinois her Granddad Darby insisted
she take along after reading Landon's announcement
set as headline in the morning paper—Sheriff To Pin
Awards, the article going on to detail that Bitterroot
County Sheriff Landon Reid himself was to make the
awards presentations at the Center Fire Club Bonfire
Bash on Saturday afternoon, the where and when. It
went on to list the times of the scheduled events.

"This is a very special dog, Jessica Marie," her
Granddad Darby had told her. "He knows his stuff."

He was also a very valuable dog—one of their top
Malinois stud dogs, three-and-a-half-years old, full of
boundless energy, and chocked full of skills in the
take-down. Jessie had spent the early morning hours
when she'd usually be running bonding with him, her
granddad coaching her in the finer points of working
him …and he was like a quickening flame. Kennel

named Yoda, he was dark fawn coated with a black mask, and, right now, he was all eyes and happy excitement as he sat watching deputies coming and going.

"We need to go over to the armory," Landon said, coming up on her, Britta giving a two-stroke wag as they approached.

"Okay."

She got up and headed for The Rhino, Acer, Sumi, and Yoda coming to heel beside her. "Everything a-okay between you and Dad?" she dared ask as they strapped in.

Landon's head dropped. "Yeah."

That didn't sound promising. "Glad."

"I have never in my life respected a man as much as I do your dad, Jessie," he said softly.

That made her swell with pride. "Thanks."

"Thanks for sharing him. It's got to be hard."

It was. She was managing, though. "You think this op is going to work?"

"I hope so."

Over at the small shop that was the S.O.'s armory, Landon got fitted with a full body plate, him flinching as the sergeant there adjusted it to snug around him. Done, he was breathing hard, his face muscles ridged.

"You didn't take a pain pill this morning, did you?" Jessie chided.

"It makes my brain giddy or cross, depending, so, no. I need to be clear-minded, especially today."

"Right."

"Deputy Anderson?" the sergeant said.

She turned to. "Yes, sir?"

"Your turn."

"I've got—"

"Your turn."

She rolled eyes back to Landon. He stood there eyes telling her 'no argument'. *Platzed* the dogs and stood to. "Yes, sir." Got fitted, too, her regular plated vest handed over to Landon who handed it back once she was done. "Just a bit of overkill," she muttered.

"Not hardly," Landon muttered back. "Back to the S.O., please."

"You bet."

*

THE NORSE berzerker, Deputy Amy Vandertil, was sitting in his office when he returned. She stood to attention as he, Britta, plus Jessie, and her three dogs, one Landon didn't know, trooped in. "As you were," he grumbled, and the woman sat back down. He introduced Jessie and Amy to each other—formally introduced them.

"My dogs would like to introduce themselves," Jessie said. "Is that okay?"

Vandervil gave a thumbs up. Said nothing, and Jessie led her dogs up, them sniffing the woman once Jessie did some sort of hand signs to the dogs.

"So I guess it's you and me on flank," Landon heard Jessie say.

"Howie says you're top marks with weapons," Deputy Vandertil replied.

"Oh, I'm an okay shot."

Landon smirked, looked down at his desk. *Right.* But now he knew what Howie had refused to tell him last night or this morning—babysitters galore. Sighed. And there would be no arguing. *Waste of assets needed elsewhere.*

*

LANDON TOOK off. Perfect opportunity. "I'm, um, not privy to all the deadly details of Captain West's plans," Jessie said. "Anything you can share?"

"Thought you'd never ask," Deputy Vandertil said.

Jessie grinned as they put their heads together while the boss was gone. By the time he came back, they were on a first name basis and, Jessie guessed, heading toward friendship.

*

"LEAVE TACTICAL to Tac, please, sir," Howie growled when, unable to stop himself, Landon walked himself over to the Tac Quonset hut to try to reason with his captain.

"We're short staffed for this kind of op. They outnumber us, what with Halloween and—"

"Leave tactical to tactical, please, sir," Howie repeated, eyes flinty.

"Sir, yes, *sir,*" Landon snapped, all snark.

Howie didn't even blink. Just said, "Thank you, Sheriff Reid, sir," and carried on with his sergeant and his corporal as he had been before Landon had interrupted.

...Stalked back to his office, stopping on the way to check under the counter after the front desk deputy again removed 'the embosser'.

Landon pulled out the fist sculpture—a bronze. Pulled out the special pen Judge Laird had given him and signed it. Put it, front and center, before his desk deputy whose face was now beat red, and said, "You can leave your *embosser* on the counter, Deputy. No need to hide it any longer." Touched the man on the shoulder, smiled as wickedly as he could manage, then headed for his office.

Found Jessie and the Norse berzerker in cahoots. Groaned as they shut up, secrets leaking out their eyes like smirks. Sighed and sat down. *Outmaneuvered and outnumbered on all counts!* And it was *his* plan!

***

45 – Bonfire Bash

THE BONFIRE BASH started at one with a barbeque, and the weather was sunny and fifty degrees with a briskly sharp wind kicking up. Kids ran and screamed. People sat around and talked, sipping sodas and eating pulled pork, baked beans, mac and cheese, and salad, with cake and ice cream for dessert.

Nerves twitched. Eyes watched. Then came the year-end awards ceremony.

By prearrangement, Britta was to stay at Landon's side, Deputy Vandertil acting as Landon's helper up on the portable stage. She handed him the medals as Landon pinned the achievement awards on, first, the youth members, then the adults. Jessie expected the attack to happen then.

Before the actual awards presentations, Landon made a speech—a nice one that made people laugh and applaud as it lauded the accomplishments of the group and its benefits to both youth and community heritage. And, of course, he tied it all together with praise, which was actually a call, to continue to uphold the high moral values historic to the Bitterroot.

"Leave it to Landon. It's always the duty, honor, and valor cards pulled out and flashed around," Jessie muttered, giving strokes to the dogs on down-alert from their perch on the open backend of The Rhino. She was ready to send them.

And, one more time, taut-nerved, she checked her SIGs, wondering when. The seconds, the long minutes ticked by. When would they strike ...or would they?

*

ASKED TO, Landon accepted the honor of lighting the bonfire, the huge stack of splintered board ends collected from construction jobs and remnant log ends donated from logging cleanup. He called up the kids who were top markspersons to help him, having them space themselves around the stack to stick their burning firebrands under it when he did.

The first sparks caught and began to crackle. Then, in moments, the fire flared up into a blazing inferno. Fire, a ritual as old as the first tribes to master it—Landon felt the history of the primitive ages of man as it began to burn. *We've come a long way, but are we any better for the journey?* He hoped so.

He looked around. Saw his deputies, all of them on edge. Felt his own nerves twitching. It was his plan. And he worried. Tonight, if they all survived this ordeal, he was taking them all out to The Hereford, every one …on his dime. They deserved it. So did he.

He touched Britta's head, and the dog nudged his hand with her cold, wet nose. It made him feel better. He turned eyes to his shadow, Deputy Amy Vandertil. She winked. Finally, he sighted Jessie, and she gave him the thumbs up.

He nodded. Stressed. Prayed …again.

***

D. L. Keur

46 – Reinforcements

THERE WERE SEVERAL ways to hunt—stalk your prey, still hunt, waiting and hoping it came in range, or lure your prey with bait. He was the bait. So were his deputies.

When hunting a predator, luring your prey was safest, and that's what Landon had chosen. But would the predators take the bait? And if they took it, when would they strike?

Hopefully after the kids have gone home. He'd been pointed in including those times in his announcements in the paper, on the radio, on TV. He hoped the enemy had taken the cue. *Don't hurt the innocent. They're non-combatants. This is between me and my deputies and you.*

And, yet again, Landon prayed.

*

STROBING LIGHTS incoming—Jessie saw them from the corner of her eye—city cop cars, eight of them—and leading the pack was Harvey Mueller's unit, Captain Dirk Compton's right behind it. They had help.

Jessie saw Howie jog over to meet them. Saw Landon watch, but stay in his place—relief.

Howie huddled with Captain Dirk Compton at Harvey's unit, then stepped clear, Compton heading back to his car, Harvey easing forward to park between two S.O. units.

Then Harvey came to join Landon, Jessie asked to move over to let him in. Reluctantly, she did as asked.

*

"YOU DIDN'T think we were going to let you get all the glory, did you?" Harvey asked. Arm in a cast, Harvey was decked out in full formal dress uniform, a modest smile on his lips as he accepted a chair.

It was just about the first time Landon had ever seen Northridge's Chief of Police smile. Retired from the FBI, Harvey was an expert administrator, a glorified pencil-pusher, and PR man all rolled into one, though Landon knew he'd once, long time passing, been a field agent when in his prime.

"A little wide of your jurisdiction, aren't you?" Landon asked.

"Jerome's range is technically within the city limits."

"This field, too?"

"Debatable."

Landon wanted to chuckle. It wasn't, and they both knew it. Swallowed it and just nodded.

"Besides," Harvey said, "we're just returning the favor for all the times you've backed us up."

"I appreciate it." And Landon truly did.

Cars began leaving—one parent or another taking kids home as planned. It was now just before four. Landon breathed relief as the last car drove off. Sundown was at around 5:30. The bonfire crackled, wood shifting and settling, sending off sparks that flew upward toward the sky. According to plan, if something came down, the remaining civilians, all adults, all crack shots, would take cover. They were told not to engage. Did he believe they wouldn't? No. And that was okay.

"I should have brought marshmallows," Harvey quipped.

And they sat there, waiting. A half an hour passed. "I guess they didn't accept the invitation," Landon said, squinting as the sun sank lower. It would be another half an hour before it slipped behind the mountains to the west, a half hour after that, official sunset. Then a full hour of twilight. The bonfire bash was officially over at 7PM—dark. Two-and-a-half-hours to go.

***

47 – Incoming

ACER'S EARS PRICKED. So did Yoda's and Sumi's. Moments later, Howie's voice came through her shoulder mic: "Incoming from the archery range, due west. They're coming out of the target bales." And, of course, the sun was just above the mountains west of them.

Of course they'd wait for the sun to blind us. "Smart. Predictable. And we should have had the dogs clear the field." Jessie hadn't thought of it. Neither, it seemed, had anybody else.

If should'ves were did-its, they'd have this done and dusted. Instead, they had an imminent engagement.

The dogs stood. Jessie pulled sunglasses out of her day pack, her hands shaking. *Quit. Ice down*, she scolded herself. And her hands stopped their quivering on command. Yes, she was getting better.

She was out of position for protecting Landon. *Darn you, Harvey Mueller.* She pulled her right SIG. Cleared the chamber. Swapped out the magazine for the one Howie had given her with rubber bullets. *Please don't foul.*

*

FIVE QUICK CHIRPS through the mic—Howie. His deputies, twenty-two of them, moved into position behind their units. So did Mueller's sixteen officers, seventeen with Compton. Landon and Mueller stayed where they were, Deputy Vandertil beside and Jessie behind them.

The dark-clad figures of the shooters came forward at a steady pace. They seemed in no hurry.

A buzz ...like wasps. "What is that?" Landon muttered, looking, looking.

"Incoming UAVs,"—Howie, again.

Then he saw them—a whole hoard of flying dots—drones like Jessie flew. There had to be another van!.

"Unarmed," Howie said. "Spy birds only."

So that's how they're filming this. Landon had wondered that. Now he knew. And, yes, there was money behind this whole criminal game.

*

DRONES—Jessie had to admire that touch. Then, behind the approaching shooters, figures running, dogs beside. *It's Dad!*

Scrambling, she got out binoculars and focused. Yes. It was her dad, center, the four prowlers running before, Numa at his side. And her granddad on his left flank, three Malinois running at heel. And John with two GSDs. And Twilla with two Malinois. And Stan—GSDs. And all the rest of the Anderson Dog trainers—Bob, Jeff, Rennie, and Pablo, pairs of GSDs or Malinois with them, as well. And, along side, were the men and women who came in once a month to train in the pit. Including Tank. Jessie wanted to cheer. Heeling beside those men and women were more of the dogs Jessie worked with on a regular basis. *We've got them surrounded. Boxed in.* And she grinned. *They're outnumbered. They're done.*

***

48 – Melee

SHERIFF LANDON REID waited until the assailants were within range, them walking calmly, steadily toward their targets, him and the law enforcement officers present. And he knew they knew that, until and unless they engaged, law enforcement wouldn't fire. They also knew he and his wouldn't and couldn't use deadly force. And they were armored …just like the law officers waiting for them were.

He stood up. Beside him, Harvey stood up, too.

The shooters stopped, stood, their helmet-clad heads looking straight at him.

He waited.

Behind them, Oli and the dogs were coming in range as planned. *Now*, he told himself. Picked up the bullhorn. Flipped the switch to turn it on. Raised it. Spoke. "Drop your weapons. You're under arrest."

*

"YOU ARE SURROUNDED. You cannot escape. Drop your weapons. Lie down, face down on the ground, arms over your heads, feet crossed. *Now,*" Landon growled., the bullhorn making his deep, slow voice resonate.

And the shooters stood there for long seconds, Jessie watching for any movement, her SIG steady on the one closest to Landon.

Then, as if cued, the shooters did as told, and Jessie was amazed. A wash of warmth went through her, from her cheeks to her shoulders to her hips and down. *They're complying.* They were complying.

Behind them, her dad and his company of people slowed, the dogs, too. Jessie watched the dogs recall and come to heel beside their assigned handlers. *Good, good dogs.*

She took the cue. Whispered to her dogs and Yoda, the dogs going to standing stay.

"Deputies, shackle them and read them their rights," Jessie heard Landon say through the bullhorn as law enforcement officers approached—not fast. They were very wary, guns drawn, but pointed low.

Jessie held her breath. Behind her, the fire crackled.

*

HE SHOULD HAVE anticipated this. This, Landon realized too late, was all for cinematic drama. But he hadn't. Neither, it seemed, had anybody else.

His deputies and city officers were all but on them, the still bodies on the ground, and, as they approached, those bodies snapped up their weapons and, screaming like demons and banshees, sprang to their feet, running, weapons firing, running directly into the men and woman who were nearly upon them.

Flying bodies of dogs attacked from behind as the sun began to sink below the mountain horizon west of them. There were screams. There came the sound of more weaponsfire—his deputies returning fire.

Then, seeming to spring from the earth, a face, the same face he recognized from before, plus three others. And the one that he recognized screamed, "YOU'RE MINE, LONNIE TUUNZ! ALL MINE!" Then his dog leapt as she fired her gun, paint splattering him, face and torso. And it hurt.

*

JESSIE SHOT rubber, targeted to torsos, but the bullets didn't do any good. The dogs did, though. The attackers went down, Britta, Acer, Yoda, and Sumi grappling them. Then she saw the woman who seemed bent on taking Landon down slip her jacket and the dog. She pulled a real gun—a .9mm, not a Stinger®.

Jessie shoved her way through, the chief of police tumbling. Amy beat her there by a stride, knocking Landon flat, the butt of her rifle slamming up into the woman's torso as Britta went for a second take—the bared gun arm.

The assailant went down, crying out, and, that fast, the big soldier stepped in over the now downed Landon, her body towering over him, to bring the business end of her weapon to bear on the woman's throat. "Ready and willing," she said, and Jessie swore Amy was wearing a smile. She'd fire.

*

IN THE FINAL throes of the melee, Jessie wiping his face and checking him over—"Broken nose, Landon"—it was the dogs that had brought the assailants to bay. It was the dogs. Landon knew that without any doubt. Quicker, cannier, much more agile, and, best of all, non-lethal in their attacks, the dogs had won the day. It was over.

***

D. L. Keur

EPILOGUE

THIRTY-ONE PEOPLE, all women, all of them dressed in padded black gear and cheap body armor, their helmets stripped from their heads, were handcuffed, leg shackled, then escorted to the jail's prisoner transport bus, the only secure vehicle big enough to accommodate them all at once.

"Thirty-one!" Howie said. "Holy moly! An army of criminals, and we already have a bunch in custody."

"Did you pick up whomever loosed those drones?" Landon asked.

"Not yet, sir."

"We found out where they're staying," Deputy Angela Murphy said, handing Landon a couple of key fobs that had 'Heart Realty' printed on them.

"Do pay them a visit," Landon said.

"Deputies have secured that subdivision …which, by the way, is mostly still under construction except for the twelve model homes already completed. City is bringing in the owner and the realtor, both, sir."

"Excellent. Let's get some answers."

...But, by mid-November, with the investigation ongoing, Landon was frustrated by the lack of progress. They had a total of sixty-one people either out on bail, in custody, or in a psych ward—one— and, other than Reasoner, still, nobody would talk, though they now had forty-seven of them positively IDed.

There were no solid answers in the case. Just pay-out receipts for housing, and travel receipts, all paid for by—Landon guessed it right—Actuator Films and RealTake. Both LLCs were privately held, registered in Delaware, making finding out who owned and controlled them nigh on impossible, at least until the corporate transparency law took effect. But it was Andy Newsome's problem, now, because Landon had finally turned it over to the FBI. It was now a federal case.

In Georgia, the same corporations were behind the similar action that had come down there ...on the same night—October 31st. The clincher was the name 'Lonnie Tuunz'.

The hard drives and cams told the story, the SD cards with each players' actions recorded there ...including the hits on Homer Garrison, Cornie Parker, Richard Orr, Brown, the Mastiff, Wes and

Glen Briggins, John Heppert, and a hoard of others. And, of course, 'Lonnie Tuunz'—Landon Reid and Harvey Mueller, in this instance.

In the previous season's airing, 'Lonnie Tuunz' had been the chief of police, Chicago and his counterpart, a woman, in L.A., Terri's computer sleuthing and hard work paying off big-time dividends.

Landon gave her a commendation, a promotion, and a raise. She was now Deputy Sergeant Terri MacLeod.

Jessie, of course, threw a party to celebrate and Landon was invited. Jedidiah came with Jessie, the two of them laughing and dancing together the entire evening.

*

JESSIE INSISTED that Landon help cut the ribbon, cameras flashing and TV cameras taping the opening of the new Bitterroot County no-kill facility. Jessie didn't make it through in one piece though. She floundered, tears breaking loose, and, Jed taking her under his arm, Landon stepped in to salvage the moment with his usual flair of saying just the right words. Then everyone was given a tour. Next, it was on to the Landon Reid Charity opening, and Jessie was thrilled, because people really, really seemed to like, not just the offerings, but the reason for its existence. Landon actually blushed hot in the face, and it was Jessie's turn to rescue him by speaking up when he literally choked up, his voice failing him.

The day was a huge success.

*

"DNA RESULTS came back on that body found in pieces," Martin said, walking into Landon's office. "It's Nicholson."

Landon looked up. Frowned. A shock hit him at that news. "You're kidding."

"I'm not. Somebody, probably one of his rich customers, took their revenge," Martin said. "Looks like they took a page from his book and dropped him from the sky. Couldn't have happened to a nicer guy."

"It's murder, Martin."

"It's Agent Andy Newsome's problem, not ours."

Landon dropped his head. Thought about it. Raised his eyes to his undersheriff and said, "Good."

It wasn't even an hour later when the next surprise dropped in Landon's lap. A man walked into his office after getting the go-ahead from Red. He was a stranger. That stranger took a piece of paper out of the inside pocket of his jacket. He laid it down on Landon's desk—a check made out for a three with a lot of zeros after it.

Landon looked up at the guy. "What's this?"

"Drop your investigation into Actuator Films and RealTake."

Another piece of the puzzle. Landon touched a button on his desk phone. "Red. Send in some deputies, please. And get Andy Newsome in here, too."

Looked back up at the guy as his deputies walked in. "You're under arrest. Attempting to bribe a law enforcement officer, for starts. You have the right to remain silent...."

*

"THE MALINOIS are smaller, tidier-looking, perhaps," Judge Regina Laird told Jessie's dad.

Jessie smiled. Knew what her dad would do, and, sure enough, at Oli's signal, her Granddad Darby let one of them loose.

On command, the dog leapt to the boards on the wall and climbed up like it was nothing, crossed a truss to the middle, looked down, then, at Darby's signal, swapped ends and came back down to sit, happy and panting, staring up at Judge Laird.

"My, my," Her Honor said, her eyes wide.

"They're very energetic dogs and require a *lot* of exercise," Oli told her. "German Shepherds are much more mellow, but, of course, still require exercise. Just not quite so exuberantly."

"We'll go with the German Shepherds, please, then?" Regina requested.

"Certainly. I think it's a wise choice."

"And you really think two?"

"I do, Your Honor. One as a personal protection dog that doesn't leave your side. One to guard the premises—your office, courtroom, and home, both to be with you at all times."

"And they'll get along with each other, and won't bite someone, like you demonstrated with those kind people over there?" she said, nodding to Jessie, Twilla, and Stan.

"Oh, they'll attack and bite, for sure, even kill, but only if someone has malintent upon you and yours …or on command."

"Very good. I'll take the two as you recommend. When do I begin my lessons with them and …acclimation period, I think you called it?"

"Whenever you choose."

"Right now, then. Let me write you a check."

"Excellent." Oli turned. "Jessie?"

*

10:00AM SATURDAY MORNING, showered and shaved, all chores done and laundry in the wash, Landon, happy and comfortable in his bathrobe, cats on his lap, had just settled in with Sol's treatise on the criminal mind. He was somewhere in Chapter Eleven of the huge tome, a book that was written in a dry, no-nonsense academic voice, a book that included references to studies that included everything from background histories of families, statistical data, and even brain scans of the various subjects. It was tough going and required Landon to keep an unabridged dictionary and a medical reference at hand so he could look up words he didn't know and couldn't even properly pronounce.

Britta looked up just before surveillance announced the arrival of 'Jessica Anderson'. Within moments, Sol came pounding down the stairs. "Jessie's here!" He headed for the door before Landon could even scoop up Pine Tree and Owl.

Moments later, Jessie bounced in, dogs flooding in around her. She stopped dead in her tracks and stared at him. "You're not even dressed yet, Landon?! It's after ten!"

Indignant at the suggestion that he was remiss, he told her straight out, "It's my day off! Tomorrow, too."

"Well, your guests will be here in less than four hours, so we'd best get this place ship-shape, don't you think?"

*

THE LOOK on his face—Jessie couldn't help but laugh, especially when the brows did their crinkle thing.

"What guests?!" Landon asked.

"It's your Early Thanksgiving dinner today. Did you forget?" ...which, of course, he knew nothing about. A giggle escaped her, but she smothered the rest. Watched him start shaking his head, his face blanching.

"It's okay. We've got it under control," Sol said. "Be right back."

And, as planned, Sol disappeared up the stairway to the upstairs light switches, ear to the now open original great room staircase.

"Who's coming?!" Landon demanded, recovering himself.

"Red, Martin, Howie, Sol, Tank, Kins, Terri, Tom H., Judge Laird, Dad, Gram, Granddad, and me. And their and my plus ones, of course."

And, again, she had to stifle her laughter at the crestfallen, now turning panicked, look on his face.

"Ah—"

"So, hurry up. Get yourself into some jeans and an old tee so we can get this place clean."

The eyes pleaded. "I don't have anything thawed to feed that many people, Jessie!"

"Oh, no worries. An Anderson is always prepared, remember? Turkeys are in the oven at our house, the rest of the food either already done or ready to bake when the birds come out. Gram, Dad, and Granddad are handling transport. So get going, please."

"This place won't hold that many people."

And Jessie could tell he was now getting really upset.

"Landon. Calm down. I'm way ahead of the game. Okay?"

His face looked beyond tragic.

Going to the wall, she opened the stereo doors, slipped her fingers into the notches in the dry wall, pulled and shifted the first piece of four by eight gypsum board. Then, Landon standing there, mouth open, eyes shocked, she stepped to the other side, and shifted the other, leaning them both into the nearest corner.

He came up beside her, his breathing quick and audible—stressed. His hand touched the carved, polished, waxed wood of the big, handmade double doors, something that had taken Jessie hours to get cleaned and shiny. That hand shook. She watched his eyes. Grabbed the handles and opened the doors, pushing them wide.

The lights came on, Sol having caught the timing perfectly. The room came alight, candle-bulbed chandeliers with their garlands and strings of tiny Christmas lights twinkling.

Jessie waited, breath pent.

He just stood there and stared. Then, his hand grasped the door frame as he swayed on his feet.

"Landon?" she called gently. Touched a careful hand to his shoulder.

He turned shocked eyes to her. Just stood.

"Landon?" And fear rising—she'd gone too far, this time—she said, "It's okay. I'll call everyone, and we'll have it at our house instead. I—I'm sorry. I thought—"

"It's just …like …my grandmother—" He huffed out a breath. And another. Swayed more, then leaned against the door frame.

Tears welled in his eyes as she watched. A hand moved to his mouth, the back of it pressing into his lips. Then the hand came away. "It's just as it used to be." Then, whispered, he said, "It's just like…." Turned his eyes to her again. Swallowed. Then, surprise, he said, "Thank you." Stepped forward and crushed her in a bear hug. "It's the way it was …used to be. Just like it used to be."

*

HE WANTED to know how she knew.

"I snooped. Even found the family albums with the pictures that showed how it used to be decorated."

He wanted to know how she hid doing it.

"When you were at work. Sol helped when he could. So did Dad."

Landon was okay with it. He was more than okay with it. And what Jessie had thought—that Landon had boarded it up—wasn't true. "Granddad and I did it after my grandmother died. He insisted. I helped him. I've never had the guts to open it back up. …I wanted to, but I just never…. It was too much. Too painful."

"It's okay that I did it?"

"Yes. …But I wish you had let me help."

"You wouldn't have allowed it, Landon. It's the way you are."

And, for once, he didn't argue the point.

*

THE DINNER had been full of laughter and merriment. His cats had a ball. So did the dogs—his dog, Jessie's dogs, Oli's dogs, even Judge Laird's new dogs. It was a houseful, a houseful that included good company and good cheer—his first real Thanksgiving in the place since …forever, celebrated the weekend before the actual holiday, Christmas music playing on the old stereo, tiny Christmas lights twinkling on the decorated garlands Jessie had hung along the walls, on the old wagon wheel and antler chandeliers, across his grandmother's piano, and around the big double bay windows, now freed of their plywood barriers. His house was becoming a home for the first time in years …since his grandmother died and his grandfather went into perpetual mourning, then died two years after. The house was coming alive again, all due to a meddlesome, platinum blonde minx. And he loved her for it …loved her. Knew it.

Her laughter chimed out, and he turned. She and Jed were arguing about how to properly cut the tiered spice cake. He turned back to the window. He was glad she was happy. He was glad Jed was happy. But, somehow, the thought made him melancholy.

"Here you go, Cowboy,"—Oli.

He took the tumbler. Sniffed—rum. Touched glasses with Oli.

Again her laughter rang out. Again he turned. They were dishing the cake out on plates, Judge Laird shifting plates onto trays, Jessie's grandmother, Ana-Mari, helping. The two ladies seemed to get along well.

Jed spied him watching. Raised his glass in toast, and Landon acknowledged, then turned his back on them and, more sadness welling, gazed out at the night with its waxing moon.

Oli stepped nearer. "Hear my words, Landon, and hear them well," he said, his voice going quiet. "Sometimes in life you have to pursue your goals. The game won't come to you."

THE END

I know you hear this beg at the end of every one of these books, but, honestly, without reviews, a book dies, so would you please take a moment to leave your honest review for me? Even a one liner would be appreciated, and, if you are interested in knowing when new books and audio versions of novels in The Jessica Anderson K-9 Mysteries series are available, you can sign up for my newsletter via my website, DLKeur.com. Thank you. –Dawn

(And, no, the series doesn't end here.)

ABOUT THE DOGS

MITCH, THE MARVELOUS MALINOIS

Mitch was found on the streets of Miami by ABMR (American Belgian Malinois Rescue) in October 2017. They guessed that he was born sometime in July.

In November, he went to his foster home in Orlando. His foster mom is a police officer at the Orlando Airport and her K-9 is a bomb specialist.

Ann's daughter saw Mitch online, and, after an intense series of interviews and a home visit. Says Ann Davis, "It was like I was adopting a child. They agreed to let us adopt Mitch and his gotcha day was officially February 2nd."

MILO, QUEENIE, OSO, ACER, AND THE REST

Milo is modeled after my beloved Bailey. And, yes, he really was that elegant and tall. A wonder mutt, Bailey, for me, was extra special. I so wish he were still with me.

Queenie is modeled on an Irish Setter I inartfully nicknamed 'Red'. She was a windfall who wound up going on to win all sorts of awards, both for her conformation—the judges drooled over her, in fact—and for her startling skills. This dog had a soul of boundless joy and was responsible for finding a lost six-year-old.

Oso, the Elkhound, was a dog I had as a kid, and, yes, I named him Oso, because he looked like a fuzzy bear. He wandered in one day in the middle of winter, starved and sick. We took him in …as we did all strays, got him the veterinary help he needed, nursed him back to health, and kept him. Ultimately, because he was an Elkhound, a breed known for their air scenting skills, he was responsible for finding people lost in an avalanche in our mountains during Christmas break one winter. His very best friend was Erasmus, the Philosopher Piglet, my pet piglet that grew into a thousand-pound Yorkshire boar. Their friendship lasted their lifetimes, the two of them dying within weeks of one another.

Acer, Britta, and Sumi are all based on various German Shepherds that I have known or that have been part of our family throughout my life. Within these novels, you'll get to know them all and more, along with other notables …like Chauncey, the Briard …but that's another story.

D. L. Keur

*

ABOUT THIS SERIES

The Jessica Anderson K-9 Mysteries began life near the end of December 2020, during the Covid-19 pandemic which reference I have purposely omitted from the stories, because, like all of us, I hope to put that behind me and begin, once more, to live a more normal life.

In all, I have more than a dozen books planned for this series, four already heavily researched and in various stages of draft. I plan to write and release these novels on a regular schedule for you (and me) to enjoy. And joy is, in fact, the main reason for writing them, for, while there is drama and trauma, there is a quintessential heroism in these marvelous animals. In writing these novels, I wanted to share that joy, inspiration, and unique richness that is a life with animals, specifically dogs, and of living in "God's Country."

Within this book and all the subsequent ones of the series, all the places and events, as well as all of the persons' names, save one (with permission), are completely fictional. That said, though, the bases (plural of basis) for the elements of the stories are very real and true to the land, the climate, and, most importantly, to the animals and people who call this great, but often misunderstood, part of rural America their home.

*

ABOUT THE AUTHOR

As an author who delights in writing stories that I myself would want to read, this is the first novel and series of novels that I've written under my real name. For decades, I've cloaked my identity under pen names,  even once deciding to self-publish instead of continuing the traditional publishing route. Convinced to by another author who became a close friend and writing confidante, I decided to unveil my identity and allow readers to connect me with some of my fiction work.

Writing is my passion. Though, among other things, I'm an artist and musician, writing novels is where I lose myself in The Zone, immersed for hours, even days, into the worlds that birth themselves in my brain to emerge out my fingertips. May you enjoy the results of my creative travels as much as I.

Dawn Lisette Keur

OTHER BOOKS BY D. L. Keur

Writing as D. L. Keur

The Jessica Anderson K-9 Mysteries

Death Scent **(Book 1)**

Stray Trouble **(Book 2)**

Grim Track **(Book 3)**

Dire Traces **(Book 4)**

Dead Falls **(Book 5)**

Troubled Pursuit **(Book 6)**

Game Trail **(Book 7)**

How to Write a Good Book in 17 Days, Get-it-written self-help for serious writers by D. L. Keur, non-fiction

Dawn's Flute Notes, Practical Advice for Flute Players from Practice Room to Stage by D. L. Keur, non-fiction

Writing as E. J. Ruek

To Inherit a Murderer, paranormal suspense, set in N. Idaho, this is the story of a godmother saddled with guardianship of her deceased best friend's son, a twelve-year-old who is a murderer. (Controversial)

Old Hickory Lane, the story of an Idaho veterinarian

Created Evil, mythic epic fantasy. Get ready for a whole different take on the Apocalypse.

Slightly Disturbing Stories, a nerve-tingling anthology of short stories that end well for the innocent and good. They will stick with you, each a slightly disturbing ripple in your memory, because it's not what's shown or told; it's what's left unsaid that echoes …forever.

Writing as Aeros

A Gathering of Rebels by Aeros, a 2 volume Science Fiction epic space opera in the most classic tradition of Frank Herbert.

[Title Withheld] (pending publication)

Writing as C. J. "Country" James

Through Better & Worse, a Montana Love Story, Western Family Saga/Romance by C. J. "Country" James

To Have & To Hold, a Continuing Montana Love Story, Western Family Saga/Romance by C. J. "Country" James

All of them are exclusively available at Amazon everywhere in the world.

And, in Joy, I hope we meet again.

***

D. L. Keur